Finding Anna

Finding Anna

Hidden Series Book One

LM Terry

Finding Anna

Published by LM Terry

ISBN-13: 9781790765478

Dedication

To my Husband and Children

To my husband, thank you for loving me unconditionally. Thank you for supporting me in making my dream become a reality. To my children thank you for listening to my endless chatter and always cheering me on. Your love will always be the backbone of my success.

To my Beta Readers

Thank you ladies for taking time out of your busy lives to give my story a chance. For your advice and most of all your words of encouragement. You kept me going on the darkest of days.

To my Parents and Sister

To my number one fan, my sister, thank you for being the first person to be brave enough to dive into the story. To my dad for teaching me to work hard. And, lastly to my mother, she instilled a love in me for words and I will forever be grateful. I know that you have been an angel on my shoulder from page one,

Table of Contents

You fall, you rise, you make mistakes, you live, you learn. You're human, not perfect. You've been hurt, but you're alive. Think of what a precious privilege it is to be alive – to breathe, to think, to enjoy, and to chase the things you love. Sometimes there is sadness in our journey but there is also lots of beauty. We must keep putting one foot in front of the other even when we hurt, for we will never know what is waiting for us just around the bend. ~ unknown

Preface

Anna

I woke up wondering why I couldn't smell my mom's gourmet coffee. My parent's routine is usually like clockwork. Something feels off this morning. "Mom, Dad," I say as I round the corner to the kitchen. It's empty. My heart rate picks up as I slowly spin, a little niggle of fear creeps up my spine.

My eye catches a white envelope left on the center of the table…with my name written on it. Well, the name that used to be mine. I have been living a dead girl's life ever since mine was taken from me. It is my name! I slowly reach for the envelope, half expecting it to vanish before my eyes. I snatch it, running down the hallway back to my room, locking the door behind me.

My hands tremble as I stare at the envelope. With my back against the door I run my finger across the familiar, beautiful, wispy handwriting that was my mothers. Not the dead girl's mom but my mother…Anna Velazquez's. I whisper the name to myself, "Anna Velazquez". I have not spoken nor heard it since I was ten.

I hold the letter to my chest. What does this mean? Are my parents finally coming for me? Sophia, my nanny told me they would come as soon as it was safe, that I would stay with the Madronos. I needed to pretend that I was their daughter. Just for a short time she said. That was nine years ago.

I look at the envelope again. I have been waiting for what seems like an eternity for this, for answers. I run my finger under the seam, ripping it open unevenly. Inside is one piece of paper with a handwritten letter from my mother.

Happy Birthday Dearest Anna,

Is it my Birthday? I look up on the corkboard above my desk to the calendar. Yes, my nineteenth. How could I forget? I shake my head. It is because they have not allowed me to acknowledge my previous life. I have been celebrating Sarah's birthday as my own for the past nine years…nine years. I focus my attention back to the letter.

If you are reading this, then I have been successful in keeping you hidden. I hope that the Madronos treated you well. Lila was a dear friend of mine. When she lost Sarah in that horrible drowning accident I knew you taking her identity was the only way to keep you safe. My dream has always been for you to be happy and I pray that you are.

Please know your father and I both love you very much. You are our world. By now I am sure you realize that this is your life. It is important that you do not try to locate us. It is far too dangerous. I asked the Madronos to give you this letter on your nineteenth birthday. An account has been set up for you at the Hearthside Bank in Sarah's name and you are now the owner of the ranch. The Madronos are on their way to enjoy a much-needed getaway. Don't worry over them as they have been compensated for the promise of seeing you safe. I'm sure that this has not always been easy for them. I know that they missed their beloved Sarah as I missed you.

I want you to be free, free of your father's business, free to live a life of your choosing. As long as you keep Sarah's identity and do not try to find us you should remain safe.

I love you, more than you will ever know…Love mom

The fire of anger radiates through me. It's like a small ember has been smoldering in the pit of my stomach for the past nine years. I have been waiting for something, anything, and this is all I get, no explanation as to what they thought I needed to hide from. "What the fuck," I whisper.

I remember my mother, elegant and quiet. Always keeping me herded within her skirts. I was safe and protected on my father's estate. Then she sent me away, sending me off across the border with only Sophia to accompany me. I have not felt safe or happy since that day. All I feel is empty and alone. It's more than just a feeling…I am alone.

I crumple up the letter in my fist and toss it in the wastebasket by my desk. Well, now what? I guess the only thing to do, put one foot in front of the other. That is what I have done my whole life, one foot in front of the other.

I push myself off the door, turning to unlock it. I hesitate as I step back out into the hallway, poking my head out to make sure the unknown monster I have been hiding from is not waiting for me.

I stop outside my parent's room. I place my ear up to the cool wood and listen, nothing. It's not like the Madronos were ever mean, it's just I always had the feeling they didn't want me. I think they did in the beginning, hoping that I would somehow fill the void that was Sarah. I push the door open letting my eyes roam, stopping on the closet, empty except for a few stray hangers scattered along the carpet.

I guess that is that. I am alone. Alone with my fear of the faceless monster. One foot in front of the other I repeat to myself, one foot in front of the other.

Chapter One

Anna

It's been two weeks since my birthday. I guess I am coming to terms with living alone and the fact that no one is showing up for me. Maybe the faceless monster has given up too.

I have been feeling guilty for being so angry at my mom. I am not naïve about the life I left behind on the estate. I remember the guards and the guns. My mother tried to distract me from them and my father's business. I'm not even sure what his "business" was.

My father was always locked away in his office. The only time I ever really spent with him was during meals. Even those times were interrupted, he constantly had to take a call, or a guard would come in and whisper to him. He would give my mother that apologetic look as he rose from the table.

I do not know if my parents are still alive. I have considered getting a passport to go back across the border and search for them. I don't. I can't. Every time I park at my local post office to fill out the paperwork, I end up sitting in my car for hours, picturing my mother's fear. She was so afraid the day she whisked me away.

I wish I had a face to put on the unknown monster. Was it a disgruntled business partner? Was my father doing something illegal? I do not understand what I have been hiding from and that is what makes me hide from everything and everyone.

My anxiety rises as I pull up to my job. It's a little bookstore in a quiet community a few miles from the ranch. I was home-schooled, my parents encouraged me to take a position in town to help me socialize. I picked this place hoping that it would limit my contact with others. People go into a bookstore for an escape. They are looking for another world to meld into. They spend much of their time there with their nose in a book. It's the perfect place for me to work. I don't like being the focus of attention and here I am not.

I am an avid adventurer through novels myself. Stories are my only outside understanding of life. I have had exactly two realities, one on my father's estate and one here on the ranch. That is okay with me, I have traveled the globe going as far away as other galaxies, time traveling to different dimensions all while in the safety of my bedroom.

I take a quick peek in the rearview mirror before getting out. Contacts check, hair up check. I look into my eyes again. Even they belong to Sarah, a deep warm brown. My real eyes, the one hidden beneath these dark depths are blue. I have worn contacts since I was ten. Sarah and I were similar but our eye color was not. My new parents insisted that I wear them.

I have always tried to blend in, fly under the radar so to speak. Around the time of my thirteenth birthday it became harder and harder as I observed boys taking notice of my curving figure. I started wearing my hair up, no makeup and the least form fitting clothes I could find, it has seemed to work this far.

I make my way across the street to the bookstore casing the area as I do. I'm always watchful never able to let my guard down. I tell myself that it is silly after nine years what am I afraid of? Whatever monster my mother thought was after me has vanished. Vanished just like Anna Velasquez.

The door dings upon my entry and two gray heads peek up at me over the tops of their books. "Good morning Frank, morning Irene." I smile as they both rise from their seats coming towards me for "hugs". I brace myself for the contact.

"Good morning Sarah how are you?" Irene says pushing me back to gaze into my eyes. "Honey, are you sure you are up to working today? You seem a little pale. Frank does she look pale to you?"

"I think she looks fine, don't make her self-conscious." He winks, flashing me a warm smile.

Guilt consumes me for lying to them. The day I found my mother's letter I called them, telling them I was sick with the flu. I told them my doctor had advised that I take a few weeks off. I would have taken more time, but I know that they have plans in Dallas tomorrow, a big book fair of some sort.

They have spent their entire lives here in this store. They even live in the small apartment above. I envy them, having each other to lean on, so comfortable in the world they carved out for themselves.

"I'm fine, really. I wouldn't want you to miss your trip. I needed to get out of the house, the walls were closing in on me." It's a lie, I could hide away in my room forever.

They seem to accept that I am feeling better and make their way to their perch behind the counter. Just like two peas in a pod they put their noses back in their respective books.

I sigh sauntering over to the coffee nook, drawn there by the comforting smell of rich beans brewing. It's in a little space in the corner of the store. They set small tables for customers who want a quiet place to work or study. There are big picture windows letting in the warm sunlight. It was a nice addition they added shortly after I started there.

I notice a laptop open on one table. I turn to my employers. "Do we have a customer already this morning?"

Neither look up from their book, Irene nods in response. I stare out the window seeing a gentleman on his phone standing on the corner. I notice the car in front of the store, Kansas plates. He could be in town on business.

I turn to walk away, then it hits me out of nowhere, an overwhelming urge. I nonchalantly walk over to the open laptop. The screen is still lit. He must have just received the call and stepped outside to take it. I look out the window. The man has his phone up to his ear, absently looking off in the distance across the street.

I quickly without giving it much thought click on the Internet button and type Manuel Velazquez, my real father's name in the white search box. I hit the return key. Waiting as the computer does its thinking I peer up to determine if either my employers or the man from outside is watching me.

He is no longer standing on the corner. He is making his way up the steps to the bookstore. I see that my inquiry has brought something up. There is no time! I quickly click out of the browser and step back towards the counter retrieving my freshly poured coffee just as the door dings his arrival.

I shake as I pull the cup to my mouth using both hands. What the hell was I thinking? Part of me is ashamed that I invaded a stranger's space. The other half is humming from the thrill of doing something so daring.

I hear the man pick up his things behind me then stop to ask Frank for directions to the nearest motel. I glance over as he picks up a business card off the counter. With the snap of a finger he is gone.

My pulse slowly returns to normal. I scold myself for being so stupid. But, I know deep down it was an opportunity I couldn't pass up. A computer that could not be connected to me. One that could have provided answers if only I would have had a minute longer.

Chapter Two

Anna

The next morning, I head to work early. I check my phone seeing a text from Frank letting me know they hit the road for Dallas. I smile to myself, besides my parents Frank and Irene are the only other people I communicate with. I told myself that I need to make friends here. I have just been waiting to go back to the life I once had, with old friends and family.

I park in front of the store. I promise myself that I will try putting myself out there. I have wasted too much time waiting. No one is coming for me. Now that my parents and Sarah's parents are gone I am finding myself craving human interaction.

I glance around as I cross the street. It seems like there is more traffic than usual in the sleepy little community. I shrug off the thought grabbing my keys from my bag going in and starting the morning coffee.

I sit behind the counter pulling my phone out of my back pocket. Last night I downloaded an app for the Hearthside bank, sure enough there was an account set up in Sarah's name. I log in again. Current balance two million dollars. Two million dollars. I have always known my parents, both sets were wealthy. I have never wanted for anything, but I can't wrap my mind around the number.

I close out of the screen shoving the phone back in my pocket. The large amount in my account just adds to the unanswered questions. If my real parents had cash like this then why did they need to send me away? Why couldn't they have used it to keep me safe? That and with the money I am sure they provided the Madronos that should easily have afforded me protection.

Maybe they didn't want me. Maybe it was easy for them to send me away. The letter, the account set up all those years ago tells me that my mom never planned for me to return home. The Madronos seemed to have had no problem walking away either.

My throat tightens, I force myself to push the thoughts out of my mind. I don't cry. I haven't cried since the day I said goodbye to my mother, and I refuse to start now. One foot in front of the other. I repeat my mantra in my head as I get up to organize a box of newly arrived novels.

The door dings heralding a customer's arrival. I look up seeing a police officer and another man wearing a suit and tie. I leave the pile of books and walk over to greet them at the counter putting on my best customer service smile. "Good morning, how may I help you?"

"Good morning. Yes, I am Detective Liam Sharp, and this is Officer Gallagher." He opens a little black case showing me his badge. "Could I please speak to the owner or the supervisor here?" he asks.

"I'm afraid the owners are not in today," I tell them. "Is there something I can assist you with?"

"Possibly." He pulls a business card out of his jacket setting it down on the counter in front of me. The police officer heads over to the coffee area, seemingly uninterested in our conversation.

"There has been a murder across town, at the Midtown motel. We found this in the room where the crime was committed. We hope that you can provide us with any information you may have regarding the victim." He places another item in front of me, a picture of the guy whose space I invaded. "Do you recognize this man?"

I pick up the photo in front of me trying to control the shaking of my hand. "Umm, yes he was here yesterday morning. He asked Frank, the owner of the store, for hotel recommendations. I saw him pick up our card on his way out."

Detective Sharp cocks his head to one side giving me an inquisitive gaze. "Can you tell me anything else about this man? Did he happen to say where he was from? What he was doing in town? Anything you can remember could be of help."

I am certain he is curious about my obvious state of anxiety. "I'm sorry this is just so shocking, a murder here? It doesn't seem possible." I shake my head.

The detective remains silent, patiently waiting for my response to his questions.

I continue, "I recall he had Kansas plates. He did not say why he was in town. I assumed he was here on business. He didn't speak except to ask about the hotel." I lay the photo back down on the counter as I finish my sentence.

"Did this gentleman purchase anything here? We did not find any books in his room, so I am curious why he visited your bookstore."

I glance over to the coffee nook and point. The officer standing there takes a swig out of his cup. He looks up, probably questioning why I am pointing at him. I look back to the detective. "He was sitting over there. He was working on his laptop." I swallow hard as I say the last word.

"Hmmm, interesting, we didn't find a computer in his suite or in his vehicle." He squints down at me with interrogative eyes, wondering if I am telling him the truth. "Are you certain he had a laptop with him?"

I nod my head in confirmation. The air is being sucked out of the room. The officer in uniform comes back to the counter asking how much he owes for the coffee. I tell him it's on the house. He nods his thanks and turns to walk out.

The detective hands me his own business card. "If you think of anything else please let us know Miss?" He pauses waiting for me to give him my name.

"Sarah, Sarah Madrono," I say sucking my bottom lip between my teeth.

He jots it down on a small tablet he retrieved from his jacket. "I'm sure this is an isolated incident but please be cautious of anything that seems out of the normal."

I nod my head again in understanding. In the back of my mind I ask myself if I even know what normal is.

I do my best to get through the rest of the day. I had thought about locking up early to run home and lock myself in my room but that might look suspicious. I realize that I am not the one that the police are looking for, but I can't help thinking I have that man's blood on my hands. I only did a single search and shut out of the browser as it was opening. This is all just a coincidence I tell myself again as I close the store.

I stop at the gas station on the way home. There are two old guys at the pump next to mine, their conversation catches my attention. "I guess it was gruesome," one of them says.

"Ralph told me he was tortured, fingers cut off, blood everywhere. Probably caught up with a drug cartel. He must have really pissed someone off." He half snickers to himself, acting like the man from the hotel got what he deserved.

I cover my mouth with the back of my hand, my lunch suddenly crawling up my esophagus. I click the lever on the pump, not even filling my tank. I do not want to be privy to any more of their conversation.

Somehow I make it home. I am so anxious at this point that my ears have started to ring, I am on the verge of hyperventilating. I throw my bag on the couch and head to my room. I just need a nice hot bath. None of what happened is my fault. It's a coincidence I tell myself for the twentieth time today.

I run the bath tossing in one of my lavender bath bombs to help quell my nerves. I sink into the warm fragrant water and push all thoughts of the stranger out of my mind. Instantly my body reacts. I take a deep breath. Everything is fine.

I close my eyes and focus on what I should make for dinner. I am missing Mrs. Madrono. She was a wonderful cook, me not so much. I'm feeling better as the water cools in the tub. My stomach grumbles signaling me to leave my retreat in search of something to eat.

I tuck the towel in above my chest as I walk down the hallway to the kitchen to turn the oven on to pre-heat. Frozen pizza it is. I head back to my room to dress. My heart stops. On the table is the letter I received two weeks ago from my mother.

It is wrinkled but flattened out as if someone was reading it. They had to have pulled it from the trash. I glance down the hallway. Did the Madronos return? My head tells me it could be them, but my heart tells me a different story.

I quietly make my way into the living room and retrieve my purse from the couch. I fumble in search of the business card the detective gave me earlier today. I'm not sure if he can help me. I have no one else.

I try to enter Detective Sharp's number on my phone, willing my hands to get the numbers right. I feel like I'm in a nightmare. You know the ones where you are trying to dial for help only to keep clicking on all the wrong buttons.

I sense something. Before I can turn a hand slams across me with a cloth covering my nose and mouth. I cannot breathe! There is someone, a large someone behind me like a brick wall. I buck and claw at the hand over my face trying to draw in a breath. A darkness swallows me, the fight within me vanishes.

Chapter Three

Dylan

I'm gripping the phone so tight in my hand I can feel the thin shell bend slightly. "What the fuck do you mean they got another one?"

"I know it's fucked up. I should have put someone on the girl. I didn't think they were here for her. That they would take her. How could I have known, Dylan?"

"Who is she?" I say irritated that Liam couldn't stop them.

"Her name is Sarah Madrono. She is not their usual type. I questioned her two days ago in relation to the murder. She worked at a bookstore that the murder victim had visited."

I run my hand through my hair frustrated. Another girl is victim to these assholes. "So, do you have a location?"

"Not yet, but we do at least have a country now. Venezuela. They are being tracked as we speak. Their risk coming into the states just may help. Unfortunate for her, but for us, this is what we have needed," Liam says. "We are close, we will find your sister, man. We will, I promise."

I hang up the phone without a response. I shouldn't be so hard on him. He has worked harder than anyone besides myself to locate my sister. He busted his ass to get a position within the FBI, hoping that it would gain us more leverage. He loves her too I remind myself.

The guilt I feel for leaving my mother and sister sits like a boulder in the pit of my stomach even though many years have passed. I won't stop until I find her. I must save her. I know it may be too late, but I can't quit until I get answers.

I pull up a map on my phone and zoom in over Venezuela. Eight years is a long time. If we find her alive, she is more than likely dead inside.

I'm putting my trust into the FBI and Liam to handle this one. Every time my guys and I get close to the man behind it all, Oliver Wright, he slips through our fingers. I hope that this time we can end this and annihilate him.

When we got word that some of his men had shown up in the states we thought this may be our last chance to find my sister. Why they were here, we really don't understand. The guy they murdered gave no clues.

My thoughts wander back to the young woman they took. What did Liam tell me her name was? Sandra, no Sarah, Sarah Madrono. They usually get their girls from outside the United States. The poor thing must have caught their attention somehow. My stomach churns as I fear for her. One day just a plain simple Texas girl working in a bookstore and the next…I force the images from my mind of what they might do to her.

My guys and I have found cells of their operation over the years. We took a shit ton of the assholes out. Saved as many girls as we could. Their faces haunt my dreams. At least we were able to have saved some of them.

I looked up the word save once in the dictionary. Save-to keep safe or rescue (someone or something) from harm or danger. We may have freed them, but I knew a few would never truly be saved. They had left their physical bodies too much, drifted too far away from what was happening to them. Many just shells of their former selves.

My sister could be in the same condition when we find her. If we find her. It doesn't matter I tell myself. I will save her. I will pull her up from the depths she has retreated while in the hands of these monsters. "Please hold on Sophia, we are close. Liam and I are getting close," I say under my breath.

Chapter Four

Anna

I'm floating in darkness. Every time I begin to break through I feel the hand and cloth over my face, once again cocooning me within.

Awareness is returning. I am careful not to move, not to let them know I am coming out of the fog. But I cannot control the shaking of my body.

My head is splitting. I cannot move my arms or legs. I am tied down to a hard surface. My wrists forced at my side. Ankles strapped. The most terrifying thing is that I can tell that I am naked. I shudder uncontrollably, I cannot discern whether it is from being cold or sheer terror.

"Boss, she is coming to again. Do you want me to set her up in a cell with one of the other girls? Doc just checked her saying she is clean, still a virgin. He gave her a birth control injection, so she is good to go," a gruff voice says from across the room.

I notice someone move close as I try to process the words I just gathered. I jump as they touch me under my right ear and drift down my jaw, my throat, running between my breasts finally stopping just above my naval. A palm rests there, I can feel the warmth of their skin a contrast to the coolness of mine. I hear a whimper, realizing that it is my own.

"No, I have something special planned for this one. Once she is fully awake bring her to me." His tone sounds silky with a hint of menace behind the words.

The hand glides off my stomach and I pick up the sound of a door opening and then closing. The voice beside me chuckles. "I don't know what you did to piss the boss off little lady. You better put your big girl panties on." He laughs again. "Oh, wait you don't have any panties do you now?" He snorts at his own joke. I do nothing but shake.

I hear the door again. I stall a few minutes making certain I am alone before opening my eyes. I blink at the bright light above me, I am in a small gray room. I'm strapped to an exam table. I lift my head cursing to myself as it pounds its disapproval and glance down at my naked form, not seeing any injuries. The headache must be from what they used to drug me.

I lay my head back down to control the shaking and take a few deep breaths. Tears stream down the sides of my face pooling in my ears. I can't be here. I can't do whatever this is. I fight the urge to call out for help, knowing no one here will save me. I think back to the day I said goodbye to my mother, the fear I saw in her eyes. I want to kick myself for how stupid I have been.

I need to figure out where I am and why I am here. Then I will decide on a plan. I must face the monster, he has me and I have no one to blame but myself.

The silky voice belongs to him. He put his hand on me. I have never been touched by a man like that. In fact, I can count on one hand the number of men who have ever laid a finger on me. None of them touched me the way he did, he was stroking me as if I was a family pet.

A doctor examined me. To the extent of knowing I was a virgin. They gave me an injection all while I was unconscious. The thought of someone touching me while I was unaware causes bile to rise, burning my throat.

I need to keep calm if I have any chance at getting away. My mind spins. The detective, will he be looking for me? Will they put the man that was murdered in the hotel and my disappearance together? You're fooling yourself, Anna. No one is coming, you need to figure this out alone.

The door opens interrupting my thoughts. A large man with shaggy brown hair enters the room. My hands jerk in the restraints a natural desire to cover myself. I turn my face to the wall, tightly closing my eyes not wanting to watch him assault me with his. The guy laughs, I realize that this is Mr. Jokester.

"Come on doll, I know you have been awake. You can't hide in here forever."

I inwardly laugh at this. I have been hiding for nine years and I messed it up by one search. Maybe that was a coincidence, but something tells me it wasn't. I put on my *big girl panties* and I shift to face him. "Hiding, is that what you call this? I'm fucking strapped to a table. I would call that kidnapping," I seethe.

He clicks his tongue. "Girl, I will say this once. You better watch that mouth of yours. Mr. Wright is not someone to mess with."

I turn to stare up at the ceiling. Mr. Wright, the monster has a name now. How ironic his name is Wright. Nothing is right about what is happening, this is all wrong…very wrong.

As the man approaches I try my best to stay still, keeping my eyes trained on the light. He releases my feet from the straps and then moves up to my wrists. As he reaches over to release the last strap he sighs. "Listen and listen close. Do not run, keep your eyes down, mouth shut and do what he tells you. If you do these four little things, no one will hurt you. Up," he orders once I'm free of the restraints.

I sit up immediately and wrap my arms around my chest. He grabs my legs at my knees helping me to turn on the table. He lets me adjust to the upright position for a few seconds then takes me by the elbow to help me off the table.

When my feet hit the floor, I wince at the pain that shoots up my calves. I have no idea how long I was out. It seems like I haven't stood on my own two feet in a very long time.

"You got it?" he asks.

I nod my head thinking how strange it is to have this big burly guy act like he is my nurse maid. He tugs at my arm urging me to take a step towards the door. My feet may as well be cemented to the floor.

"Let's go, doll, no use prolonging the inevitable," he urges.

One foot in front of the other, one foot in front of the other. I take a step and allow him to lead me like a sacrifice. My heart beats faster with each moment. I keep my eyes lowered as we walk just as he instructed. We pass a few men in the halls, no one seems to take an interest in the naked girl being led to slaughter.

He leads me up a set of stairs to a main floor of a house. We must have been in a basement. The air is less humid on this level. We cross through an entryway past a door that might lead to freedom.

He notices my slight hesitation as we pass the door and jerks me tightly close to him. "Don't even think about it." He continues pointing us towards a large beautifully crafted staircase that spirals upwards towards a landing.

We reach the top, then he leads me down another hallway with elaborately carved wooden doors running its length. I haven't been in a home this luxurious since my own as a child. Except this one does not feel cozy like my father's estate. Here I can almost taste and smell fear. My eyes watch the designs in the carpet as we walk. It reminds me of patterns in an adult coloring book. We stop abruptly.

I glance up and see two large doors before me. I peek at the man who brought me here. Staring down at me he quietly whispers, "remember what I told you." He waits for me to acknowledge him.

I slowly shake my head lowering my eyes back down to the floor. He knocks, and I hear the same silky voice from downstairs. "Come in." He opens the doors and gently nudges me from behind into the office. The room is cold. My earlier trembling begins anew.

He pushes me in farther then stops, directing me to sit in a chair facing the front of a large wooden desk. "Here she is, boss, anything else?"

I don't hear a response. Maybe he nodded his answer, I can't tell because I'm focused on my trembling knees. I feel Mr. Jokester leave my side and hear the door close behind me.

I'm alone with the monster, frozen in my seat. I can't look up at him. After a few seconds I realize that I have been holding my breath, I slowly let it out.

I can sense his eyes on me. Unmoving like a large cat waiting to jump on his prey. I try to focus on my breathing keeping my vision locked on my knees. Is he wanting to see what I'll do, if I will run? The more I ponder the more I want to turn and study the door.

It's not that far behind me and he is sitting at his desk, it would take him a second or two to get to me. But, once I make it to the exit there is a brick wall with shaggy brown hair on the other side. Just as I'm almost ready to submit to my urge to flee, the man stands.

He comes towards me slowly. I fight the urge to scamper away as he gets closer. He places a chair directly in front of me and sits. I watch out of my peripheral vision not giving in to the increasing need to make a run for it.

He reaches down, grabbing the leg of my chair, yanking it close to him, forcing my legs to settle between his long ones. The heat radiates off him and seeps into me. It does nothing to stop the invading tremors. My stomach hurts from the constant racking of my body.

Reaching out he grabs my wrists and drags my arms away from my breasts. I watch his hands as they guide mine to rest in my lap. He has fair skin and long fingers, reminding me of talons on a bird of prey. My shaking intensifies.

We sit for what seems like hours, but reality is it is mere seconds. My mind races, fretting over what this man wants from me. Finally, he speaks. "Are you cold?" His words slither up my spine resembling a snake coiling up a pole.

I open my mouth to respond, but nothing comes out. The shaking still wracks me to my core. He reaches out placing his hand under my chin and gently forces my face up towards him. I keep my eyes lowered.

"Look at me," he commands in a stern voice.

I had spent years imagining the monster hunting me. My mind always conjured up an ugly fowl creature. The mirage in front of me is that of an angel. He has short dark hair, cut to style as I would imagine most wall street businessmen would, chiseled features with sharp lines along his jaw, cheekbones and nose. His pale skin and blue eyes make him appear gentle.

I quickly drag my eyes away, frightened by the way he looked at me. He dove clear down into the depths of my soul. He wants to destroy me. I can feel it. His mannerisms are laced with tenderness all the while emitting a quiet violence.

He laughs. "What is your name?"

I know he knows my name just as surely as he knows his own. He knows everything about me. I am certain. I respond in barely a whisper, "Sarah."

I can't be Anna right now. This cannot be happening to Anna. I must remain as Sarah if I am to survive whatever this is.

He laughs louder this time. "Kitten," he purrs. "We need to establish something here. I know everything. More than even you do, I am sure. I can give you the answers you seek but make no mistake, I will not tolerate you lying. You realize that I already know so why don't you tell me?" he coaxes.

The shaking is so bad now that my teeth are chattering. I swear it must be thirty degrees in here. I can't be Anna. I won't let him hurt Anna. "My name is Sarah."

He stands and slowly lays his hand on the top of my head. He is going to kill me. I don't wish to die but I can't do this. I want to go back to my life on the ranch. Tears threaten to spill now. I should just tell him, he already knows.

He yells out loud, spurring me jump. "Brian!" The door opens and then the man standing before me says two words. "Punish her."

"How do you want me to do it?" Brian aka Mr. Jokester asks nonchalantly as if he were asking him how he would like his coffee.

"I trust your expertise in this matter as long as she realizes that she should never defy me again." He takes his hand off my head and gently cups my cheek for a brief second before walking back to sit down at his desk.

Brian comes forward. I jump up and rush towards Mr. Wright. "Please, I'll tell you." I am full out crying now. I place my hands on his desk begging for him to look at me, his attention on the papers in front of him. "Please."

Brian's large hands grab my arms hurting me as he forces them behind my back, he shoves me towards the door. I scream craning my head back to look at Mr. Wright. "Please, my name is Anna. My name is Anna," I cry out as Brian pushes me past the threshold closing the door.

"You should have listened, doll face," he says in my ear.

I should have. I don't know what Brian has in store for me. Whatever it is, it can't be good.

He takes me into a room a few doors down, one with the elaborate wood carvings on them. He opens it driving me inside past the bedroom furnishings into an attached bathroom. I wriggle in his hold, but it is nothing to him. I am small prey. He releases me and reaches down to turn the water on in the tub. I try shoving my way past him, but it is useless. He is literally like a wall, towering over my petite five, five. He could break me in half if he chose.

"In," he says as he shuts off the faucet. He smiles at me menacingly, showing me a glittering gold tooth. I guess someone could consider him handsome if he wasn't so damn frightening. "In," he grates out again.

I cautiously step into the tub and sit down. Water comes up slightly over my ribs. Brian licks his lips as he stares at my breasts. Self-consciously I cover them with my arms. Then just as quickly as lightning strikes he reaches out, pushing me back, submerging my entire head under. I grasp for the hands that are pressing me down, kicking my feet, raising my hips, spraying water all over the bathroom.

He pulls me up, allowing me to catch my breath. Before I can utter a word of protest, he pushes me down again. I fight with all my might. He is killing me. I am going to die. I am going to die with no answers.

Brian repeats this over and over just letting me up long enough to gulp in a few breaths. My mind wanders. A peace comes over me maybe from the lack of oxygen, I don't know. Is this how Sarah felt right before she died.

I see her now. She waves from the side of the beach. "Anna," she says excitedly. "Let's build a sandcastle." Her eyes that of a ten-year-old squint in the bright sunlight. I walk over and sit down next to her in the warm sand. "Help me finish the castle," Sarah says in a soothing voice, placing a hand over mine. "Don't worry it will be over soon."

Chapter Five

Anna

I feel someone smacking the side of my face. I don't want to go. It's so nice here on the beach with Sarah. I have missed my friend. Whoever it is insists that I leave my haven. I hear her say as her voice fades, "you're okay I will be here when you return." And then I am choking, spitting water as gruff hands pound on my back.

Brian laughs as I peer up at him, wet hair plasters my face. "We done here?" he asks. Like I have a say in the matter. He gets up when I don't answer leaving me alone.

I pull my legs up and hug them. I have a choice I realize. I can fight, or I can submit. Two choices, one will give me pain and suffering, one may lead to answers.

I'm not sure if I am supposed to stay put. The water is so cold. The insistent chatter of my teeth begins again. I rest my forehead on my knees. How did I end up here? I try not to let my mind wander to what they will do. They gave me a birth control injection, the implications of that I cannot deny. A voice startles me from my thoughts. I look up seeing Mr. Wright lean against the doorframe of the bathroom.

"What is your name?" he asks gently as he walks towards me and crouches down beside the tub.

"Anna," I say barely audible to even my own ears. I stare at the water trying to decide if I am happy that I lived through the violence that just happened.

He brushes the wet hair off my face. "Good girl," he says as he reaches to help me out. He takes my hand and leads me back to the double doors. I'm leaving footprint marks in the patterned carpet. He doesn't seem to care that I am dripping all over the expensive softness.

We go straight through the room he initially interrogated me in, to another. It is large with a big four-poster bed in the middle. The windows are covered in rich burgundy colored curtains, matching the coverlet.

He guides me to the attached bathroom. I stop at the threshold. Is he going to torture me again? I'm so tired, I won't be able to take much more.

"No one will hurt you in here."

I think about it for a moment. He doesn't seem like a man who does his own dirty work, nor does he want it done in his presence. Yes, I am safer here, in what I assume is his space, than anywhere else in this house.

He walks over to the shower and turns on the water. "Here this will help you warm up," he says.

I accept his offer, not fully understanding why he is being so nice. At this point I don't care. I am cold. I need to stop the shaking. The muscles in my stomach clench tightly at the onslaught of the never-ending chills.

I step in as he shuts the door behind me. "Everything you need should be in there. Take your time. I will see about getting you something to eat. Are you hungry?"

I stare at him through the glass and nod slightly. He nods in return. I watch hesitantly as he leaves, breathing a sigh of relief as the latch clicks shut, thankful that he has left me to shower alone.

I stand under the spray of water to soak up the warmth. Tears stream down my face. So much has happened in the last few weeks to bring me to this moment. He said he would give me answers. That is all I have ever wanted. They will come at a price, a price I'm not sure I am willing to pay.

I finish washing my hair and body, appreciative of the fact that the shaking has subsided. I shut the water off and step out of the shower, grabbing a towel hanging nearby. Am I supposed to wait for him to return? I do not want to let myself get chilled again. I wrap the overly large cloth around myself reveling in its softness. I open the door to peek out.

Mr. Wright is setting a plate down at the small desk set off to the side of the room near the windows. He looks up and smiles at me. He is a beautiful man, tall and slender. If I had to guess I would say he is in his early thirties, possibly older it's hard to tell as his skin is flawless. He is dressed in dark-colored dress pants, a crisp white button up with the sleeves rolled up and the top several buttons undone.

"Anna, come relax and eat. It's not much the cooks have all retired for the evening. I did manage to find someone to wrestle you up a sandwich." He makes a grand gesture ushering me towards the table.

After I sit he pushes the chair in closer as if he were my date and we were eating at a fine restaurant. My eyes drop down to the meal before me, my stomach chooses to growl at that moment. I look up hesitantly at him.

"Go ahead, I didn't poison it I promise." He gestures with his hand drawing an x across his chest as he speaks. He leaves me to eat and sits on the edge of the bed.

I pick up the sandwich devouring it in four bites. I don't care what this man thinks of my appetite. I'm a little beyond that point. I try to remember my last meal and stop mid chew to worry over whether someone shut my oven off at the ranch. How silly, none of that matters now. I gulp down the water and set the glass back down on the desk. I don't take my hand off it. I tap the side of the glass lightly with my index finger. Mr. Wright reads my mind.

"Anna, I don't think you are the type of girl to take someone's hospitality and throw it in their face," he says. He looks the least bit worried that I will throttle the glass towards his head.

I turn to glare at him. I slowly remove my hand from the glass. "Thank you for the shower and delicious meal," I say in my sweetest voice.

"You're most welcome," he replies, ignoring my sarcasm.

He leans over and opens a drawer in the table next to his bed. I watch him intently, half expecting to see him pull out a gun. He retrieves a brush and something else. He stands walking towards me and I quickly turn myself away from him.

He pauses behind me then reaches around my shoulder, pushing the plate and glass back. Then he places a small case directly in front of me on the desk. I stare at it as if it is a snake ready to strike. It is a contact lens case.

I feel him gather my hair into his hands as he runs the brush through my dark long locks. He is gentle, holding it tight, so it does not pull at my scalp. I know what he is asking of me. He is stripping me of Sarah, leaving me with no place to hide.

I reach for the case slowly opening each side, left and right. I raise my hands to my eyes, carefully removing each dark lens and place them in the liquid filled little cups. I screw the lids on tightly. At least I don't have to pretend anymore.

He wants Anna. A small part of me warms. No one has wanted me to be her for a long time. Nine years to be exact. I scold myself. This man kidnapped me, stripped me and had me punished. He runs his hand down my hair and I lean into his touch. I can't allow myself to be lulled by him. I'm so tired I can hardly keep my eyes open.

The warm fuzzy thoughts are shattered as quickly as they creep into my mind as he whispers into my ear. "You are being such a good little kitten, if you learn to keep your claws in maybe we won't hurt you so much. What do you think?"

He sets the brush down and pulls my chair out instructing me to stand in front of him. He tilts my chin up forcing me to meet his gaze and strokes my cheek with his thumb. "There you are. No more hiding from me and no more hiding those magnificent blue eyes. I have been looking for you for a long time, do you know that? You are about to make me a rich man, well a richer man that is." He winks and releases me to take a small step back.

"Brian found you a room with the other girls. We should head down there so you can rest."

Thank god, he is not expecting me to sleep in here with him. But, it confuses me. I still don't know his intentions. He thinks I will make him money. Maybe he is going to hold me for ransom or worse than that he plans on selling me. Everything inside me screams he is in the sex trafficking industry. How does this relate to my father's business? Was he…

I don't have time to ponder this thought as he suddenly pulls the towel away from me. His eyes roam over my body. I feel the blood rush to my cheeks. He lets out a long breath. "Beautiful, you look just like your mother."

My heart stops. I watch the enjoyment on his face at my shock of hearing him compare me to my mom.

"Let's go, you will be sharing a cell with someone. I am sure she is going to be excited to see you."

My mind runs wild as he drags me through the house, downstairs to the lowest level, past the exam room. I am shocked silent. A bubble of excitement enters my veins at the thought of seeing my mother again. This is why she didn't come for me. She was being held prisoner.

He stops at a door and pulls a set of keys out of his pocket, slowly he reaches out to slide the selected one into the lock. When it is inserted all the way in he turns to smile at me. Turning the key, he pushes the door open. It is dark in the room. He reaches around the frame to flick a switch. A bright light comes on in the center of the ceiling illuminating the tiny cell. There is a twin-sized bed, a bedside table and a toilet.

He steps inside the cell. I follow behind him eager to see my mom. Instead, I spy a petite young woman curled up naked in the corner of the cement room near the foot of the bed. Mr. Wright crouches down in front of her. He touches the top of her head much the same way he had done to mine earlier, saying, "sweetheart, I brought you a friend." The girl looks up at him. It's not my mother, but it is a face from my past.

"Sophia?" I ask, shaking my head in disbelief. She appears thinner than I recall. The expression in her eyes when she sees me will haunt me forever. It is a mixture of sadness and horror.

Mr. Wright stands and pulls Sophia to her feet. He turns with a smile. "You remember," he exclaims. "Good, then there is no need for awkward introductions. Sophia, you recognize your little ward Anna don't you?"

"Yes, sir," she replies emptily.

He clasps his long fingers together in front of him before saying, "my work here is done. I'll leave the two of you to become reacquainted." He walks out into the hallway leaving us standing in the tiny room. Before he closes the door he says, "I would get some sleep tonight Anna, tomorrow will be another fun filled day." I hear the clang of keys as he locks us inside.

I rush to Sophia and reach out for her. She stands still, flinching slightly as I near. I slow my movements down, taking in the marks, bruises and the dark circles under her eyes. I wrap my arms around her ignoring the fact we are both naked. She seems shorter than I remember. I think to myself that it is not that she has gotten smaller. It is I that has grown.

I hold Sophia like this for a long time until I hear a tiny sob escape her. I pull back to look at her, I walk her over to the bed. She gets in lying down and curls up to face the wall. I shut the light off then get in the bed beside her pulling the thin blanket over the both of us. I draw her into my embrace. I feel her sobs coming stronger and faster now. I cradle her in my arms. What can I say to ease her pain? I see from her body she has endured far more than I have, guilt washes over me, this is my fault.

I want to ask her a million questions. I can't bring myself to speak. I let her cry, this isn't about me, it's about her. After a while her sobs subside. She whispers in the dark, "I'm so sorry, Anna."

I don't ask her to explain. What could she possibly be sorry for? I decide that it is an apology for the situation we are in and leave it at that. My eyes are so heavy I could not respond even if I tried. After everything that has happened my body is forcing a shutdown. I drift to sleep comforted by the warmth of my nanny Sophia beside me.

Chapter Six

Dylan

I cram the last of my shit into my suitcase fighting the urge to turn around and punch Liam right in the face. I'll be damned if he thinks I am staying away.

"Dylan, you know I can't allow you to fly to Venezuela."

He tries to reach over to take my bag away from me. I knock his arm and shake my head. "Fuck you. I promise I will stay back and let your team go in, but I need to be there when you get her out."

Liam sits down on the edge of the bed. "You realize she might not be there," he breathes.

"Do you think I don't fucking understand that?" I growl.

"I can't let you leave. Wright and his men know who you are. They know what you look like, they have eyes everywhere. If one of them spots you, they will be gone without a trace again."

I stop. He is right. When he showed up here in Dallas with news they had a location, I couldn't get my shit together fast enough. I sit down on the other side of my bag flopping myself back onto the bed to stare at the ceiling. Defeated. Liam has always been the voice of reason.

"We are finishing up the last of the logistics. We should be ready to move in soon. We are shooting for two weeks. Any longer and we risk them moving."

"You're certain Wright is there?"

"Yep," he replies as he rises. "We have a plane ready to bring Sophia and any other girls we find back here. I also have Dallas Memorial on standby letting them know what they might encounter."

I mull over what he says.

"I see it's tough for you to sit this one out but there is no other alternative. Once we have the fucks in custody, then…well you and the boys will think of a way to get to them. Let's just find her first, then we can deal with them later."

"Oh, I will get to that motherfucker even if he is in prison. When I do, he will pay," I grit out.

"I know you will, brother. Tell the guys what I told you and stay the fuck put. I got to go. I'll call as soon as I locate her."

I watch him turn to walk out. He will find her. He loves my sister. Loves her so much that he has been carrying around a goddamn engagement ring in his pocket for the last few years. I helped him pick it out one day. We thought we were close then too. We lost them. We've failed more times than I care to admit.

We are all ruthless killers. Liam used to be a part of the team until deciding to give the FBI a try. Dustin, Mark, Anthony and I have all done unsettling things to get to these fuckers. Well unsettling to most civilized human beings, to us it is just another day at the office.

I sit up and pull my crap back out of my bag. I want to say fuck it and get on a plane. I can't, Liam is one hundred percent correct. If any of Oliver Wright's men see me they will know I am there for them. I have been hunting and killing his men for the last eight years. In the beginning it was not Oliver that led the scum sucking traffickers, but a man named William Ramirez.

I hate Ramirez just as much. I have learned that he had health issues. No one has seen nor heard from him. I hope he is dead. Before he disappeared off the face of the earth, he passed his business dealings down to Wright. Wright is the one who ordered the massacre at the Velasquez estate.

Mr. Velasquez was a private investigator who worked to find girls that had been kidnapped or somehow ended up in the sex trafficking world. He was the best in the field and made himself a great fortune. He put a large target on his back in doing so. He saved my mother from Ramirez. He also saved my mom's friend Annette Velasquez. Annette ended up marrying Mr. Velasquez, it was quite the love story. But they are all gone, killed in the massacre.

The guilt over my mother's death sits hard on me, crushing my soul. No one knows why Wright came with such vengeance. The theory is that he was trying to impress his predecessor by taking out the man that had caused so many headaches for them. Wright took the young girls from the estate that day, my sister included. I have been working to find her ever since then.

Mr. Velasquez was like a father to me, to all of us. We were all in the states when the attack came. He was providing the best training money could buy so we could work for him. My mother was so proud of me the day I left. I was eighteen. She was happy with the man I was becoming under Manuel's tutelage.

Sophia was seventeen when I left. She was a year younger than me. She had also worked for the Velasquez's as a nanny for their daughter. She loved the job so much. I can picture her pushing the little girl on the tire swing, both laughing happily in the sun. Sadly, the girl died the year before I left for training in a drowning accident at a small pond on the property.

It shook everyone. Mrs. Velasquez had been entertaining friends of hers and each of their two daughters snuck away to the lake to swim. Sophia was off that day, running errands in town. I remember Annette coming frantic asking me to go find my mother for her.

After, the funeral my sister briefly went with the couple who had been visiting back to the states to help with their daughter. I guess the girl was so shook up due to watching her friend drown that they wanted her to have someone to turn to until the grief eased. Anyhow, she returned a few weeks later. She didn't like to talk about any of it. She mourned for Anna. Her and the dark-haired little girl had become friends despite their age difference of six years.

I shove my clothes in a drawer. So much has changed since then. If only we could all go back to the early days on the estate. Mr. Velasquez had me listed as a benefactor. No other living relatives left. I am now the reluctant owner. I can't bring myself to return. Someday. Maybe when we get Sophia, I can take her home and try to glue all her pieces together.

The guys are whooping and hollering in the kitchen, back from their shopping trip to the store for beer and steaks. I need to fill them in. We need to be ready when shit hits the fan. I smile thinking of the many ways I will tear the bastard, Oliver Wright, to shreds with my bare hands.

Chapter Seven

Anna

I wake up to Sophia shaking me fiercely. As soon as my eyes open, she is pulling me to the ground beside her. I slide down hearing keys clang together. She tells me to keep my hands behind my back and my head down. My brain doesn't even have time to comprehend what is going on as the door opens sending a bright light skittering across the floor of our tiny cell. Black boots enter my vision and stop in front of Sophia.

"Good morning ladies," the man with the boots says. He has an English accent. "Sophia, I see you have a new friend."

The sound of a zipper grates over my ears. "You know what to do, baby, aww yeah just like that." His accent rains down over Sophia as she gags. I know what is happening next to me. I may have never been with a man this way, but I am not stupid. Tears creep down my cheeks. Somehow I need to get her out of here. This is all my fault.

The man takes notice of my tears. He laughs lightly. "Honey there is plenty to go around, don't worry I will let you have a taste too." Before I can leap up and run, he fists a handful of my hair shoving his cock into my mouth. "Don't bite," he says through gritted teeth. I try to turn my head away, but he has my hair pulled so tightly I can't move as he pumps in and out.

"What the fuck," a man bellows. The asshole let's go of me abruptly making me fall backwards onto my ass. I peek up to see Brian standing in the doorway. "You stupid son of a bitch. This is Wright's girl."

"I'm sorry boss, I didn't know."

I glance at the guy. He looks like a punk rocker from the eighties. He has spikey blond hair and black eyeliner highlights his shocked eyes. I can see that he is afraid. He knows Mr. Wright will hear about his poor judgment.

Brian steps close to him towering over the man. "The hell if you didn't you jack-hole. You were all given specific instructions not to touch this one," he yells and points down at me.

"I'm sorry, she looked so innocent with the tears and all. I wanted to let her in on the fun. I would have pulled out." He tries to leave but Brian grabs his arm. "Anna, follow me, Sophia go down to breakfast with the other girls."

I hesitate but Sophia shoots me a pleading expression and pushes me out behind them. I agree but all I want to do is throw up. I wish I could curl up in a ball on the bed and pretend none of this is happening.

I follow Brian through the house, making note not to stare at the door to the outside world as we pass by this time. He is angry. I do not want that anger directed at me, not after what he did yesterday.

He knocks like the previous day. "Come in." Mr. Wright stands as we enter, I can tell he was not expecting us to come with punk rocker in tow. "We had an incident boss."

I purposely hide behind Brian. Mr. Wright might blame me for what took place. I know Brian is mad at the punk and not me. What if Mr. Wright doesn't see it that way? The man who assaulted me keeps his head down.

Mr. Wright passes by Brian and holds his hand out to me. I reluctantly take it. He pulls me around to face Brian and Mr. Punk Rock. "What happened?"

Brian looks at the punk to respond. When he doesn't, he hits him in the back of the head with a thud. My assailant spills, pleading his case. Mr. Wright grips my hand tighter with each word that comes out of his mouth. I wince and must make a whimper of protest because he lets go only to wrap his arm possessively around my waist.

The punk finishes with, "I am so sorry Mr. Wright. I don't know what came over me. She is just so…"

Before he can finish his sentence and before I have time to process what is happening, Mr. Wright reaches behind him. He pulls out a handgun from the back of his waistband. He aims it directly at Mr. Punk Rock and pulls the trigger, putting a bullet right between his eyes.

I scream as blood sprays. I turn to run from the gruesome scene before me, but he catches me around the waist and pulls me close to him. He picks me up off my feet hauling me into the bathroom and into the shower.

He reaches out to twist on the faucet. I watch as bright red mixes with the water swirling over the stone tile floor. He removes his clothing and tosses them into a pile outside the door. I must be in shock because I don't move. I stand as still as a statue. He washes my body running his hands over me then turns to wash the blood off himself.

I glance up at him as he closes his eyes to rinse the soap out of his hair. The old saying devil in disguise enters my mind as I study his angelic like features. I'm numb. I don't know what I should think. One day he orders Brian to punish me, the next he is putting a bullet in a man's skull for touching me.

How many people have died because of me? The man in the motel, the punk rocker. Who else has suffered at the hands of this man? Something tells me he has hurt many lives to get to me. And then there is Sophia, she is nothing but a shell of her former self. This is all my fault. All of it. Why does this man want me so bad?

The steam from the shower is closing in on me. I feel as if someone is sitting on my chest. The weight of everything weighs heavily upon me. I can't seem to draw in enough air. I see stars and they send Mr. Wright to a blur in the distance.

His strong arms wrap around me as he picks me up and removes me from the shower, setting me on my feet. I reach out to him to steady myself as he quickly dries me off. He is carrying me somewhere else now. Oh shit. He is taking me to his bed.

My senses come rushing back as I try to sit up. No. I am not ready for this. He sits on the edge and pushes me down. He has a hold of my arm. He is shushing me, telling me that I will be okay. "Breathe in and out, kitten. Slowly. Everything is going to be fine. No one will hurt you."

He wraps something tight around my arm and before I can ask him what he is doing, I feel a stick. I look down to see him inject a needle into my vein. Immediately I sense a warm fuzzy sensation that starts at the top of my head and slides down until it reaches my toes. My body appears relaxed, but my mind…my mind is crying out.

"There you go, breathe in an out. Good girl. I'm sorry, I am not a man of patience, I should have waited to kill him but...did he hurt you, kitten?"

I wish he would stop calling me that. I am not his damn pet. I hate him. I want to return to my cell, to get away from him. When I don't respond he stands up, I watch him go to his closet to retrieve some dry clothes. He watches me watching him. He pulls on his boxers and tosses something at me. It lands at my feet. I slowly sit up. It is a blue sundress, the same color as my eyes.

"Do you need me to help you?" he questions. I sense an undercurrent of excitement in his voice.

I stay sitting on the bed and pull the dress over my head. My movements are slow, my limbs seem heavier than they should. Having clothing makes me feel somewhat better, but whatever drug he has given me has taken full effect. My mind wanders to a place far from here.

If I listen closely, I can hear her humming. It is comforting knowing she is waiting for me on the other side of consciousness.

I want to slip away to her, but Mr. Wright crawls up on the bed behind me to brush my hair. I can't protest, I sit there silent. "I have a surprise for you today, kitten." I shiver at his words. I do not need any more surprises. Watching a man die before my eyes, his blood spraying over me is enough for one day.

He finishes with a kiss to the top of my head. Before I can process what is going on, he drops to a knee in front of me. He opens a small box with a diamond ring inside. He grabs my hand and slips it on my wedding finger. I stare at it. It is heavy upon my hand. I raise my eyes to him.

"Soon you will be mine. No one will look at you let alone touch you unless they have my permission." He is holding my hand running his thumb back and forth over the top as he speaks, a frightening smile slowly spreads across his face.

I want to pull away, but I don't. None of this seems real. I am floating, watching this all happen to someone else. Is he proposing? No, this isn't a proposal this is, well I'm not sure what the fuck this is. He killed a man before my eyes. Now he is slipping an engagement ring on my finger. I shake my head to clear my thoughts.

"I have another present for you." He stands retrieving a book wrapped in a beautiful red bow with an engraved pen attached to the top. The writing on it is my name, Anna, written in delicate calligraphy. "Sophia told me you like to write poetry, consider it an early wedding gift. Something to fill your time."

I take the book from him. "Why?" I don't know what else to say. I am floating like a helium balloon in a windstorm, threating to break free never to be seen again. The only thing that anchors me to the ground is the constant hold he has on me.

"You will understand shortly, kitten. We have a special guest coming for lunch today. He should arrive soon." He kisses my hand and urges me to lie back down. "Sleep for a little while and I will come get you when he arrives."

My eyes are heavy, I am confused, nothing makes any sense. Why would this strange man want to marry me? My thoughts come fragmented now. He kidnapped me…he knows things about me that no one else does…he has Sophia…he thinks I resemble my mother…"

"Anna." Sarah's voice is calling me. I think I should stay and figure out this puzzle, but she is giggling. I can't help myself. I need to go find out what she is doing. "Look, I found a toad. Come help me catch him." I follow her running, splashing along the edge of the lake.

Chapter Eight

Anna

"Anna. Anna, it's time to wake. Come now, our special guest has arrived." Mr. Wright is standing above me gently shaking my arms.

"What? Where am I?" My mind is so foggy that I panic.

"Kitten, everything is fine. You are here with me right where you should be." He sits on the side of the bed and helps me to a sitting position. "Why don't you freshen up. I left a toothbrush and other items for you in on the counter. Make yourself pretty, hmm." He pulls me up patting me on the backside as he ushers me to the bathroom.

I stand looking in the mirror. I was right the dress he gave me matches my eyes. I look tired, my pupils are dilated. This has been a roller coaster ride from hell and it's not over. In fact, it has just begun. I brush my teeth trying to eliminate all traces of Mr. Punk Rock. I brush so hard that I make my gums bleed. Gaging I spit into the sink.

I splash cold water over my face as I struggle to control the waves of nausea that have come over me. I hear a knock on the door. It opens without even giving me enough time to respond. It is him.

"Everything okay?" His eyes meet mine in the mirror. I shake my head yes.

"I would prefer that when I speak to you from now on that you answer me with words." I see the threat in his gaze.

I lower my eyes and then force them back up to his and say, "yes, Mr. Wright. I am fine."

"Oliver, you can call me Oliver. I only allow the others to use sir. But you, you are special and if we are to be married, it is fair to let you call me by my name." He moves behind me and brushes my hair to the side to place a feather-light kiss at the nape of my neck.

He watches in the mirror for my reaction. A single tear slips down my cheek. He reaches around and whisks it away with his thumb as he smiles at me. He seems to get pleasure from my discomfort.

"Let's go shall we, it would be rude to keep our guest waiting." He takes my elbow and picks up the book he gifted me then leads me down to a dining room.

The room is painted the color of a crisp blue sky. All the furniture is a rich wood or white. It is bright and cheerful with four large floor to ceiling windows on one end. There is a long table in the center. I can see that someone set it for three guests.

He pulls a chair out for me then places the book and a small box of tissues beside me on the table. "You might need these, this will be a special reunion, kitten. If you excuse me, I'll be right back." He kisses the top of my head and leaves the room.

I glance around wondering to myself who this guest could be. He is toying with me. I am learning that he loves the game of keeping me in the dark, leading me to think one thing while presenting me with another.

I feel void. I don't even care what is about to happen. It could be the drugs I don't know. I'm hungry and nauseous. There is water on the table. I take a drink savoring the coolness as it runs down my throat. I need to keep my shit together, so he doesn't drug me again. I need a clear mind if I am going to get Sophia and I out of here.

I hear voices and swivel to see Oliver help an older gentleman to the dining room. "Anna, come I have someone I would like to introduce to you."

I rise accessing the older man as I do. He is not as tall as Oliver, but he is slouched slightly so maybe he isn't that much shorter. He has a dark complexion and eyes black as night. The same feeling comes over me as when I first met Oliver. This man is ill, but I imagine in his glory days he was just as ruthless as the younger version next to him.

Before Oliver can introduce me, the older gentleman stops and looks at me as if he has seen a ghost. "Annette?"

I halt mid step towards them. He called me by my mother's name.

Oliver gently urges him closer. "She looks a lot like Annette does she not?" He cocks his head to one side questioning the old man. "Remember, I told you I found your daughter? This is Anna."

Wait. What did he say? I back away until my butt hits the table stopping me from any further retreat. The older man gets a renewed sense of energy and rushes forward wrapping me in a giant bear hug. I can't move. I don't return the embrace leaving my arms hanging at my side. I watch over his shoulder, wishing I could slap the smugness off Oliver's face. That or stick a knife in his chest, either would make me happy at this moment.

The man pulls back and his eyes roam over my face. He is unrecognizable. How can I be his daughter? I didn't hear Oliver right. I am drowning in the blackness of the old man's scrutiny. He draws me into another tight embrace before finally letting me go.

I slump into my chair. I'm done. I am literally fucking done with this shit. Fuck Oliver, fuck whoever the fuck this is, fuck all of it. Oliver helps him to the place setting across from me and then takes his seat at the head of the table. He reaches over to grab hold of my hand.

I peer up at him. He smiles at me before turning to the other man. "William, she is just as beautiful as her mother is she not?"

"Even more so, her dark skin compliments her eyes. She has her mother's eyes you know?" He pulls something out of his jacket pocket and hands it to Oliver. Oliver takes it holding it up to the side of my face comparing. I realize it is a photo. "Amazing," he says as he passes it to me.

I accept the photo with trembling hands. It is a photograph of my mom. Tears sting the corner of my eyes. Oliver pushes the tissues closer. I glare at him, defiant, refusing to take anything he offers me.

"William is your father, kitten. I'm not sure if your mother ever told you." He knows damn well that this all comes at a shock. "She ran away from him when she was pregnant with you. He has been searching for you ever since." He speaks the words like he harbors intimate feelings for me, as if we were not complete strangers. "When he became ill, I took over running his business and his search for you."

"Oliver, I don't know how I can repay you. You have been so loyal. After I got sick, I thought I would never get to lay eyes on my child," my new father says reaching for the box of tissues.

"Well, now that you mention it Anna and I have grown fond of each other." He flashes me a smile and a wink. "I would like to ask you for her hand in marriage." He pulls my arm across the table so that William can observe the huge rock on my finger.

The man claps his hands. "My dear boy, yes! This is perfect." He pauses as he places his hand on his chest, a small flash of pain quickly passes over his face. "You will get married soon will you not? I would love to walk Anna down the aisle. Who knows how much time I have left." His obvious anguish does not hinder the excitement in his eyes.

A woman comes out from a swinging door dressed in a black and white maid uniform. I watch silently as she places a beautifully arranged plate in front of each of us. My earlier hunger has vanished. My mind reels from all I learned. My whole life has been a lie. As I slowly put the pieces of the puzzle together I realize that I am the daughter of a sex trafficker.

I can feel the blood pump in my temples. The man I thought was to blame for my situation was not the reason for me having to hide at all. William is the reason my mother sent me away. The one responsible for me having to live as Sarah for the past nine years. He is the monster. It is his business that my mom was trying to protect me from.

"Anna, I know all of this comes as a shock to you, kitten, but you need to eat." I stare down at my plate. Oliver squeezes my hand painfully as a warning before letting it go. I pick up my fork and take a bite, forcing myself to chew and swallow.

"I cannot tell you how happy your daughter has made me and yes, we will get married soon. I would not want you to miss it. I was thinking next week. What do you think, Anna?" He leans over and gives me a peck on the cheek.

I don't answer. He has already decided. I have no say in any of this so instead I look at the man who is now my father and ask in a quiet voice, "William? Would it be okay if I kept this picture?"

He looks at me, I can see he is happy. The thought should warm me, but it doesn't. I know he is evil. He admittedly had my mother against her will. They said she had run away. "Sweetheart, anything for my daughter and call me Dad, honey."

I place the photo inside the front cover of the book that Oliver gave me and ignore my new father's endearments. I decide in this moment I will do whatever it takes to get away before this wedding happens even if that means I do not make it out alive. My mother found the courage to run and so will I.

"Thank you," I say as I force myself to offer him a small smile.

Oliver drops his napkin in his lap and leans back in his chair. I can sense that he reads my mind. I do not look at him as I pick up my fork and continue eating. One foot in front of the other as a plan slowly unfolds.

Chapter Nine

Anna

Oliver keeps me close to him during the daytime hours for the next few weeks. He knows I am planning my escape. He does however still let me go downstairs to sleep with Sophia which makes me happy. She doesn't ever say anything, I hold her and let her cry each night.

I don't see William, my father, much. When Oliver demands, I visit him in his room. We don't speak. He just stares at me, maybe making a brief comment about how I look like my mother. The last few days I haven't had to sit through the awkwardness thankfully, his health taking a turn for the worst. As cruel as it sounds that makes me happy too.

I remain quiet through all of Oliver's meetings and business dealings. I pretend not to listen all the while writing feverishly in the notebook he gifted me. He reads through it at the end of each day before releasing me to the tiny cell.

"You are talented." He peers up over the leather-bound book at me.

"Thank you," I reply. If only he knew how talented of a writer, I really am. I smile as he hands me back my musings and turns to pour himself a drink.

"I set the wedding for Saturday." He studies me over his shoulder, fishing for a reaction.

Two days. Two days is all I have left. I wish I could take them all with me but right now I need to focus on getting Sophia and I out. I won't forget the others. There are many. Oliver has girls not just here but in several countries. I listen as he is on the phone arranging buyers for them, planning auctions with what I assume are very wealthy and powerful men. The names familiar to me.

I nervously eye him. "Saturday?" I lick my lips as my mouth turns dry at the prospect of marrying this man. I stare at the book in my hand. I have one last thought. I need to know something before I enact my plan. "After I marry you will you allow Sophia to leave?" I ask meekly.

He pulls up a chair in front of me and sets his drink down on the desk. He reaches out taking a strand of my hair twirling it between his fingers. "If I agree to let her go would you come to me freely?" he asks.

I swallow hard, shaking my head yes. My original plan is to run, but it is dangerous. I don't know if Sophia is well enough in her mind to go along with me. I hate to risk her life so if I am able to spare her I will. It is the least I can do considering she is in this situation because of me.

He clicks his tongue. "Words Anna, remember your words."

"Yes," I say. Somehow this day is taking an unexpected turn. I am not sure I can finish what I started.

"Show me."

I freeze. I wasn't expecting him to react this way. I assumed he would just give me a simple answer. He hasn't touched me the last few weeks, busy ensuring my father's lawyers had changed his will. William is leaving everything to my new husband and me.

He has made it very clear my nights with Sophia will end once we are married. Ironic that a sex trafficker has been waiting to sleep with me until our wedding night. He likes to toy with me. I suspect he gets great pleasure watching my nervousness over the whole situation.

He laughs and is about to get up calling my bluff when I reach out and place my hand on his leg.

He stills and looks at me lustfully. I can do this. If he will let her go, then I must do this for Sophia. He pulls me into his lap and takes my mouth so forcefully his teeth graze across my lips. I taste the metallic flavor of blood mixing with his gin and tonic. His hand glides up my thigh under the sundress I am wearing. I close my eyes tightly as he reaches my most intimate spot.

He nuzzles the side of my neck all the while keeping his palm stilled on me. I tremble. No one has ever touched me there. I was not prepared for this. I hear Sarah's familiar voice calling me back to the lake. I can do this. I will run and hide with Sarah until this is over.

His lips deliver light kisses along my throat then he whispers in my ear, "Kitten, do you think I am a fool." His finger slips slightly into me. I plead with my body to stop shaking and brace myself for his violation. Abruptly he dumps me off his lap onto the hard floor.

I land with a thud my dress coming up in a very unladylike manner. He tilts his head back and laughs. He glares down at me with menacing eyes, terrifying me to the core of my being. "I cannot do that. Sophia knows too much. You know too much. Don't think for one second that either of you will ever be free of me." He stands then whistles, signaling Brian to come and escort me to my cell.

When we get downstairs, he opens the door and follows me inside. I go to the bed scooting to the corner as far away from him as I can. "Doll, I realize that this isn't your idea of a good time but trust me you got it better than some of these girls. Don't do anything stupid." He looks around the room, my breath hitches. He knows. "I mean it, if you run, and he catches you it will not end well."

He walks out as another man, the skinny one brings Sophia back. She gives me a look of concern as Brian slaps her on the ass. "Talk some sense into your friend Sophia, tell her there is no way out."

She stares at me with wide frightened eyes. He closes the door. She rushes to the bed, speaking for the first time since our initial reunion. "You are not planning an escape are you?" She doesn't let me answer, her words continue to rush out. "There is no way out, Anna."

"I can't stay here. He wants to marry me Sophia." Tears fall as I continue to relay my plight to her. "Manuel is not my father, a man named William Ramirez is. He is here." I sob heavily now. "He is or was a sex trafficker just like Oliver."

She sits quietly and puts up her hand to stop me. "I know, I'm sorry, Anna, this is all my fault."

"No. I am to blame. They took you to get to me. None of this is your doing. I'm getting you out of here Sophia. I'm getting us both out." I hiccup in between sobs.

She stands going to the door and leans her back against the metal running her hand through her hair. "I told him, Anna. He didn't know you were alive until I informed him. They thought you had drowned. Your mother's plan worked, but I ruined it." Her head falls as she speaks burying her face in her hands.

I sit unmoving on the bed. I'm not sure what to say. "Sophia, it's okay. It's not your fault."

"It is. They came to the estate, they killed everyone except the young girls."

My heart drops to my stomach. My parents are dead?

I whisper, "they are *all* dead?"

"Yes, except the girls. They took us. He sold the others. I shouldn't have told him anything. I didn't think they would find you. I thought I could bargain with him for my release." She bangs her head harshly on the door as if trying to punish herself. "I didn't tell him everything, only that you were alive. He has been waiting for you to make a mistake."

And I did. I get up going to her. She tries to push me away, but I pull her into my embrace. "It is okay Sophia. None of this is your fault."

I hold her tightly and whisper into her ear, "I am getting us out of here tomorrow. I need you to be ready."

She pulls back and looks at me, shaking her head feverishly. "You can't escape him Anna, you can't." She quickly slides by me and shuts off the light then jumps into bed leaving me to stand alone in the dark.

I walk over to the bed and reach under the mattress to pluck out the rope that our captors mistakenly left tied around Sophia's neck one night. I tuck it under my pillow and get in pulling Sophia to me. "It is not your fault," I whisper to her again as I allow myself to drift to sleep. Tomorrow I am running. I am bringing her with me whether she likes it or not.

Chapter Ten

Dylan

I top my piece of shit little rental car to one twenty, slamming my fist into the steering wheel. Nothing went as planned. Not a fucking thing. I am going to get my revenge and she will help me.

Liam told me she gave the FBI a lot of helpful material. She relayed information on other cell locations and buyers. She was keeping tight-lipped on everything else. The other girls say she is engaged to the fucker. How the fuck could anyone want to marry that bastard. I don't really care to figure it all out. She isn't my end game. I'm just going to use her to get to him.

All I can see is red as I make my way swerving in and out of traffic. Liam better not be late. I am done letting his bureau investigate this. I'm taking matters into my own hands. He told me she planned a service at two this afternoon. I am hoping to meet up with him before then.

He might try to stop me. He is always stopping me from one stupid thing or another but not this time. I am going fishing. I'm dropping a line and she will be the bright, enticing lure at the end.

I turn off the freeway and make my way to the small town near her home pulling into the Midtown Motel. Liam and the girl are on the road back. Nobody knows about our connections to Sophia. He has had to keep his shit together. His superiors would freak if they learned he had any ties to the case. I feel bad for him but there is no time for that. The mission may have changed, but the end will be the same. Oliver Wright will die.

I kick open the door to my room and throw my bag on the end of the bed. I need to get some sleep. Sleep has eluded me ever since receiving Liam's call telling me everything fell apart. I failed her and there isn't a damn thing I can do to bring her back.

I feel alone. I shouldn't. I still have my guys. They are like family, but Sophia was the one person who knew me before. Before all this shit. I used to be a good man, not anymore. I will do anything to get to him. Even kidnap a girl? I crack my knuckles and weave my fingers together placing my hands behind head. Yes. I would hijack the pope himself if it brought Oliver Wright to my door.

A knock brings me out of my dark thoughts. I peek out of the small opening in the closed curtains. Good, he isn't late. I need to get as much information as I can before I take her. She is going to tell me everything I want to know while we wait for her fiancé to show up. Maybe she knows where he is, and this will go faster than planned. I need Liam to inform me of what he knows about her.

I open the door and sigh at the sight of him. He is worse off than I am. He puts his hand up before I can say anything coming in grabbing the whisky out of my bag. He opens it slamming a third of the brown liquor down.

He slumps down in one of the rickety motel chairs. I sit across from him. He hands me the bottle. I take a swig and hand it back. He needs it more than I do. "Where is the file?"

He reaches into his briefcase on the floor and tosses a folder on the table. "What are you going to do?" he asks.

"Better you don't know." I grab the folder and open it. Everything I ever wanted to learn about Sarah Madrono inside.

Liam takes another swig. "She is innocent, Dylan."

I laugh. "Innocent? I thought you said she was engaged to the fucker?"

"That's what the other girls told us. You don't understand you didn't see her. She was just as frightened as the rest of them." He closes his eyes.

I feel bad for him I do. I may not have been there this time, but I have rescued my fair share of young women. I realize what they've been through. "So, you think she was a reluctant bride to be?" I toss the folder on the table. I will study this later.

"Yes, I do. She is smart, Dylan. She must have been privy to his private conversations. She had a whole notebook of information. He monitored what she wrote so to the reader it looks like poetry. But, she had laced it with words and letters to help her recall the names of buyers and towns. Brilliant really. She will save a lot of people. So, whatever your plan is, remember this." He shakes his finger at me as he stands going to the bed to lie down.

"What about Sophia? What is Sarah's tie to her?" I ask as my chest tightens.

"I don't know, she said they shared a cell together. She asked for two things in return for the information in that book of hers, one was for a new identity and the other was for…" His voice cracks, he takes a moment to control the wave of emotion before continuing. "She wanted to know if they could release Sophia's body to her, so she could give her a proper burial."

I look at my watch, Liam had told me that the girl had planned the service for two. I don't want to miss it. "Are you going?"

"I can't, Dylan, if I go I won't be able to hide my feelings for Sophia." He gets up and heads to the bathroom.

As he walks away, I grab the whiskey and take another long drink. I put the folder away, walking out of the room leaving the alcohol on the table for him.

I toss my bag in the back and peel out of the motel lot. I head to the edge of town checking my phone to make sure I'm headed in the right direction. I see it now. A small cemetery on the side of a hill. My heart sinks as I spot a tent rising out in contrast to the surroundings. A minister of some unknown denomination stands there looking at a book, a bible I'm guessing.

I pull up behind a grove of trees a short distance away and get out to crouch down by some bushes. A small silver car arrives, and a young girl gets out, walking up to the minister. She shakes his hand. He reads as they stand side by side near my sister's casket.

It is beautiful with the sun shining on it. Their reflections peer back at them in the black onyx. It has silver handles with a design etched into it. At least Sophia is being cared for at the end. I pick up a leaf and crush it into my palm watching the pieces fall slowly to the ground.

I look back up to see the minister give the dark-haired girl a hug. He gets in his vehicle and leaves her alone with my sister. She takes the rose in her hand carefully setting it on the casket.

Then she does something unexpected. Something so intimate it pulls at my heart. She places her palms face down on the casket and lays her head down between them so that her cheek is flat against the smooth black surface. She is speaking but I am too far away to make out what she is saying. My chest tightens at the intimacy of the moment.

I can see that she is crying, her body shakes slightly as the sorrow escapes. She stays like this for a long time before she slowly turns to walk away with her head down. As she enters her car she pauses and looks around as if she can sense my eyes upon her.

I want to go to my sister, but I need to watch the girl. I need to know what her plan is. I will come back tonight when it is dark. I get in my car and wait until Sarah turns onto the road then I follow.

She makes three stops before heading to her ranch. One at the bank, a local relator and finally the little corner bookstore. Eventually she makes her way home. I see the lights come on and observe as she goes to each window checking the locks before closing the curtains.

I pull away. Tomorrow we meet. She will tell me what she knows but for now I need to pick up Liam. We both need closure. It's time to go to the tiny little cemetery on the hill and say our goodbyes to Sophia.

Chapter Eleven

Anna

I walk in and throw my bag on the couch. I avoid turning around remembering how this nightmare all started, I'm half expecting Brian to be behind me. It was him. The man who took me. I trudge to the windows to check that they are all locked, it's a silly thing to do. When Oliver comes for me nothing will stop him, not even locked doors or windows.

I can't shake the feeling that someone is watching me. I know it is more than likely too soon for him to be looking for me. He could have connections here in the United States and they are already tracking my every move.

It doesn't matter. Next time I will not go easily, I'll fight until they kill me, I won't surrender. I walk down the hallway to my room. I stop in the doorway. How many years did I hide in here? I flop face first onto my bed. The FBI game me a new identity. I can't remember what it. It is irrelevant. I don't know why I even asked for one. He will come, different name or not.

I reluctantly stopped at the bookstore on the way home. I didn't want to. Frank and Irene have been worried to death about me. They wanted me to stay with them. I'm not putting anyone else in danger especially them. They are the only people I have left in this world. I cannot remain here. I told them I was leaving tomorrow to go into the witness protection program.

It's partially true. I'm running far away from here. I've gifted the ranch to a local shelter for battered women. The ranch is large with many rooms, they can house up to twenty ladies here. I guess there have been studies done that show people can heal being around and working with horses. They were thrilled with my offer. I'm happy with the thought it might benefit someone. I'm glad for the horses too, Frank has been caring for them since my abduction. I couldn't help Sophia. Maybe this will make a difference.

I purchased a small cabin in Colorado. The drive to the nearest town almost two hours away. He will find me there but at least I will be far enough away he can't hurt anyone else.

I think about the man they killed at the motel. It seems like years ago, but it has only been a little over a month. After purchasing the cabin and paying the expenses for Sophia's final resting place, I still have over a million dollars. At least now I know that it is legitimate earnings from my father, well my stepfather.

I pull out my phone and pull up the go fund me account for the family of the man. I study the pictures of his wife and daughters. Tears spill from my eyes. I make the donation anonymously…one million. This won't bring their dad back but hopefully this makes their life a little easier. I stopped at the bank, so they would know the transfer was legit. I pulled the rest out in cash. I don't want to hassle with setting up a new account in Colorado.

How long will I have to wait for him? I know that he will come. The expression in his eye as Brian hauled him away to run and make their escape, told me as much. When he finds out I gave information to the FBI, he will be furious. He will kill me. That is what I am banking on, anyway. If he doesn't, then I fight him until he has no choice.

I set the phone down, rolling over onto my back. I look at the rope marks engrained in the palm of my hands. I clench my fists. Nothing went as planned. Tears sting at my eyes. I miss Sophia. She was like family and now she is gone, and it is all on me.

That morning, I had a plan, and it was working. I waited in the dark for the skinny man to come and get us up for the day. Waiting, running the rope through my fingers. The adrenaline was intense, coursing through my veins. When I heard the clang of the keys, I put my finger up to my lips to remind Sophia to remain quiet.

She tried to talk me out of my crazy plan the night before, but she couldn't. She gave up after seeing how scared I was at the thought of marrying Oliver. She pulled the blanket over her head. When he walked in I slammed the door shut and wrapped the rope around his neck then jumped on his back before he knew what was happening.

I pulled tightly. The rope cut into my hands as he bucked like a wild horse. He slammed me into the cement wall knocking the air out me. My back scraped against the rough concrete. He reared his head and hit me in the right side of my face but still I held on. I could feel the rope giving, cutting into his neck. Then just as quickly as it began he slumped to the ground with me falling on top of him.

Sophia scrambled to the ground to retrieve the gun from his holster. Our eyes locked. "Holy shit," I said in hushed tones. "I killed a man."

Then we heard it. Guns going off on what sounded like the floor above us. We rushed out then slowly climbed the stairs. When we reached the main floor, I saw men in swat gear crouched down near the front door. The door I had wanted to escape from every time I walked by. It was then I looked up and my eyes met Oliver's.

He was staring at me over the banister. Brian was tugging at his arm trying to pull him the other direction. He stared at me and mouthed the words, "I will find you." I spun to Sophia as men in gear rushed in. One of them spotted us and yelled to run towards him…towards freedom.

"Sophia, it is happening we are getting out of here! Let's go!" I ran for the door and then I stumbled as a blast went off behind me. I turned back my ears ringing. She had shot herself in the side of the head with the gun she had retrieved off the man I had just killed.

I remember little after that. I recall sitting in the rear of an ambulance asking the detective, the one from the bookstore, if I could go back in. I needed the book that Oliver gave me. He wouldn't let me, but he sent one of his men in to retrieve it for me.

Detective Sharp offered to drive me home from Dallas. I argued that he didn't have to that I could just get on the bus. He insisted. They made me stay a few days at Dallas Memorial hospital but there wasn't really a need for it. I am bruised, my hands and back are cut up but other than that I am fine. They detected the drugs in my system and wanted to run blood tests. They were making sure I hadn't contracted anything from possible dirty needles.

Brian was right. I was lucky compared to the other girls. We were all brought to the same hospital and put on the same floor. I listened as they cried and screamed out from nightmares. I haven't had any nightmares. I haven't been able to sleep.

I'll rest when I get to my cabin. Tonight, I need to pack up whatever I am taking with me. I drag myself out of my bed to make coffee. It will be a long night. On the way to the kitchen I stop in the hallway and back up to bathroom.

I stare at my reflection. The bruise on my face is turning a lovely shade of purple and bluish green. I run my finger over it before pulling my hair up into a bun. I open the medicine cabinet and take out a new box of contact lenses. Popping one in each eye, I study myself in the mirror.

Sarah is starring back at me. I need to be her. It will help me get past what happened back in Venezuela. At least for a little while, until Oliver finds me, and forces Anna back out.

Chapter Twelve

Dylan

Liam and I stop at the liquor store to pick up another bottle of the hard stuff before we head to the cemetery. It's dark, but the moon is full tonight, illuminating the lines of white stones. The tent is gone and so is the casket. Funny how you never see the grave diggers. They are illusive characters.

We make our way up to the pile of raw dirt. I am surprised to discover a headstone already set. If that girl is anything she is efficient. I sit down in the grass and crack open the new bottle. I watch my friend walk to the stone and pull something out of his pocket, setting it on top. I catch the diamond glint against the moonlight. So many dreams being left here tonight.

Liam runs his finger along the newly etched writing. Sophia Lorenz, twenty-five years of age. The dash reflects so little space between her birth and death. How did Sarah know her birthday? It doesn't seem like something one would bring up in captivity. I want to ask him more about her, but I don't interrupt the moment.

He sits down beside me. I hand him the bottle. He rests his forearms on his raised knees and lets it dangle in his hands before taking a drink. "I can't believe she is gone."

"Yeah, me either." I lay down and look up at the stars. "She is in a better place, better than this shit show." I spread my arms out showing him I mean everything… life.

He sighs and takes another long swig before passing it to me. "What's your strategy, Dylan?"

"I told you it's best if you don't know."

"I'm not stopping you, not this time. I want him dead," he grits out.

"He will be," I say. I'm not going to let him in on my plan. He has enough to deal with. I don't want him to lose his job, it is all he has left.

"I can't put my finger on it but there is something about Sarah that I'm missing," he says. He lays back and joins me to watch the celestial show.

"She didn't give you any information? Does she have Stockholm syndrome? I guess I don't understand how she could be engaged to him."

"I asked her several questions, but she didn't talk. She just stared out the window on the flight back from Venezuela. It wasn't until after they saw her at the hospital that a nurse called telling me she was asking to speak to an agent."

"That's when she requested the deal with the information from her book?"

"Yep. I tried to get more out of her but all I got were names, locations, dates and times. All helpful but she wouldn't talk about Sophia or Wright." He sits up and reaches for the bottle. "One thing I found strange was when I asked if I could call her parents. She said no, they were vacationing, and that they couldn't be reached."

"That's fucked up," I respond feeling a bit of empathy for the girl. "So, what about Ramirez? I bet that was a surprise finding the motherfucker there."

"Yes. I wish he would have been alive. That bastard got off easy having a heart attack in his bed."

"Are you heading back tomorrow?" I ask. Hoping he heads out early so I can introduce myself to Sarah. The excitement of the hunt creeps through my veins. I shouldn't feel this way, but I do. Does it make me any better than them? I shrug it off.

I let my mind wander to the girl. She was standing in this spot earlier. I pick up the rose in front of my sister's headstone. The diggers must have placed it there. She had gently set it on the casket, her dark hair blowing in the wind. I wonder how she smells. I raise the flower to my face inhaling the fragrant scent. I shouldn't be having these thoughts. But none the less I am enthusiastic that tomorrow I will find out.

I'm taking her. I'll do whatever it takes to make her talk.

Chapter Thirteen

Anna

I watch as the folks from the women's shelter pull out of the driveway. I wave to them and then brush my hands together. Well, that is done. Everything is locked up and they have the keys. I look around, my suitcases are sitting on the ground in front of my open trunk. I reach into the driver's window and pull out the map I had tossed on the seat.

I know I could use a map program on my phone but there is something I love about having an actual map. Kind of like the feel of having an actual book in hand. I open it and set it on the hood of my car. I study the red x where my new cabin lies. I trace my finger over the highway that will take me north and then west into Colorado.

"Where are we headed?" a deep voice says making me jump.

He is right behind me. The heat off him seeps into my backside. How did I not hear someone walk up behind me? I reach up and pull my sunglasses off the top of my head setting them down calmly on the car. That was fast.

"We are not going anywhere," I say. I'm not going back to Oliver.

The man slowly reaches around me. I watch as his large tanned hand grabs the map. As soon as he has the map in hand, I scramble up on the hood hoping to jump off the other side and run. He grabs me, pulling me off kicking and screaming. He is as big as Brian, no, bigger.

I dig my nails into his arms and buck my head back. It does no good. I am only banging into his solid chest. He walks around to the back of my car lifting my feet high off the ground and forces my legs into the trunk shoving me down slamming it shut.

I scream at the top of my lungs, crying, gasping for breath. Panic consumes me. I kick at the trunk yelling for him to let me out. The car door opens and shuts. It sounds like he tosses something in the backseat. Then I hear another door open and close as the engine starts. No, no, this can't be happening. It's too soon. My screams are drowned out by the sudden blare of the radio.

Dylan

Jesus, I enjoyed that way more than I should have. I reach down to my crotch adjusting myself. What the fuck, maybe this is a bad idea. Where is Liam when I need him? I need him to talk some sense into me.

At this point I don't know if that would even be effective. I've touched her, smelled her. She smells like a field of lavender. I listen to her scream. Part of me enjoys her terror, the other lets the scream tug at my heart. "Fuck." I slam the palm of my hand on the wheel.

I drive for a while then find myself wondering what she is thinking. Her cries stopped about an hour ago. I glance at the empty passenger seat. I was just going to make the whole twelve-hours and leave her back there, but I want to see her. I want her next to me.

I stop at a little station with no attendant and pull up to top off the tank. I wait listening to see if she will scream again. Nothing. I grab my bag as the gas pumps plucking out a pair of handcuffs. I finish up and glance around me. We are in a remote location but with all the damn cameras in the world I decide it's best if I let her out down the way.

I get in and drive for another hour, debating where to pull over. Finally, I spot a road leading to a grove of trees. Perfect. I turn off and drive down the dirt road looking in the rearview mirror at the dust rolling behind the car. I drive off the road into the woods, hiding the car from the highway about a half mile back.

I shut the engine off and stick the pair of the cuffs in my waistband. I make my way to the trunk, lightly knocking on the top.

"Fuck you," she yells in a flat tone.

I chuckle. I'm pleasantly surprised at the fight in her. Most of the girls we find have no spirit left in them. Then I remember who she is, the fiancé of the man I am going to kill. A darkness settles over me. I am better off leaving the bitch in the trunk. I get back in, but I don't pull away.

I drum my thumbs on the wheel and reflect on her placing her face against my sister's casket. Curiosity wins out. I get out and pop the lid. She covers her eyes blinking at the bright light. She doesn't look at me. I reach in and pull her out keeping my hand around her wrist as she steadies herself.

I let go for a brief second to grab the cuffs from my waistband. She skitters away like a frightened deer. I smile slowly…and so the chase begins.

Chapter Fourteen

Anna

I don't know where I am running but I am determined to get away from him. He locked me in my damn trunk! Lucky for me I was able to keep it together. Fighting the claustrophobia, I slipped away to the lake with Sarah. I pondered for a long time why he didn't drug me like Brian did. I wish he would have. It would have been easier.

I stop briefly to catch my breath, hiding behind a tree. We are in a wooded area. I can't see any signs of civilization. Maybe he is someone that was sent to murder me. I think about the information I gave the FBI. The thought spurs me to run again.

I don't hear him. Just as I assume I may have gotten far enough away he comes from behind and slams me to the ground face first. I cry out as I land on the hard dirt.

He doesn't get off me. He has me pinned. I try to push up off the ground with the palms of my hands. Sticks painfully poke and scratch at my arms and legs. The only sound is my harsh rapid breathing and his. But, his is not as labored as mine. This pisses me off. This was never a fair chase. But then again, life isn't fair.

"You may as well kill me now," I say through gritted teeth, struggling to suck oxygen into my lungs.

He lifts his weight off slightly to allow me to gulp in more air. "I'm not going to kill you," he says above me as he buries his nose in my hair.

I squirm to slide my way out from under him.

"Sarah, stop," he growls.

I detect something pressed against me. He is getting turned on by my movements, that or the chase I'm not sure. His erection is pressing against my ass. I instantly still. I realize something else. He called me Sarah. Why didn't he call me Anna? This and him not drugging me earlier makes me wonder if he is even one of Oliver's men. If not, who is he?

When he speaks the low rumble of his voice vibrates against my back and stirs something inside me. "I'm not going to murder you," he says again.

Who am I dealing with? When he moves off me I turn over to get myself into a sitting position. My mind is swirling with a million questions. I slowly peek up at him. He towers over me.

If I had one word to describe him, it would be magnificent. He is tall, so tall and fit. His arms are bigger than my thighs. He is nothing but solid muscle. His hair is dark with wavy curls that hang just below his shoulders. I can see the golden highlights in his hair when the sun breaks through the trees. His eyes are smoky and dangerous, the look he gives me rockets adrenaline through my veins.

He runs his hand through his hair. I cannot take my eyes off him. He reaches out to help me to my feet. My body reacts without thought sending my hand out to accept his. As I am about to let him latch on I notice the scab on my palms have ripped open.

I quickly pull my arm back. I stare down at the blood pooling in my palms, then for some unexplained reason I cry. Why now, no, no not now…but I can't stop.

He crouches down beside me and takes my hands in his large ones. "I said I'm not going to kill you," he says gently.

I shake my head. I'm not crying because I think he will kill me. I'm crying for Sophia, the man at the hotel, my parents, all the girls who have been taken and for everyone who died at the estate. I even weep for the man I killed and most of all for myself.

He doesn't say anything and tugs me to stand by my wrists. He then wraps his arms around me, hauling me in tightly to his chest. I'm not sure what is happening. I don't fight him, I just cry.

After a few minutes, he lifts me and carries me back to the car. I keep my face buried in his chest, drawing from the stranger's strength. He sets me on my feet as he opens the passenger side door. I sit, he takes my hands in his and turns them over to exam my open wounds.

He goes to the backseat grabbing a duffle bag. He crouches down in front of me and opens it pulling out a white first aid kit, a bottle of water and a t-shirt. He opens the water pouring it over my palms then carefully drying them with the shirt.

I focus on the top of his head, while he tends to my wounds. I resist the urge to reach out and run my fingers through his hair. What is wrong with me? I'm just tired, I haven't slept in several days and my mind is playing tricks on me.

He puts ointment on my palms and wraps gauze around each hand. I watch mesmerized as he rips the first aid tape with his teeth securing the bandages. When he finishes his ministrations, he looks up at me. His eyes lock on mine.

He is the most frighteningly beautiful thing I have ever seen. He reminds me of a wolf, gorgeous to look at but deadly. He is wild, free I can see it in his eyes. He answers to no one. I am positive this man would have nothing to do with Oliver Wright.

"I'm serious, I'm not going to kill you." He wipes the tears from cheek with his thumb and then stands.

I swing around in the seat and pull my legs inside the vehicle as I do then he shuts the door. It seems weird to be sitting in the passenger side of my car. I don't think I have ever sat here. I watch him in the side mirror as he puts his bag in the back.

He opens the driver's side and gets in. He has the seat moved all the way back, but his long legs still appear cramped. He is so big he fills the space. I face my window, suddenly feeling very small.

He starts the engine and backs out of the grove of trees turning on a dirt road leading to a highway.

I shift to peek at him. I have a question burning a hole in my mind. I am frightened of his answer, but I need to know. "Where are you taking me?" I squeak out.

He reaches behind my seat, hands me my sunglasses then the map I bought for my trip and points to the red x.

"We are going to wherever your treasure map leads us, x marks the spot, does it not?"

Dylan

Plan C, I hoped I would be able to use Sarah to lure Oliver Wright into my web. But, the moment I saw the first teardrop run down her cheek that idea went right down the toilet. She is mine and I will not let him anywhere near her.

Fuck. I don't understand what is happening. I have rescued all sorts of girls and I have never once found myself attracted to any of them. There was always empathy yes, and anger at those that had hurt them but this, this is something I've never experienced. Could it be guilt for not saving Sophia? That doesn't change how I feel. I'll never be able to give Sarah up.

The way she skittered away from me in the woods, asking to be chased had me so fucking hard. By the time I finally had her trapped underneath me I was ready to ravage her body. It took so much self-restraint to keep myself at bay. She is frightened of me I can see it in her eyes, but I also sense a current that runs alongside that fear. She is curious about me and in a good sense. I could easily take advantage of that, make her bend to my will, but it will be sweeter watching her come on her own, and she will.

She is beautiful and exotic. She seems familiar, like I have known her my whole life. She reminds me of someone. I can't put my finger on it. The minute we locked eyes I recognized she wasn't the type of girl to fall for Oliver. She assumes I work for him. She is frightened of going back.

There is no way he will get to her. I will make sure of that. I'll call Liam and figure out another means to get to Oliver. My little fishing lure did her job, but it wasn't him that she snagged it was me. Things are never going to be the same.

She has yet to tell me where her x on the map is leading us. My guess is it's where she was going to set herself up and wait for Oliver to come for her. She has been quiet since I released her from the trunk, looking out her window the entire drive. I can see that she is fighting sleep, her head keeps bobbing, but she refuses to let herself drift away, lulled by the moving car. She is a fighter.

I myself am having a tough time staying awake. I could stop for coffee or…I could just get a hotel room and curl up next to that warm little body of hers. Would she scream alerting everyone? I guess it's a chance I'm willing to take because now that the notion is in my head there is no letting it go.

"We still have about six hours till we reach your x. How about we stop and get some sleep?" I stare straight ahead as I ask, watching out the side of my vision for her reaction. I see the expression on her face and recognize the flicker of hope, hope that this might be her opportunity to escape.

I could let her go. I should let her go. If I keep her I'm no better than the men I hunt. But how can I? I realize she is in danger and I am the less of two evils. The prospect of letting her go tears at my soul. To protect her, I will have to scare her, it's for her own good.

"So, what do you think?" I ask again, watching her mind reel at the possibilities.

She shrugs trying to seem indifferent. "You are in charge. I don't know what my opinion matters."

"You are right, I am in charge." I reach behind the seat and grab one of the guns I brought setting it on my thigh. "So, here is how this will go down. I will get the room and if you are quiet the whole night, no one will get hurt."

I'm taking a chance, hoping that she won't do anything stupid. I know she would risk herself. She told me so by asking me to kill her after she ran from me. But, if she thinks I will harm innocent people, she will be good.

I look at her. Yep, that did it.

"I'll be good," she says sadly.

There it is, that damn tug. I will tell her the truth of who I am when we get where we are going. I don't want her thinking I work for that ass-hat Oliver any longer than necessary. But for now, this is how it has got to be, she must listen.

Chapter Fifteen

Anna

The dark stranger pulls off the highway. Before heading into the little town, he draws a pair of handcuffs out from behind him. He doesn't use them on me, he just sets them in the cup holder. He looks at me in warning. I understand. I can't do anything, I'm not about to risk anyone else's life.

I thought he might not be one of Oliver's men but now I'm not sure what to think. I'm so tired. The prospect of stretching out on a bed and getting some sleep is overriding my thoughts of running away anyhow.

He seems satisfied with my reaction. We pull into a gas station and he points to the young woman working. He doesn't say anything, but I nod my understanding. He gets out and I fight myself to stay sitting. He goes inside coming out with a couple of sacks and tosses them in the back.

"Good girl," he says as he bends himself into my tiny car.

I shiver at his words, good girl…if he calls me kitten I will stab his eyes out. I reflect on our encounter in the wooded area and how he called me Sarah. When I was rescued in Venezuela, I debated the entire plane trip home on whether I would come clean and give detective Sharp my real name. He was so kind. He would have helped me, but I couldn't bring myself to do it.

It would have been a perfect moment to start my life back up as Anna but so much had happened. I need time to come to terms with it all. I also didn't share with him the fact that the man who died in his bed from a heart attack was my father. It's something I never want anyone to discover. I don't know why I'm ashamed. He is the one who did the evil, but I am his daughter none the less. Some of that evil lives inside me. I killed a guy with my bare hands, well my bare hands and a rope so the apple doesn't fall far from the tree.

I study my bandaged palms and then the stranger. He so tenderly cared for me. Yet he kidnapped me. Much like Oliver, but it seems different. It's not though. Tired, Anna, you're just tired.

We continue down the block to a tiny little motel. He gives me that look again, and I nod. He gets out and goes into the office. I watch as he and the old man inside laugh both looking out to the car. I wonder what he is telling him. Is it that we are lovers and needing a place for a secret late afternoon tryst? As I roll the image around in my head I notice a warm sense of arousal stir in my core. I fidget in my seat trying to force the reaction go away.

He comes out and gets in smiling at me. I fidget again as a blush finds its way up to my cheeks. I twist to stare out the window. That smile. Oh. My. God. It is a make your panties melt off kind of smile. Not good. Anna, you need to focus, what the fuck is wrong with you?

"Maybe we should just keep going, I'll drive if you would like. I promise I will be good," I say in a rush of words not turning to face him.

He pulls away from the office and parks in front of a door to a room giving me a little chuckle. I swear I can feel his laugh rumble right through the car up through my seat zoning in on my crotch.

"Sarah, I know you would be a good girl. You will be good either way. But, I see you are tired and so am I, so we stop. We can wake up early and get a head start but I need rest."

Calm. Anna, breathe. We are just going to sleep here. It will be okay. One foot in front of the other. Before I realize it he is out unlocking the door to the room. He looks at me through the windshield and beckons me with his finger.

I should run but I don't. It's like there is unseen magnetism pulling me towards him. The outside world is slipping away, and it is just the two of us. I slide in past him and pause on the other side of the threshold. There is only one bed. The parking lot is empty, surely he could have gotten a double room. He laughs and turns to go back out leaving me in the room frozen, staring at that damn bed.

He comes in carrying all our bags. He sets them on the floor and walks past me again to close the door. The lock click echoes through the room. It's dark now with the curtains closed to block out the late afternoon sun. He flips the light. "Have a seat."

I turn to face him as he points to one of the hotel chairs. Grabbing the sacks from the gas station he sets them in front of me on the table. "I figured you might be hungry or thirsty. Go ahead, nothing in there bites I promise."

I open the bags finding gas station sandwiches, bottles of water and chips.

"Not much, I would take you out for dinner, but I'm not sure if I can trust you yet." He looks at me and searches my face with those frightening eyes of his.

I grab a water and sandwich watching as he picks up my small travel bag and dumps it out in the middle of the bed. I feel violated seeing him run his hands over my things picking them up examining them.

"Just making sure there is nothing in here that you could shoot, stab or strangle me with." He furrows his dark eyebrows keeping his eyes on me.

I swallow hard, did he know the guard I strangled? I laugh nervously.

"Umm, first off I didn't realize someone would kidnap me today. I was a little unprepared, I left my weapons at home. Second, I couldn't strangle you if I wanted."

"Do you want to?" He picks up the book that Oliver gave me. I don't know why I kept it, but I did. He sees the pen tucked inside and opens it to the last page of my mussing's.

I try to distract him. "You should eat, I promise there is nothing in my bags you should be worried about."

"You didn't answer my question, Sarah." He twirls the pen through his fingers and looks at me in all seriousness.

"No, I don't want to strangle you."

"Perhaps you should." He studies the calligraphy on the pen. "So, who is Anna?"

I glance down at my lap. "I don't know. Oliver gave me the pen along with the book. I assume it was a pen he picked up along the way."

"Hmm, it doesn't appear to be a pen that is just picked up along the way. It looks like someone had it made for an Anna." He stares at me tilting his head down slightly. His intensity terrifies me and excites me at the same time.

I shrug and pick up my sandwich taking a bite.

He drops the subject. He hasn't though, I can see it in his eyes. He didn't flinch when I mentioned Oliver. My heart sinks. Obviously he works for him. But he doesn't know who I really am. I guess Oliver didn't tell anyone. As far as I know only four people know my identity. Well now, we are down to the two of us since William and Sophia have passed.

He opens my larger bag and sifts through my clothing. Satisfied that I have nothing to kill him with, he gathers the items from my travel bag and carefully puts everything away. He pushes it and my suitcase by my feet.

"After you are done eating take what you need, and you can shower," he says joining me at the table.

I quickly gobble down the rest of my sandwich, gather a few things and practically run to the bathroom locking the door behind me.

He unsettles me, his presence is so large I feel like I'm being swallowed up. He must have been sent by Oliver to keep tabs on me. I was hoping for some time. Time to spend in my new cabin…alone. I haven't had a chance to process everything and now here I am forced to deal with this larger-than-life man.

A knock on the bathroom door makes me jump.

"Sarah, you can shower by yourself, but you need to keep this door unlocked."

I stare at the doorknob. Do I unlock it? What if I do and he insists on coming in? Crap. I can't bring myself to turn the latch.

"Sarah," he growls in warning.

I reach out and slowly turn the lock stepping back to wait for him to open the door, but he doesn't. I hear his footsteps retreat. He kept his word. I quickly undress and hop in the shower washing as swiftly as I can, listening for him. I dress just as fast and walk out in my sweats and tank top.

"I thought that would speed the process up," he says as I pull the towel off my head to dry my hair.

I glare at him as I walk over and grab my brush. He doesn't move. He never takes his eyes off me. I'm suddenly self-conscious. "Do you need help?" He stands following me as I sit on the end of the bed.

"I'm fine, thank you." I am worried about him touching me. If Oliver finds out, he would kill the dark stranger and that makes me sad for some reason. "Oliver doesn't like anyone to touch me," I whisper.

He takes the brush from me and sits down beside me. "I don't give a fuck what Oliver likes. You don't belong to him anymore. Your hands are injured, and you need help. Besides you belong to me now."

I'm so confused, did he say I "belonged" to him? Did Oliver sell me to this man? No, that can't be, he wouldn't receive my father's inheritance. I am so tired of all the guessing and uncertainties. This guy could just be stupid and thinks he can get away with this. When Oliver finds out, he will put a bullet in him.

"I don't think you understand," I say with urgency, needing him to listen to what I am saying.

He runs the brush through my hair leaning in to smell it. "No, I don't think you understand, Sarah. You are mine and Oliver Wright can go fuck himself because I'm not letting him near you ever again."

"He killed a man…for touching me," I exclaim, pushing his hand away from head.

"Awe, you like me don't you? You are worried about me that is sweet." He goes right back to running the brush down my long locks.

"You obviously don't know him." I guess if this idiot wants to get himself killed who am I to stop him.

He stops, I detect his restraint, his anger comes to the surface as he has the brush paused in my hair. "Oh, I know him, he is a dead man walking."

I don't move, apparently I'm in the dark here. I have no fucking idea what the hell is going on. Something tells me to drop the subject and just let him finish. He starts the brush again and I keep my mouth shut.

When he is satisfied with his work, he stands and grabs the handcuffs out of his bag. I crawl back up on the bed as he follows walking alongside, hovering over me. "Two choices here, one I handcuff you to the bed or two you join me in the bathroom while I shower. Either choice will be appetizing." He leans his hand up against the wall over me while waiting for my answer.

"Handcuffs," I say uncertainly. I don't like the idea of being tied up, but I also don't…well maybe a small part of me does, want to see him naked.

"The lady has picked her poison." He smiles clipping one side of the cuff to a post in the headboard and the other he clicks gently around my wrist. He runs his hand lightly over the palm of mine before letting go. "When I'm done, I'll look at these and put more antibiotic on them." He takes a few steps back and runs his eyes along the entire length of my body starting at my feet moving all the way up until reaching my face.

I shift uncomfortably at his intense scrutiny. I am chained to a bed, a bed I am sure he expects us to share. He backs up not taking his eyes off mine until he reaches the bathroom door, he winks before leaving me alone.

My anxiety rises as I hear the water start. I pull at the cuffs but there is no way to free myself. "Anna," my friend Sarah calls out to me. I have missed her. Tears threaten to spill again. My mind flits to being tied up to the exam table at Oliver's.

Why does everything have to be so hard? I want to be free. I have found myself captive by not one dangerous man but now two. What is it about me? I guess Oliver wanting me makes sense. He desires my father's money but this guy what does he want? He wants all of me. I shiver at the thought.

The water shuts off as I work myself into a frenzied state. I can't breathe. I need out of here! I pull at the cuff and feel it cut into my wrist. I ignore the pain. I need to get free. He opens the door coming out in nothing but his boxers. I halt my movements.

He rushes to me when he spots the trickle of blood running down my captive wrist. "Sarah, what the fuck are you doing?" He reaches over and grabs the key off the table quickly unlocking the cuff.

My breath is quick and shallow. The all too familiar stars rush in and force me into a dark hole. He wraps his arms around me. "Sarah you need to breathe slowly. In. Out. That's it, baby."

Eventually, the tunnel recedes, as I focus on his words, his warmth, his smell, his touch, he envelopes me. Nothing else exists. I push away embarrassed that I have broken down twice in front of him in one day.

"I'm sorry," I say as I struggle to unwrap him from around me.

"Are you feeling better?" He lets go and looks at me with serious eyes.

"Yes, I'm sorry. I haven't slept for a few days. I rarely cry. The handcuffs just reminded me of something that is all. I wasn't trying to escape I promise."

He runs his fingers through his hair sighing. "I haven't slept much either." He gets up and brings the first aid kit back to bed. "Let me put some of this on your hands and wrist, then we will sleep."

I allow him to take my palms in his, but I sense the edge of my anxiety as he applies the antibiotic. He must also sense it because he gently reminds me to breathe. He finishes and then shuts off the light, leaving the room in darkness.

I don't move as I feel the bed shift from his weight. He reaches for me and pulls me into his arms. "Lay down, I will not hurt you we are just going to sleep." He situates so he is behind me, cradling me. He continually whispers in my ear to breathe.

"Tell me about where we are traveling, it looks like it is in a mountainous area. What is there?"

I am stiff as a board lying beside him. I have never been this close to a man in bed. It reminds me of the days in my cell when I comforted Sophia, letting her curl up next to me, telling her it would all be okay.

"It's a cabin," I say into the darkness.

"A cabin, hmm, that sounds nice. Does it belong to you? A place you visit often?"

I don't know why I am compelled to answer, but it keeps my mind off my situation. "I bought it. I have never visited there. I have only seen photos. I gave the ranch away to an organization that helps battered women. So, I guess it's my home now, at least until Oliver finds me."

"He won't find you. If he does my guys and I will take him out before he so much as looks at you," he murmurs sleepily in my ear.

"Who are you?"

"I'm the man that will tear you apart and put you back together, but you can call me Dylan. Hush, you need to sleep. We have a lot of driving ahead of us tomorrow." He buries his nose into my hair and pulls me tight to him.

Dylan, I likc that namc. Sophia had an older brother named Dylan. He is gone though. They are all gone. Tears prickle behind my eyes. They slip out and drop onto the cheap hotel pillow. My thoughts are dark, but my body slowly absorbs Dylan's heat. Focusing on the rhythm of his breathing I finally relax and drift to sleep.

Chapter Sixteen

Dylan

I jog back to the hotel from the little donut shop across the street. I didn't cuff her, but I don't think she will run even if she wakes. I couldn't bring myself to lock her up after her reaction last night. I need to read over that damn file, so I can see what I am dealing with. She is strong, but she is also scared and hurting.

I woke early and found myself excited to begin the day. That hasn't happened in a very long time. Knowing I will have her all to myself and that we are going to a cabin in the woods has my blood pumping with new vigor. Yesterday, taking her, I can't describe it, it's like I had been living in black and white. Now it is suddenly full of vibrant color.

As I open the door, she wakes to the sound. She covers her eyes at the bright early morning sun pouring into the room, casting dust rays to the bed.

"Good morning, sunshine," I say as I set a coffee and a box of donuts on the bedside table. She sits and draws herself into a ball.

"I need to make a call but dig in. I'll be back in a few minutes."

She nods hesitantly and waits to see if I will cuff her. I take my cup and walk out of the room. I sit on the hood of the car punching Liam's numbers into my cell.

"Dylan, what's up, man? Where are you?"

I search around. "I don't know some podunk town in the middle of nowhere," I reply.

"You took her didn't you?"

I can hear the tension in his voice. "Yeah, I should have known you would figure it out, but…"

"You can't do it?"

"No. Well yes but no. I was planning to use her to lure Oliver, but I can't do it, but I also can't give her up." Fuck how am I going to explain this.

"What do you mean you can't give her up? Dylan, you can't keep this girl, she has been through too much already. Just let her go and I'll see that the FBI assigns someone to keep an eye on her."

"No, I'm keeping her, she is mine. I don't expect you to understand because I don't. I need you to tell me anything new you found out about her. I will find another way to get to Oliver."

All I hear is silence on the other end, so I continue, "Liam, I realize you don't like this. If it makes you feel any better, you can join us and see her for yourself. We are headed to Colorado. She bought a cabin there to hide from him. I'll call the guys to come out and set security up at her place."

"This is not good, Dylan. There is something about her I can't figure out. You don't need this shit. We need to take Oliver out and move on."

"Did you learn anything new?"

He sighs on the other end. "No, but I remember something. I thought she looked different when we rescued her in Venezuela. I assumed it was just because she was thinner and in distress. I was looking through my copy of her file and I noticed on her birth certificate that her eyes are listed as brown."

"They are brown, so what?"

"Well, that's what I thought as I reflected back to the first time I met her but no, when I interviewed her at Dallas Memorial they were blue."

"They are brown. I'm with her now. You were all tore up about Sophia, you aren't remembering correct."

"Dylan, listen to me man, they were fucking blue. They weren't just blue they were stunning blue, like sapphires. Don't make me out to be the crazy one. You can kiss my ass. You are the fucking crazy one for kidnapping a girl who we just rescued. Think about what you are doing."

"I'll send you the location. I need you to come and convince her I don't work for Oliver. Then you will see for yourself that she has brown eyes and that I'm not torturing her."

"I want nothing to do with this crazy town crap you got going on," he yells into the phone making me pull it away from ear.

I smile saying, "see you soon."

"Fuck you, Dylan!"

I hang up, sipping my coffee eager to get back inside to her. When I walk in she is dressed and sitting by her packed bags, cappuccino in hand. "So, you ready to hit the road? I'm impatient to visit this cabin of yours."

She stands and reaches for her suitcase. I stop her movements, bending slightly, forcing her gaze to land upon mine. Yep, I was right brown eyes. She quickly looks away. I grab her things and open the door waiting for her to exit in front of me.

As I follow her to the car and toss the bags into the back, I remember seeing a couple of boxes of contact lenses in her bag. Maybe she has poor vision, but I didn't see any glasses. Usually people who wear contacts own a pair of glasses. Looks like we have a few mysteries to unravel when we get to Colorado. Ah, I feel more alive than I have in a long time.

She spends the entire trip staring out her window, not speaking. I thumb through the radio stations. Before I know it we are in Colorado, the mountains come into view in the distance. "We are getting close."

She glances up through the windshield and straightens in her seat, excited. Then she smiles. My heart stops, a fucking smile.

"I love the mountains. I have never been to the Rocky Mountains," she exclaims. "They are beautiful, even from here."

I watch her, mesmerized by the light in her expression. It's as if a whole new person morphed into her body. Everything about her changed.

"Yes, there is something about them isn't there? Just wait until we get up there and you breathe in the fresh air."

She turns towards me with that fucking amazing smile. "You have been? I haven't traveled a lot." The smile leaves her face as she drifts off somewhere else in her mind. "Actually, Venezuela is the only other place I have been besides the ranch." She stops to look down into her hands. "I didn't get to see much while I was there."

And then she goes back to staring out her window.

I can't wait to tell her who I am, I need her to understand I'm not part of that whole operation. "I don't work for him."

She stiffens at my announcement. She doesn't turn to face me as she says, "how do you know about him then?"

"Fair question, I've been hunting Oliver Wright and his men for the past eight years. He abducted my sister."

She spins and searches my face for the truth of what I am saying. "So, you took me hoping that I would lead you to him?"

"Yes, I learned that you were engaged to him. I expected he would come for you and then I would strike." I focus on the road ahead of me. "Every time I get close he changes locations."

She shakes her head. "But you said you wouldn't let him near me, you said I belong to you. I don't understand."

"My original strategy was to take you, wait for him to appear and then kill him. But that plan has changed so now we go to your cabin and I make sure he never gets near you again."

"So, are you kidnapping me or are you helping me? Dylan, I don't understand!" She sits agitated in the seat next to me.

Shit, I should have waited for this discussion. "Calm down, the answer to both of your questions is yes."

"So, you are kidnapping me, and you think this somehow helps. Stop the car!" she screams.

"I'm not stopping the car. You need to settle down." I reach over and grab a fistful of her hair, forcing her to quit flailing. A flicker of fear skitters across her face. "We will talk about all this when we get to the cabin. Liam is joining us in a day or two and you can ask him yourself whether I'm telling the truth."

"Liam Sharp?" she questions, her voice quivering.

"Yes, he and I are friends." I calmly let go of her hair and wait to see if she will sit still. I hesitantly move my hand back to the wheel when she doesn't move.

She says nothing else the rest of the trip. I should have kept my mouth shut.

Anna

I watch as the mountains grow large as we get close. Soon we are on winding roads heading higher. I can feel the pressure in my ears as the altitude changes. It is beautiful. I am happy with my decision to come out here, but this was not how I envisioned it. I was going to be alone. I would hide here for as long as I could with my nose in my books.

I steal a glance at Dylan. I know who he is. He seemed familiar and now I realize why. He is Sophia's brother. After he told me about searching for his sister I was certain. I wonder if Sophia knew he was alive. She said everyone at the estate was murdered. She might have fought harder and wouldn't have ended her life if she knew he had been out here looking for her.

I didn't know him well. He was always hanging out with the older boys. My mom kept me away from everybody except for Sophia and her mom. My mother and Sophia's were best friends. I'm sure he doesn't recognize who I am…yet. Part of my agitation earlier stemmed from fear. His family is dead because of me. I am terrified what he will do when he finds out.

It won't take him long. I have the feeling he is determined to find out everything about me. Before I thought he was just one of Oliver's men but now, this changes it all. I know what he wants, and it's not my money or my father's inheritance it's me. All of me, he demands to peel my layers back and have me bare my soul to him. That can't happen. I have been living life as someone else for a long time. I can't let anyone in. I will break.

I could tell him who I am, then he would lose interest. I am sure he will hate me for the pain I have caused him. My heart constricts at the thought of him hating me. No, I'll have to get away as soon as I can or try to keep him at bay until Oliver comes. He said he knew agent Sharp, I'm not sure the connection there but, it doesn't help me.

My life is a complete mess. I glance up as we hit a bump throwing me off balance. Dylan reaches out to steady me.

"Looks like we are almost there, this road is crap. But hey, good job picking the most remote place in these mountains." He smiles as we bounce around in my little car. "We should invest in an SUV or something. We won't be going anywhere once the snow flies."

I didn't think about that, but I doubt I will be here that long. It's only the end of June. We make our way down the dirt road, there isn't much to see but trees on both sides. The farther we go the more frightened I become. How am I going to get away from him? Part of me welcomes him coming along for the ride. I hadn't realized quite how isolated this cabin would be.

Eventually the forest thins, and the trail leads us to a clearing. There it is. My new home, something I have always wanted, a cabin in the woods. My fear of being with this big brute of a man subsides a little. At this moment I am as excited as a kid in a candy store. I'll worry later, for now I want to go and explore.

"You said you gave your ranch away, that you bought this place? Not to be nosy but what do your parents think of all this? Do they own it or do you?" Dylan asks as he pulls up in front of the cabin.

I stare at him with my mouth open. I don't know how to answer. His question catches me off guard. It makes sense, he is friends with Agent Sharp. He questioned me about my parents too. I panic. I'm only nineteen. I worked at a bookstore. There is no logical way for me to explain owning a ranch. Then gifting it away to purchase a cabin such as this. I turn to reach for my door handle, the lock clicks.

"I asked you a question, Sarah. Here we are, there is nowhere to run. I understand what you have been through believe me but, no more running. I told you I will tear you apart and put you back together. You need to trust me. You need to be truthful and you need to do as I say." His expression is deadly serious, he isn't playing games anymore.

"It's complicated," I plead. "Let's look around and check the place out. I need a moment of not thinking about things."

He unlocks the door not taking his eyes off me. "We explore, eat and then I want answers."

I shake my head in agreement praying that he will forget the questions. I know he won't. I can't answer him. He will figure it out. I can't run, I can't hide. He will hate me when he learns who I am.

He opens my door for me. "You got the keys to this place?"

"The realtor said he would leave them under the mat. I stand by the car watching him stride up the steps. Kicking the mat, he reaches down and picks up the keys.

He jingles them in front of him to show me they were where I said they would be, flashing me a smile. When he smiles, he doesn't look near as frightening.

I join Dylan on the porch as he opens the front door. He steps aside but as I pass he quickly scoops me up and carry's me across the threshold. What the hell? He sets me back down on my feet as soon as we enter, not letting me go. I try to push away but he doesn't budge.

He takes my chin in his hand and forces me to look up at him. He is so much taller than me, the top of my head barely comes to his shoulders. I focus on the wooden beams above him, looking anywhere but at him.

"Don't. Move," he says. He states this with such authority I tremble, not sure what is happening.

He lets go of my waist and keeps one hand firmly on my chin, bringing the other towards my face. I try to squirm away, but he pulls me closer to him, moving his hand towards my eye.

"I'm fucking serious don't move." He brushes his index finger lightly over my eye drawing aside the brown contact exposing the truth.

He releases me and stares at the contact on the tip of his finger. No, no, he will figure out who I am. I run, trying to remember the layout of the cabin. I dash upstairs straight through the master bedroom and into the bathroom and lock myself in. I realize after plopping to the floor that he didn't follow me. He didn't try to stop me. He knows.

I try to pull myself together. I stare out the window, no way down. I go back to the long mirror running over the counter. One brown eye and one blue. I always thought people born with two different colored eyes were unique. I am not unique. I am just a fucked-up mess. I don't even know who I am anymore. Am I Anna or am I Sarah? Sarah's parents ran off and left me alone. Anna's parents are all dead, my mother, stepfather and even my real father…the notorious sex-trafficker.

Suddenly, I feel nauseous, I slide to the toilet and relieve myself of my morning breakfast. I squat down and look around me at the elegant bathroom. It is all stone tile and wood framing. The walk-in shower is large with a rain shower head in the center. This place is beautiful. I could be out exploring my new home but instead here I sit. I'm tired of running, tired of hiding.

What would happen if I quit running, quit hiding, quit thinking? Dylan said I need to be truthful with him, to do what he says and to trust him. I have never trusted anyone. Possibly Irene and Frank, at one time my mother but after being sent away even that evaporated. I don't know if I can do what he is asking. Then again, he isn't asking…he is demanding.

I get up to remove the brown contact then stare into Anna's eyes. What do you have to lose, Anna? Absolutely nothing, at this point all I have is this cabin and the hot yet terrifying man downstairs. Oliver will eventually come but maybe Dylan can make me forget about all that for a little while. That or he will kill me when he learns the truth of who I am. Either way, it won't matter. The end will always remain the same, I will die.

Chapter Seventeen

Dylan

I stare at the little brown contact on my finger. I tried to confront her in the car. I could see her excitement as we pulled up, but I couldn't leave it alone. It's like a scab you keep picking until finally you make it bleed. After Liam mentioned her eye color, I noticed she was wearing contacts. Then she confused me when I told her who I was. She seemed more agitated than when she assumed I worked for Oliver.

She bolted the minute she realized what was happening. She wasn't just using the contacts in vain to match her current outfit. She is hiding. She ran upstairs, she will come back down when she is ready. She knows I'm not going anywhere.

I walk outside inhaling a deep breath of fresh mountain air. I shouldn't have stolen her moment of excitement, but I don't play games. I want everything out in the open, I can't help or protect her if I don't know what the heck is happening.

I jog down the steps and grab our bags out of the car then take them inside. I will go through her shit deeper, read my file and hopefully find clues. I grab her little carry on and the folder out of my bag and head into the kitchen.

Everything is spacious in the cabin. The living room and kitchen are all one big open space with high ceilings. Large logs run up the corners, each with their own uniqueness. Ah, I could get used to this, it is beautiful, just like the owner. I open the fridge expecting it to be empty, but it is packed full, along with the cupboards. Damn, this girl is resourceful.

I grab a soda and crack it as I open her bag to dump it on the counter. The only things that pique my interest are the contacts, notebook and a ring I hadn't spotted before. It was tucked away in a little compartment. It looks like an engagement ring, the rock in the thing must be worth thousands. I put it back in the pocket. I need to remember to ask her why she kept it. Something so tiny but it makes me so angry.

I open the file from Liam and read through it. Her birth certificate has her eye color listed as brown. He didn't lie, the blue that was hiding was unique, unforgettable. I have known someone with a similar color. I pause, could it be? I study the date. The age would be correct, but Annette and Manuel's daughter drowned. I pick up her book of poetry pulling out the pen, *Anna.* No way, could this be the connection between Sophia and her? Could she be little Anna Velasquez?

I reflect on the funeral for the girl. The short casket was closed. They buried her on the estate in a private cemetery. Annette visited every day after her death, she was distraught, never the same after that. My sister traveled with her friends to help with the other girl, what were their names? Dammit, I can't remember.

I pull my phone out to dial Liam but as I do I spot something sticking out of the black book. I tug at it. I stare at the image in my hand. No fucking way. It is a picture of Annette herself. I lean back in my chair staring up at the ceiling. I put my cell away, no need to call. I am certain of who she is. How did I not notice the resemblance earlier?

Still, so many unanswered questions but now I know who she is. I'm not sure how she is alive. I can't help but speculate that this is fate. And she is mine…Anna Velasquez is mine…all mine. I smile to myself. Manuel and Annette would be pleased. I couldn't rescue Sophia and that kills me, but we pulled someone else we knew out of the depths of hell. Manuel would be so angry if he knew that Oliver had his daughter. He would be proud of us for finding her. I'm excited to tell Liam, he will shit his pants.

This explains so much. The tenderness and great care she showed for Sophia. It even clarifies why they took her. I'm not sure how Oliver figured out she was Manuel's daughter, but it shows how determined he was to take everything from him.

That is why they kept Sophia. They must have somehow found out Anna was alive and hoped Sophia could point them in the right direction. She knew the truth. A girl drowned that day except it wasn't Anna it was the other little girl. A shudder runs through me at the image of what they may have done to my sister to persuade her to give up the information.

Anna

I've sat in the bathroom all afternoon. Dylan doesn't come for me, but I know he is still here. I could hear him in the master bedroom opening and shutting drawers. I peer out the window to watch the sun sink behind the trees. My stomach is grumbling, I can smell something cooking. It smells amazing. I push off the window seal and turn to look at the door. I'm not sure what is waiting for me on the other side. I suspect that he has figured out who I am.

I need to keep it together. I'm weary of crying in front of him. He must think I'm a big baby. I don't know what to say, sorry for killing your mother and sister? He will hate me. The idea makes me miserable. I should be happy that now he knows who I am, he will be repulsed by the site of me. More than likely he will either kill me or leave me...alone. I thought I wanted to be alone. Alone to think. Alone to wait.

Let's get this over with, Anna. Let's go out and rip the band-aid off. I open the door, the scent of whatever he is cooking comes rushing at me. I'll wait until after I eat, he might deny me food once he learns the truth. Nothing to lose right? One foot in front of the other.

I stop at the top of the stairs and crouch down to see where he is. He has his back turned to me. He is rinsing something in the sink. He is in jeans and a gray short sleeve t-shirt. I watch the muscles ripple on his back from his movements and notice the tribal art tattoo peeking out under his shirt on his left arm. God, he is spectacular. He reminds me of Sophia except she was so petite. I'm guessing he is well over six feet and made of all lean muscle. I take a seat on the top stair, so I can ogle him.

"You finally decided to join me. Perfect timing, come and sit down, everything is just about finished."

He didn't turn so I don't know how he knew I was staring at him, but he did. I guess it's his training. I slowly walk down the steps over to the table that is already set. I pull a chair out and notice that in the center of it is the picture of my mother that William gave me and the pen with my name on it. I sit down and stare at my plate.

The days of being Sarah are over and that freaks me out. Anna needed a reprieve after all that happened to her in Venezuela. Dylan is not going to let that happen. He wants answers. He left these things on the table, so I would know what to expect. I'm so deep in thought he startles me when he is suddenly beside me scooping salad onto my plate.

I don't look up as he takes the seat across from me. "This place is beautiful, Anna, you have good taste. I like it. We will enjoy our time here I have a feeling."

There it is, my name, he knows.

He keeps using the word "we" an awful lot. Soon enough he won't. I'm going to tell him everything. If I can just get up the courage. Then that will be the end of the "we". I cautiously glance around the cabin. It is beautiful. Cabins are their own kind of artwork. As I run my eyes around the layout of the place they land on Dylan's. I hear his breath hitch. I quickly glance away.

"Don't," he orders. "Don't hide from me, Anna. I'm not sure what is going on, but you don't get to hide from me. We will work this out tonight and then move forward. Do you understand?"

I shake my head in acknowledgement and pull myself together to look him directly in the eye. It is hard to let him see the real me. It makes me self-conscious.

"Damn, your eyes will be the death of me."

More like he will be the death of me. Heat rises to my cheeks at his complement. Oliver always made similar comments, but it only caused me to hate him more. When Dylan compliments me or shows his possessive side, it incites a different reaction in me. I like it and that can't be good. He is just going to hate me when all is said and done.

The oven dings, he hops up and points to my plate. "You haven't even touched your salad and now dinner is ready. I hope you like chicken parmesan?"

"I like anything I don't have to cook." I am in heaven. After days of not eating much but gas station cuisine, I am starving.

I quickly poke at my salad, delighting in whatever dressing he used. It is a raspberry vinaigrette I believe. He laughs as he walks to the table loading my plate with the main dish. A man that is good looking and can cook, ah I'm sad that this will probably be the last time he cooks for me.

"What you don't like to cook? If I remember right, your mother loved to bake."

I set my fork down with a clank, suddenly feeling inadequate. My mom was an amazing chef, so was Mrs. Madrono. My mother and I used to bake together. When I went to live with the Madronos I would ask if I could help only to be shooed back to my room.

"I'm sorry," he says. "Eat. We will talk after dinner. I looked around the property, it is larger than I thought. You never got to explore when we first arrived, we should do that."

I pick up my fork. It doesn't take long to devour the delicious meal. I savor each bite not knowing if it will be my last. I stand to clear the dishes from the table. He joins me in the chore.

"I'll get this, you cooked dinner. I may not cook but I can clean." I offer him a small smile. He is being so nice. Come to think of it, he hasn't really been all that awful. Except for the whole trunk and kidnapping thing. If I block that out I can almost pretend that we are a couple just doing the normal mundane tasks of each day.

"The sooner we finish the sooner I get my answers," he says.

And back to reality.

After we start the dishwasher, he grabs my hand and leads me through the house. He shows me everything I haven't seen already. Almost like he is a realtor trying to make a sale. After showing me the two bedrooms and bath on the main floor we head outside to the wrap-around porch. When we get to the backside of the cabin, I see a pool and hot tub. I pull my hand from his.

"I don't remember seeing this in the description," I say nervously.

"It's beautiful, I love the blue lighting." He walks over to the side of the house and flips a switch. The pool turns blue along the edges illuminating the water, casting shadows on the bottom as it gently waves in the breeze.

I wouldn't have bought the place had I known there was a pool. I wasn't a big fan of water to begin with but even more so after my experience with Brian. A chill slithers over my skin. I take a few steps back watching Dylan as he bends down and skims his hand across the top of the water.

"It is heated," he says. He glances up and sees my discomfort. He doesn't say anything and leads me back around to the front of the house to a wooden porch swing. The horizon is turning a deep purple, soon it will be dark.

I sit down and stare at the stars. They are just beginning to reveal themselves in the darkening sky. Dylan sits down beside me and makes the swing tilt. He puts his arm around me to prevent me from dumping out. When it levels out, he tugs me in closer to him.

"I assume you have figured out who I am?" he asks.

I try to loosen his grip by wiggling a little, but he doesn't budge. "Yes, you are Sophia's older brother."

"And you are little Anna Velasquez." He squeezes me in jest, trying to lighten the mood.

"I'm so sorry about your sister." I swipe at a tear running from my eye. "I don't know where to start."

He sighs. "I understand, how about you tell me how you ended up using the name Sarah. I thought you had drowned when you were ten. What are you eighteen, nineteen now?"

"Nineteen, my mother's friends were the Madronos. It was their daughter Sarah that drowned. My mother saw her death as an opportunity to whisk me away into hiding, to become Sarah. I'm not sure why they agreed, but they did."

"So, it was Sarah in the casket that day. I remember the little girl you were with did not attend the funeral, but I didn't think much of it as one would assume she would be upset."

"My mother kept me in my room until the night we left, Sophia went with me and stayed for a few days before she had to leave. She told me my parents would come for me when it was safe. She said I needed to pretend to be Sarah until then. As you probably already realize they never came."

He lets out a long breath. "So, your mother felt danger was lurking."

"She did. I wished she would have let me in on the reason for sending me away. I didn't even know what to be afraid of all those years. I received a letter from my mother a few months ago. One she must have originally written when she sent me away. The Madronos left it on the table for me the day they vanished on my nineteenth birthday."

"So, they are missing?" he asks his voice rising.

"No, they left because they were done. I was nineteen. They had fulfilled their obligation to my mother."

He sits forward so he can look me in the eye. "That's bullshit, they left you? Alone?"

I peer out at the pine trees. He is angry that they abandoned me. But that is how it has always been. I've been alone for nine years, whether or not they were in the house. I'm not upset. How can I criticize them? They let me take the place of their deceased daughter. They tried to save me. I should thank them if I ever see them again.

"It's not like that, Dylan. I don't blame them, they were sad, they missed Sarah. They kept me safe for a lot of years. It was my stupid fault that Oliver found me."

He sits back and pulls me close to him again. "It's not right, I will never leave you. I promise."

I pull out of his embrace. I stand up and take a few steps before turning to him. If I run, I'm sure he will follow. His muscles are poised for a chase. "Don't say that, you don't understand. Everything is my fault, all the deaths, all the girls they took from the estate."

"It. Is. All. My. Fault," I annunciate each word trying to emphasize my point.

He reaches for me but I back away. "It is not your fault. You were a child who couldn't even comprehend what was going on. Oliver is a terrible man. None of it is your fault." He grasps at me again.

I place my hand on his chest halting his advance. "Manuel is not my father, a man named William Ramirez is. That is why they went to the estate. They were looking for me. That is why they took Sophia. Oliver kidnapped me, so he could marry me and get William's money."

He begins to shake from anger, I brace myself for the furry. But, I must continue, there is no going back now. "I thought Manuel was my father. I didn't know Oliver had everyone murdered. I didn't know he had Sophia. I knew none of it but none the less it was all because of me." I sob. Saying everything out loud makes it all too real. They are gone, my parents, Sophia…all gone.

I can't do this, why did I tell him. I jump off the edge of the porch and sprint into the dusk. I'm not sure if I am running from him or myself. I rush into the trees hoping the darkness of the forest will swallow me whole. This time he chases me. I realize as I go that I am no match for him, so I stop dead in my tracks. He skids to a halt behind me. We stand there in the dark for several minutes, the only sound in the cool night air is our breath and the occasional hoot of a nearby owl.

"Anna, I'm not a good man. When you run it brings something primal out in me. I don't think you are ready to meet the beast. One day but not today. I need you to come with me on your own accord to the house."

I tremble at his words, *the beast inside him*. I can feel it. I felt it yesterday when he let me out of the trunk, and I ran. "Why don't you kill me, and we can both move on?"

I don't turn, I'm ready to die, I'm tired and oh so exhausted.

He rushes towards me and grabs the back of neck pushing his body up against mine. He pulls my head back into his chest. My heartbeat picks up. This is it. He is going to choke the life right out of me. As we stand there warm tingly feelings sneak into me. When he grips my neck tighter my stomach rolls, not in a bad way. It feels just like when you take a big hill too fast.

What is happening? I should be terrified. My life should be flashing before my eyes. But, all I can envision is him forcing me to the ground, making me drop to my hands and knees, then taking full advantage of me. I shiver causing goose pimples to creep along my arms.

"Why, Anna, maybe you would like to meet the beast?" he breathes heavily in my ear. He loosens his grip and turns me to face him. The level of his restraint is obvious in his expression. I thought he would hate me. That is not what I see. He gleams of sheer lust. His eyes are swirling dark pools, they pin me with a serious look. The one that makes me want to run from him and surrender all at the same time.

I regard him with genuine interest as he pulls himself together. "Let's go back to the cabin. We aren't done with our talk." He puts his arm around my shoulders and leads me to the swing.

"Rules. Rule one – never ask me to kill you again, not happening. Rule two - if you run from me again I will not hold back. Rule three – never say any of what happened is your fault. There are more rules, but this is a good start, I don't want to overwhelm you."

I focus on his thigh and watch the muscle under his jeans as he pushes us on the swing. I don't say anything. The feelings that have come over me are all new. I'm used to being by myself. All the human contact over the last few months is taking its toll.

"Now where were we? Oh yes, I remember, Ramirez is your father. That explains a lot. You can't pick your parents, don't blame yourself." He rubs his hand back and forth over the top of my arm.

"I hate him, and I hate Oliver," I say vehemently.

"I know, baby. I know. I hate them too, but hey that gives us something in common." He stops the swing and tugs at my chin to force me to look at him. "I will help you, Anna. You are not always going to like it but I'm going to help you. We start tomorrow."

I stare at him. For the first time in my life I think I can count on someone, I trust him. I don't understand why but I do. It could be because he is Sophia's brother or because of the way he looks at me. I believe him when he says he will never leave me, even after he just learned the truth. I start to cry again, damn tears.

He brushes them away and leans down taking my mouth. He gently forces me to open for him. His lips are warm against mine. My head is swimming. The warmth returns to my core. He is in complete control. For once in my life I'm not afraid. I'm not sure about these new feelings, but they are as delicious as the meal he served. He pulls back and runs his thumb over my bottom lip smiling like the Cheshire Cat in Alice and Wonderland. I wonder what hole I have just fallen in.

Dylan

I wish she was stronger. I would take her here and now. I will make her mine, but I need to be patient. I read the hospital record from her file. They didn't hurt her, well they did, but they didn't rape her. The thought of anyone touching a single hair on her head makes me murderous. At least they didn't rape her, the report stated that she is still a virgin.

The idea of being her first excites me. I will be gentle the first time, we will work our way up to the hard stuff. I am going to help her and in the process I'll bind her, so she never wants to leave my side.

I about lost control when she ran. There is something about the chase that turns me on, makes me crave to let go of all restraint. But I need her to be strong. I don't want to break her. I want to heal her.

All this crap of her wanting to roll over and die needs to end. I understand where she is coming from. She blames herself for the deaths just like I do. They are gone, and we are here. I get the guilt really I do. This might be good for me too. I don't *want* to help her. I *need* to help her. After years and years of failure I demand something positive come from all of this.

She is good, so very, very good. Hmm, her lips are soft. I loved the way she opened and let me explore her mouth with mine. When I grabbed her in the forest, I could sense her fear, but I also detected her excitement. The way her breath hitched, the way the hair on her body reacted to my touch. Yes, she liked it. I knew fate brought us together.

She thought I would hate her, kill her. Nothing could be farther from the truth. I am going to rip Oliver Wright into a thousand little pieces and scatter him to the fish. I'll call Liam and the guys. Get them working day and night to find him. I will set up the security myself. I'm feeling selfish, I don't want to share Anna with anyone.

I run my thumb over her beautiful full lips. "We should get some sleep. I didn't sleep well in that shithole motel." I stand and pull her up with me. She is in a daze from my kiss. She doesn't look at me, I wonder what she is thinking. I can see that she is confused.

I lock the door and turn off the lights as we head upstairs to the master bedroom. "I unpacked for you, your clothes are in the closet or the bureau over there," I say pointing at it.

She goes to the closet, hesitating as she notices that my clothes are hanging next to hers. She turns to ask me something but stops herself. She rummages around grabbing her clothes and heads to the bathroom.

"No locking the door," I tell her. She pauses briefly but continues. I wait listening to make sure she obeyed. She did.

I strip down to my boxers and climb into bed leaving only the bedside lamp on. The dimness turns the corners of the room to dark shadows.

When she returns and spies me lying on the bed she says, "there are several bedrooms here, you can have this one. I'll sleep downstairs."

She knows better. She waits for my orders. "Nope, hop in. This is the best bed in the house. It's big enough for the two of us. It would be a shame if either of us missed out on its luxury."

She doesn't respond instead she bustles around searching in drawers.

"What are you looking for, Anna?"

"My books, I usually read before bed, it helps me fall asleep."

"They are in the trunk of the car."

She gives me an incredulous look. "Why are they in the trunk? They were in my bag."

I lock my fingers together and place them behind my head. I notice the way she licks her lips as she watches my movements, it pleases me greatly. "I locked them in there. I *said*, and I'll say it again, you are not hiding anymore."

She stands there with her mouth hanging open, unsure of how to reply. I watch as she slowly realizes what I am getting at. "I don't hide in my books." She crosses her arms across her chest haughtily.

"No?" I cock my head enjoying her standing there for my eyes only.

"Hmph." She storms to the other side and pulls the covers high under her chin.

I reach over to shut the light off, then I draw her close, spooning her in a protective cocoon. She doesn't fight as much as she did at the hotel. I smile into her hair. My little Anna, all mine.

"You are giving me the key tomorrow you know."

"Maybe we can make a deal. You give me something I want, and I'll grant you one of your other worlds." I inhale her scent locking every single detail about her into my mind.

"What do you want?" she says shakily.

"I'm sure I'll think of something." I won't, I don't want her running away from me even if it is to a fictitious place in a novel.

Chapter Eighteen

Anna

I wake up leisurely and stretch. But then I remember where I am, and I sit up straight. I look at the rumbled sheets beside me. He is gone. I hear pans bang down in the kitchen. I lay down, the smell of bacon and pancakes wafts up the stairs pulling at me to get up. I want to stay in bed all day. Or should I hide in the bathroom?

Dylan is making me feel strange things, things I don't know if I am ready for. He is all-consuming. I reflect to the kiss on the front porch, my stomach does a somersault. Damn. I sit up deciding a cold shower is what I need. I toss the covers back as I detect footsteps coming up the stairs.

"Good morning sunshine." The sexiest man alive stands in the doorway with a tray looking at me like he won the lottery. He is barefoot and wearing only a pair of sweats low on his hips that reveal a dark patch of hair over the seam. I turn my eyes away embarrassed by my brazen assessment of him.

He walks over as I cautiously grab the blanket, pulling it back up. I need a barrier of some sort between us. He carefully sets the tray over my lap. There are perfectly shaped pancakes, bacon, eggs, fresh strawberries and a cup of coffee. I've never had anyone make me breakfast in bed. "You didn't have to do this. I could have come downstairs."

"I wanted to. Another rule don't question the nice things I do for you. You have been through a lot, you deserve to be treated well, Anna."

When Oliver did nice things for me it was always a trick of some sort, a way of messing with my head. I don't suspect that this is what Dylan is doing, but it still makes me a little nervous none the less.

"Thank you." I pick up my fork and take a bite of pancakes. He sits down on the edge of the bed intently watching me.

"I like you much better as Anna," he says bending slightly to catch my eyes.

I try to distract him from looking so closely at me. "So, what is the deal with my books?"

"Oh, hmm, what could we barter? How about you tell me what frightened you most when you were with Oliver? Then I will give you a book, with one stipulation, you can only read for an hour a day."

"You can't boss me around. You don't own me." I set the fork down with a clang on the plate.

He stands up walking away. The deal off the table.

"Wait." I need a book. I want an escape from my reality even if it is just for a short while.

He returns. "One thing but it must be what scared you the most about him."

I consider his question. "Everything scared me. I can't name one thing that wasn't frightening about my time there."

He runs his finger along the bruise on the side of my cheek. I turn away embarrassed by how it must look today, every day it turns a nastier color than the previous.

"Did they hit you?"

I shake my head. "No. I got this when I attacked a guard. I jumped on his back, he reared his head and hit me in the face."

"Is that how you got these?" He pulls my hand into his and rubs his thumb lightly across my palm.

"Yes. I found a rope and surprised him when he came to get us up for the day. I killed him." I glance away leaving out the fact that Sophia tried to talk me out of it. She would still be alive if I hadn't killed him, she would have never had access to the gun.

He turns my face back towards him. "My brave Anna." He gazes into my eyes with true admiration. It warms me. He appears proud of me, something else I have experienced little. Liam gave me a similar look when I decoded my book for him. I turned over all the information I had overheard from my days spent with Oliver.

"That makes you part of my team," he says. I stare at him confused, and he explains. "My team's job for the last eight years has been taking out Oliver's men. You got one. That should merit you a mulligan, so I will give you a book. You don't have to answer my question, at least not right now." He grins granting me a spectacular view of his pearly whites.

Flip-flop goes my stomach. When he is serious he makes me melt, when he is frightening he excites me and when he smiles my heart literally explodes. If I don't give myself space from him I am just going to end up hurt. Oliver is coming. I can't forget that. Dylan says he won't let it happen. I want to trust him. But, I know that Oliver is a patient man. Look how long he waited for me to slip. He will find me. He is waiting for me to slip again.

He picks up my fork and hands it to me. "Your food is getting cold. I was thinking that I will run into town today. I need to pick up some things. We should set up security around here. I'll also stock up on supplies. I would make you go with, but I can trust you to stay. Unless you want to that is."

"You are going to leave me here alone?"

"You are welcome to come but I thought it might be nice for you to have time to yourself. To process things, explore your new home. I will be back. I will never leave you, never." He taps the end of my nose lightly. "If you are worried about Oliver, he hasn't had enough time to locate you yet. You are safe. If I didn't think so, I wouldn't take off."

"Okay I will stay," I say hesitantly. It's a trap, he is wanting to see if I'll run. Oliver used to set traps for me too.

Dylan goes back downstairs and allows me to eat in peace. I shove the rest of my food down not really tasting any of it. He is leaving me alone. Should I come up with a plan to get away? He returns minutes later setting a book down on the table beside me. He leans over to ask if I want seconds then he picks up the tray.

As he walks out he says, "why don't you go ahead and hop in the shower, I'll be up in a second."

What did he say? I'm losing my mind. Did he mean he would be up to shower with me? He must have meant he will take his after I'm done.

Surely he doesn't expect to shower with me. Anna, you are just hot and bothered, pull your head out and come up for air.

I grab a pair of shorts and tank top out of the dresser. I'll go for a walk today. My mood is slightly getting better at the notion of being able to move around without someone standing over me. I head into the bathroom and turn to bolt the door behind me, but I stop. He has made it clear I am not to lock the door. I think it's to make sure that I don't do anything stupid. After Sophia he is being cautious.

I undress and enter the shower. I turn the handles and the spray from the twenty-four-inch rain shower head falls. This was one of the selling factors of the cabin for me. It is going to feel amazing. Just as I get the water set to the correct temperature I hear the door open.

Dylan saunters in making eye contact with me through the glass. He slowly bends and pushes down his sweats.

Somehow I break the hold he has on my eyes. What is he doing? My mind is reeling, fighting hard to convince itself that he is not Oliver. That this is different. It feels different but is it? He didn't ask me if any of this okay. He demands all of it. He opens the shower. I quickly skitter to the corner farthest away from him, pressing my chest against the cool tile.

"Don't fight this, Anna. You want it too. I won't take you today, we will go slow, but I need to touch you. I need to feel that you are real and not some figment of my imagination. I want to know you are alive." His voice sounds heavy with need, but he doesn't reach for me.

I turn my head slightly and whisper against the tile, "I don't know what you want me to do."

He comes close, his heat radiates into me. Gently he tugs at my shoulders and pulls me until the spray streams along my spine. "You don't have to do anything you don't want to."

He coaxes my head back under the stream and lets the water run through the strands. I smell the familiar lavender scent of my shampoo as he massages it into my hair and scalp. His fingers move down to my neck gently caressing the knots away, I moan as he finds them.

My muscles relax. He fills his palms with more soap and begins where he left off working his way down my arms. He works harder on the tender areas, making me let out more sounds of approval. He gets to my lower back and slides his hands around to pull me closer into his body. The slickness of the soap glides between us. His erection gently pokes into my spine.

I tense, he breaths into my ear, reminding me he will stop. I just need to say the word. Hesitantly I relax against him, blindly trusting. I should stop him. My brain tells me to, but my body quietly whispers it desires this. It demands his gentle touch. It requires him to work out all the pain and wash away everything that has happened until this moment.

His strong hands roam over my stomach. Climbing to my ribs, he leaves nothing untouched. He forces every cell to life under his fingers. He moves higher yet, lightly running his hands over my breasts. My breath hitches. He groans in my ear. His voice so deep, it fires the sound that escaped him to vibrate right down to my pussy.

He cradles my tits in his palms and brushes the pad of his thumb over each nipple. I lean my head back into his chest lost in the new sensations that my body is experiencing. The outside world melts away. He pinches my nipples, shooting a brief signal of pain to my brain but just as quickly soothes his hands over them making the sensation turn to pure bliss. He does this repeatedly, pinching and smoothing until I can only concentrate on the fire burning between my legs. I find myself silently willing his hands to move, to touch me lower.

I swear he can read my mind as he leaves my breasts giving them a sweet reprieve. He pulls me in tight to him with one arm around my waist while the other hand finds its way down, rubbing lightly over me. I drive my hips shamelessly and grind into his palm seeking something more. I need more. More what I don't know but I need it. More pressure, more pain, more pleasure.

He is like a musician and I his instrument. He seems to have insight on where and how to touch my body to make me moan. He wrenches little noises from me as he slides his fingers deeper between my folds finding my clit rubbing, pinching just like he tortured my nipples. A flash of pain rewarded by the sweet tingle of pleasure.

Something builds inside me. I struggle to break away, but he holds me tight and whispers in my ear, "I got you, let yourself go, I got you."

I'm climbing, climbing and then I tumble. I cry out, closing my eyes, bracing myself against Dylan's hard torso. I grab his hand and still it on me, riding the shock waves that come as I fall into the heavenly bliss of nothing but pleasure. My body and his pressed together seamlessly.

Dylan moves his arm up and hugs me around the waist, he presses kisses against my temple. We stand there for the longest time the water falling over our naked bodies. "You okay, baby?"

"Yes." I turn to stare up at him. He towers over me, he looks worried. God, he is beautiful. I reach up and run my fingers across the stubble of a beginning beard, watching water droplets fall as I do.

He grabs my wrist to halt my movement. "You don't have to do this," he says with his serious look plastered on his face.

"What if I want to know you are alive too? I thought everyone was gone." His features soften, and he closes his eyes, releasing me. I trace my fingers along the scar on his forehead and drop them down his neck. He is so big. I think back to the hotel when he asked if I wanted to strangle him. It would take someone much stronger than me that is for sure. I rub my thumb over the hollow of his throat watching his face intently.

I grab the soap and caress my hands over him. I mimic his earlier movements over my body. His skin is tan. He is solid muscle. I watch as his muscles tremble beneath my fingers. I notice where he is most sensitive and focus my attention to those areas. His dick twitches against my stomach. My curiosity whispers to peek down at him. I take a deep breath willing my fear down. His cock is long and thick, I see it drip with desire.

He opens his eyes, staring at me intently. I sense that he is reluctant to make any sudden movements. Afraid to send me running out of the shower screaming. His words echo in my mind, *my brave little Anna*. I reach out and wrap my hand around his cock hearing his abrupt intake of breath as I do.

I peer up at him not sure what to do from here. I want to make him feel as good as he made me, but I don't know how. "Just stroke it, you can't do it wrong," he says through gritted teeth. I can see he is straining to control himself. It frightens me a little. I can't imagine what he will be like when he lifts the restraints.

I close my fist and move it down the length of him and then forward again all the way to the tip brushing my thumb over the end. He seems to approve as he tilts his head back moaning. I watch the water fall over his face.

I continue to pump my fist a little faster, wrapping it tighter around him with each stroke. He grabs my arms and leans into me placing his forehead to mine and lets out a loud groan. His cock twitches in my hand as his seamen splays across my stomach.

The satisfaction I get from giving him pleasure grows inside me changing something. I realize that I have never been so in control in my entire life. I pushed past my fear. I took control of the situation. I didn't hide. I didn't drift away to Sarah. He lifts his head looking down at my stomach smiling.

"God that felt good." He bends down kissing me hard. I open to him letting him explore my mouth. I run my hands up his torso and wrap them around his neck pulling him close.

He breaks his hold on me and smiles. "You positive you don't want to go with me today? I'm not sure if I can leave you after that."

I give him a small shy smile. "I'm sure."

We rinse off not taking our eyes off each other. When we leave the sanctuary of the shower the cool air on the other side of the glass makes the hair on my arm stand up. He wraps me up tightly in a towel rubbing my arms as he does.

I stop at the door not wanting to go back out into the real world. He knows what I am thinking. He presses a kiss to the top of my head. "When we leave this room, nothing changes. You are still mine."

After Dylan pulled away, I felt it. I assumed I would rejoice at being away from my captor. The prospect of being alone had made me happy…until he drove away.

His presence is all-consuming. Wherever we are, in the car, the kitchen…the shower. I watched as he pulled away. Slowly dread filled my soul. He says he was just going into town for supplies. He is leaving. Maybe he won't return. I will be trapped here until I die, or until Oliver finds me. I am alone.

I hyperventilated running into the house and crawled into bed. Everyone leaves me. Even Oliver left me behind. I know that sounds crazy, but it's true. Every single person in my life has left me to fend for myself. Dylan will be no different. What was I thinking in the shower? What if he didn't like it? Did I do something wrong? Did he get what he wanted and now he is gone?

I sit for hours rocking back and forth on the bed. My mantra enters my head at some point. Eventually I walk downstairs and stare at the furnishings in front of me. I peer up at the wood beams running high into the ceiling. It doesn't matter. It was all going to end the same.

Back to cooking for myself I think sullenly. I make my way over to the kitchen and glance up at the clock noticing it is well past lunch. I spot a letter on the counter. Oh god not another surprise letter. This one is accompanied by a single rose. I pick up the rose breathing in the sweet fragrance. The petals tickle my nose. I read the note from Dylan.

Anna,

I whipped up my famous chicken salad for your lunch. You will find it in the blue container in the fridge. I know you said you don't know how to cook, I thought you might like to learn. We start tonight. I will be most happy to teach you all about certain delicacies.

Forever yours,
Dylan

I read the letter repeatedly, smiling at the little winky face he drew by the word delicacies. I sense there is a double meaning there. The somersault in my stomach rolls each time I run over the words. Then the end, forever yours. Is he really mine? He keeps saying I am his, but does it go both ways?

He is coming back. I should be terrified, but I find that I anxiously await his return. I gobble up the chicken salad. I even take the chance to shower again making sure I am cleanly shaved. I then blow dry my hair and brush it, so it is sleek and shiny.

I am primping for a man. How did this happen so fast? I barely know him. He kidnapped me two days ago. What the hell am I thinking? I'm not. Dylan has done all the thinking for the both of us and I find that that somehow makes my life easier.

When I'm with Dylan, I don't have to think I just have to be. I only have to be Anna, nothing more, that seems to make him happy. He scares me and yet he doesn't. It makes little sense. I pick up my book to read as my eyes drift to the window. I set the novel down and decide to live in my reality for once. I will go for that walk.

As I'm about to step outside, I hear my cell ring. I turn towards the sound. It is right there in the living room plugged in and charging. I see that I have an incoming call from an unknown number. I thought Dylan had either hidden or taken my phone. He hadn't. I'm somewhat confused by this revelation. Kidnappers don't leave their victim with a way to contact the outside world.

Should I answer it? It might be Irene or Frank. They were very concerned the day I said goodbye to them. "Hello?"

My blood turns ice cold as I hear the familiar silky voice slither into my ear. "Kitten, I have been trying to call you. Why haven't you been picking up? I thought maybe you had gotten a new phone. Which would have been a shame since Brian was so kind to take note of your number when he found you in Texas."

I don't know why I respond but I do. Habit I guess. "I'm sorry Oliver. My phone has been dead." Is he here? I peek out the window and slowly creep my way over to the door ensuring that it is locked.

"I expect you to answer when I call. Don't make that mistake again. I will forgive you this time because how could you have known I would be calling."

"Yes, sir." I pull the phone away from ear and look at it. Could it have a tracker?

"You have been a very bad girl haven't you, Anna?"

I say nothing.

"You have made things very difficult for me but don't worry, kitten, I am a very resourceful man. I am sure that Brian will come and retrieve you soon. Why don't you tell me where you are and that should help speed up the process?"

"I'm…I'm at the ranch."

"Tsk, tsk I assumed you would know better than to play these games with me. I will find you and when I do, you will see a side of me you will not like."

Dead silence. He is giving me another chance. No way am I telling him where the fuck I am. I hoped I could wait for him to come and then I would fight him. But hearing his voice again has terrified me more than I ever dreamed possible.

"Have it your way. Take care, kitten."

The line goes dead. I study my phone and drop it onto the floor. I pick my foot up to smash it, but I stop. If there is a tracker in there will smashing it help? I am going to have to ask Dylan about it.

I peek out the window, should I still leave for my walk? I don't think Oliver knows where I am…at least not yet. I step outside and take a big whiff of the clean pine air. It is a beautiful clear day. But, I see storm clouds rolling in from the west. The similarity between the sky and my life does not unnoticed.

Chapter Nineteen

Dylan

It takes everything in me to leave her. She waves at me from the porch. I am confident she won't do anything to hurt herself while I am away and I'm sure she won't run. She isn't stupid. She is the one who bought the place specifically for the remote location. She knows there is nowhere to go.

I hadn't foreseen that she would take charge like that in the shower. Yes, I fully expected to touch every single square inch of her, but I didn't think she would reciprocate. I need to make this quick and get back to her. I need the equipment to ensure she remains safe. I can't take any risks.

I pull my cell out of my pocket to call Liam.

"Change of plans, I need you and the guys to resume the search for Oliver."

"Already started, I never stopped you dumb ass."

I laugh, he can't piss me off today. I'm in far too favorable of a mood. "Anything?"

"A private plane flew out of a small airport near the compound that night. I have my people scoring over flight patterns. The guys are ready to fly out, so we can get men on the ground."

"Excellent, no sign of them here in the states?"

"Nope."

"Good. I'm picking up supplies now. I will get the security system in place at Anna's cabin."

"Anna? Don't you mean Sarah? Did you forget her name already? Really?" he says with an incredulous tone.

"Oh crap, I forgot. Sorry, no. You will not believe this, but you were right. Her eyes are blue."

"No shit Sherlock, I told you I wasn't crazy."

"Yeah, yeah I realize you aren't the crazy one. You are my voice of reason. Anyhow, her name is Anna. Anna Velasquez. Do you remember her?" I question.

"Now who is crazy? She is dead, Dylan. I don't know what kinda crap this girl is pulling but…"

"Stop. It is her. She has a picture of Annette. It's her. Her friend, the other little girl, Sarah Madrono, she is the one who drowned. Annette talked the Madronos into taking Anna and raising her as their daughter to protect her from Ramirez."

"I'm confused here. Did Annette know that there was a threat from Ramirez and Wright?" he says.

I detect the anger that lurks behind his words. I need to tread lightly. He is tore up over Sophia. "You remember how Annette became pregnant soon after Manuel rescued her? Well, she must have already been pregnant with Ramirez's baby. He is Anna's father or at least he thought he was, I guess that much hasn't been proven."

"So, she is the reason for the attack?" he says flatly.

"It's not her fault, Liam."

"We should use her."

"What? Fuck no! Listen, one of us will kill him but we are not using her. What the hell man, you told me she gave you information, you said yourself she was innocent."

"How do you know she is telling the truth? She could be setting you up."

"Liam, I'm texting you the location, come out and talk to her yourself, you will see she is not lying. I mean it. We. Are. Not. Using. Her." I stress each word letting him know I am serious. "If anyone hurts her they are dead, do you understand?"

"Sure. I'll come, but I don't like this, Dylan. You are losing focus."

He seems to have calmed down. "Take the next flight to Denver and I'll send you the address."

"Fine," he says.

I hang up. That wasn't the reaction I was expecting. Liam is always the voice of reason but this time our conversation took a turn. I brush it off, he will come around once he gets here and talks to her for himself. He is just upset about Sophia. We all are.

The drive is torturous. The farther I am away from the cabin the harder it is to keep driving. I arrive to town over an hour later. First thing I do is go to a dealership and trade this tin can in for something more my size. I opt for a black SUV. As I transfer everything out of her car to the new ride, I wonder how angry she will be when I don't come back with it. I envision her stomping her little foot down crossing her arms giving me the big bad Anna glare. I smile, good something to get us going when I return.

I quickly run through my list and pick up everything I need. I make an unplanned stop to grab a few extra fun in the bedroom items. I'm surprised to find a sex shop in the middle of the high mountains but hey you got to do something for entertainment up here.

As I drive my thoughts swirl with excitement. I am hoping that Oliver doesn't appear for a while. Getting snowed in with Anna wouldn't be so bad, it would be plenty of time to introduce her to all sort of forbidden pleasures.

I pull up to the cabin just as evening is setting in. Dark clouds fill the sky. I hear a rumble in the distance. I will check on her before I unload the SUV. I walk in. It is quiet, too quiet. I call out to her not getting a response. I move through the house checking every room. There is no sign of her, nothing amiss, but my heart races. I shouldn't have left her.

I jog outside to look around and see a patch of trampled grass that leads out to the forest. She didn't. I follow the path she made, as soon as I am deeper into the trees I hear something. It sounds like water, a river perhaps.

I realize as I get close the sound is a little bubbling stream. There she is, sitting on a rock absently watching the current swirl around the rocks.

"I didn't run," she says not turning to look at me.

"I didn't think you had."

She turns and smiles, she knows that is exactly what I thought. "Sure, whatever you say."

I climb up beside her and brush her hair off her shoulder to press a kiss there. "I didn't think you would venture away from the house."

"I guess I'm feeling brave today." She smiles again, her cheeks flush with color.

"Brave enough to race me to the cabin and help me unload?" I joke. I study the dark sky. "It looks like it is going to rain." I stand and take a few steps thinking she will follow but I hear her speak in a whisper, barely audible over the sound of the stream.

"Do you really want to know what scared me the most about Oliver and my time there?" Her eyes are fixated on the water.

I place her hand in mine and scoot in close to her. If she is going to share something with me then I will not waste this opportunity, whether or not we get caught in the rain. "Yes, talking about it might help."

Her bottom lip trembles. "When I woke up there they had me tied naked to an exam table. They had drugged me. I had been under for a long time. I was so scared I didn't know who had me or what they would do."

The thought of her in their hands makes me want to lash out and kill. I must maintain calm for her to continue. She is finally opening up. This is what I have wished for more than anything. She stares at me searching my face, searching for reassurance. "Go ahead, nothing you say will change the way I feel about you."

She looks back at the water. "After I woke up this asshole named Brian took me to Oliver's office. He warned me about Oliver, but I didn't listen. Oliver asked me what my name was and when I told him Sarah, he got upset. He asked a second time. I replied the same. I was so stupid, I knew he already realized who I was I just couldn't be Anna not there, not with them."

Her whole body shakes. I hug her rocking her back and forth. "It's okay you are here with me now, no one will hurt you." I continue to hold her as big raindrops cry down upon on us. To hell with the storm, I'm not moving if she is talking. If we go inside, she might shut down.

"He became so angry he called Brian in and told him to punish me. I'm not sure if Brian was aware of my biggest fear, but that is how he did it."

I cradle her face in both of my hands looking into her tear-filled eyes. "It's the water isn't it?"

Her eyes widen with surprise. "How did you know?" she breathes out.

I draw her into my arms. "I saw how frightened you were by the pool. It makes sense, you watched your friend drown at ten years old. Who wouldn't be afraid?"

"I thought he would kill me. He took me to a bathroom making me get into a tub full of water. It happened so fast. He was so big I couldn't stop him, he kept pushing me down repeatedly letting me up long enough to give me a short breath." She sits up wiping at her eyes and pulls out of my arms trying to get herself together.

"Anna, I'm so sorry."

She waves her hand to dismiss me. "It's fine, it's nothing compared to what the other girls had to endure. I think I passed out, that is when he stopped."

"You didn't deserve that. What happened to you matters just as much as what happened to them. Don't discount any of it, it was real, it sounds terrifying. Anna, it's okay to not be okay. You don't always have to be strong."

She laughs, a laugh that sounds on the verge of hysterical. "No? I do, Dylan. Oliver is out there looking for me right now. I can never escape him." She stands up and scrambles off the rock as the rain falls heavier.

"Stop, Anna."

She doesn't. She runs. I clumsily try to run after her. She caught me off my game, damn her, she maneuvers over the wet slick dirt better than I can. We make it up to the clearing as the rumble of thunder moves in on our heels. It is turning into a muddy mess and I have to focus on each step as my heavy boots bog me down.

I pause to push the hair out of my face, so I can see what I'm doing. I notice she has stopped to face me. She is about six feet away, out of my reach. She points to the cabin. "What the fuck is that? Where is my car?"

I smile. Damn she is so fucking hot standing there in the rain all angry. Her blue eyes seem unworldly, bright sapphires set against a gray gloomy back drop. "I traded it in for something more my size."

I really didn't trade it in, it is in a storage unit. I bought the SUV and hid hers away. I couldn't have sold it even if I wanted to without a title. We needed a new vehicle if Oliver is looking for her, but I would not tell her all this. She is so cute when she is angry.

She stands there fuming and bends over to pick up a handful of mud. She flings it right at my face. Neither of us move. It's like a western movie where both cowboys are waiting to draw, tension fills the air.

"Anna, Anna, Anna, what have you done? First you run and then you throw mud at me?"

"What are you going to do? Drown me?" She bends down and picks up another handful holding it as a ruthless smile appears.

"Don't you fucking dare sweetheart." I realize she is messing with me. She wants me to chase her. I warned her what would happen, she is inviting me.

She flings it and turns to run. I kick off my boots swiping my hand over my face. I take off chasing her. She slips a little and throws her arms out to catch her balance, as she does I hurl myself at her knocking us both down. She crawls out from under me and picks up another pile, slinging it at me catching my shoulder.

"You've been a very bad girl, Anna." I pick up a large handful of the sludge and throw it directly at her splattering it all over the front of her chest.

She looks down and then back up at me and laughs, not a cynical crazy laugh like before but a genuine happy fun laugh. The sound is music to my ears. Her face is so lit and alive. She is beautiful even in the mud. I will never let her go. I crawl to her as she laughs harder trying to stand to make her retreat, but I grab her ankles bringing her down to the ground.

She is flat on her back as I creep over the top of her. She the prey and I the predator. She becomes quiet, watching me as I slowly crawl my way until I am over her, my wet hair drips down on her face. She blinks as her breathing picks up, her chest rises and falls faster with each second that ticks by.

She reaches up brushing my hair away from my eyes and lifts her head, kissing me lightly before laying back down on the muddy ground. “Please don’t ever leave me.”

My heart explodes. She is mine and I am hers. Nothing is perfect. We are lying in the mud in the middle of a thunderstorm. Two broken souls but in this moment I know my life is about to change forever. Good or bad we were destined for each other.

Anna

Why did I ask him to never leave me? That was so stupid! He is looking down at me with a strange look. I shouldn’t have said that. Stupid. Stupid, Anna. I’m just shook up over the phone call from Oliver and when I am with Dylan, he makes me forget.

“Anna, I will never leave you, you are mine,” he says wiping mud away from face.

I wish I could believe him. I wish we could stay here forever. I wish Oliver wasn’t lurking around the corner somewhere...but he is.

I’m safe with Dylan. When I heard him walk up behind me at the stream, I knew it was him. I could sense it was him before I even turned. There is something that draws me to him.

“Anna, what is wrong? Did anything happen while I was gone? You seem like you’re a million miles away.” He looks deep into my eyes trying to bring my focus back to him.

Just as I am about to tell him about the call a loud clap of thunder causes us both to jump. He laughs and pulls me up off the ground with him.

“We better get inside, let me grab my boots,” he says jogging back over to them.

I watch as he tugs them out of the mud. He is so damn sexy. Maybe I could wait until tomorrow. If I tell him now, he will just stew over it and spend all his time setting up the security he talked about.

I'm thinking crazy, but I need just one night. One night to be his. I don't want Oliver to be my first. The thought makes my stomach turn. I trust Dylan for some unexplained reason. I think it is more than him being Sophia's brother, I can't shake him.

He called me brave today. Am I brave enough to let him take me tonight? When we were in the shower I forgot everything. I want that again. I crave it. He is getting under my skin.

"Come on, let's get out of here before we're zapped," he says.

He smiles, his teeth look brilliantly white against his muddy face. I accept his hand as we jog up to the porch. He guides me around back by the pool, shifting so he is a barrier between myself and the water.

He takes me to an outside shower stall. "Let's rinse off, we don't want to get mud all over your beautiful cabin." He winks at me as he peels off his clothes.

I follow suit and remove my clothes rinsing off all traces of mud. My eyes roam over his body. He is solid muscle. My hands itch to touch him. He looks up and I shyly glance away as my face heats.

"You can look at me, I like to watch you too, nothing to be embarrassed about." He hangs our clothes over the fence and then pulls me into his arms holding me tight.

I close my eyes. It is so peaceful in his embrace. The smell of rain mixed with his masculine scent and the rumble of thunder. Perfect. A stark contrast to my surroundings just a few weeks ago, I shake away the thought. He places a light kiss on the top of my head.

"You're awfully quiet, let's get inside and warm up. I'll unload the car. We can have leftovers, then we can talk."

After dressing, Dylan starts a fire in the fireplace. I head to the kitchen to heat our dinner while he hauls in several large boxes and bags. He pulls out a bottle of wine from one of the sacks and hands it to me.

"You can't have leftovers without wine." He winks and heads back into the living room to unpack a few things, moving stuff out of the way, hauling some upstairs.

I decide that we should eat closer to the fire. I'm chilled after being in the rain. I've never had a fireplace. I'm dying to sit next to it. I set plates, silverware and wine glasses down on the coffee table placing the wine bottle in the middle. Viola, meal for two.

I crouch down near the fire and put my hands out to absorb the heat. I've decided to wait and tell Dylan about Oliver's call in the morning. If I have nothing else, I want tonight. He might not make a move but if he doesn't I have a plan.

One thing I'm learning about him is he is an open book. A what you see is what you get sort of guy. I like that. It is so different from how Oliver was, I never knew what to expect with him, and that was scary. Dylan is scary but in a sexy way. This morning I felt pain, but I also felt pleasure, something that confuses me, it feels dark, forbidden.

"Is dinner done?" he says from behind me.

"Um, yes. Sorry I was just getting ready to call for you," I say with a nervous laugh. I take a seat on the couch. My heartbeat picks up as he makes his way down the last few steps.

"It smells delicious," he says.

"Yes, it does, doesn't it? Too bad I didn't make it."

"Tomorrow night you will help me, and you'll see that it's not as hard as you're making it out to be. If I can cook, then so can you," he says sitting down next to me.

I give him a warm smile. "Okay but consider yourself warned. I am a lost cause. Anyway, I hope it's alright that I set us up here in front of the fire? It's just too inviting to resist."

He leans over and kisses me hard then he pulls away, smiling. "Just like you, too inviting to resist."

A blush creeps over my face as he reaches for the corkscrew and opens the bottle. "I've never had wine before. Everything is new to me." I take the glass after he fills it.

"It's okay, baby. We will take everything nice and slow." He takes a sip gazing at me over the top of his glass. He reclines on the couch and rubs little circles down my lower back.

Flip-flop goes my stomach. I'm not sure what to do. Do I really want this? Yes, I think I do. At least my body does. I'm so freaking awkward. I have never dated. I haven't even spent much time with people. I slowly let out the breath I've been holding and focus on the calming motion of his hands.

He seems satisfied that I am a little more relaxed and sits forward to pick up his fork looking expectedly at me. I pick up mine and take a bite of chicken. It is just as good as the night before. It melts in my mouth. I close my eyes savoring the flavor. When I open them, he is starting at me, fork loaded midair.

"You are so beautiful," he whispers.

Somehow we finish our meal, a tension slowly builds, swirling around us. The combination of the fire, wine, food, sound of the storm and him. Mostly him. I can't stop staring at him. I love how he makes me forget. Please make me forget, I silently will him.

I swear he can read my mind because he gulps down the rest of his wine then pushes my glass up for me to do the same. As soon as I finish the last drop he picks me up and carries me upstairs.

It's happening. I would have inspired him to chase me if he didn't make a move, but it looks like I won't have to provoke the beast. He is trying very hard to keep himself in check. He sets me down gently on the bed then steps back and unbuckles his belt. He drags it out and folds it setting it down by my feet. I shiver, am I in for more than I can handle?

He seems to be able to read my mind. "Anna, do you want this?" He stands there unmoving, the belt lying between us. I get its unspoken meaning, he said himself that a beast lives inside him. He will hurt me. He will tear me apart and put me back together again. He is giving me a choice. I shake my head yes.

"Words, Anna, use your words."

I freeze. He is not Oliver I repeat over and over in my mind as I tremble.

He climbs up on the bed beside me and pulls me into his lap. "Baby, I want you to use your words to talk to me. What if you are turned away from me and you need me to stop or need to tell me something, I might miss it. I don't want to hurt you that is all."

What he is saying makes sense. "I'm sorry. Oliver used to say that to me. I'm sorry." I try to scramble out of his arms, but he reaches out pulling me close.

"I'm not Oliver. Yes, I like things a little kinky, but my intent is not to harm or humiliate you." He turns my face to his forcing eye contact. "I will not allow him in here with us. Do you understand?"

I am about to shake my head in acknowledgement, but I catch myself. "Yes."

"Good girl," he says nudging me off his lap. "Now are you sure? Maybe we should wait. There is no hurry, we have forever."

We don't though, Oliver is coming. No amount of my silent willing him to stay away will make that happen. "Yes, I'm okay. I don't want to wait."

He pulls my shirt over my head as his hands run over my breasts. Slowly he makes his way down, gently grabbing my shorts tugging them down along with my panties.

"Scoot up, baby." I push up higher on the bed and lay my head back against the pillows. He picks up my hands guiding them to the poles in the center of the headboard. "Hold on right here, don't let go until I tell you."

I get the impression he would like to tie me up but after the incident at the hotel I appreciate that he is concerned about scaring me. He stands never taking his eyes off me. He backs up to shut off the light. The room becomes engulfed in darkness. I almost take my hands off the headboard but then he turns the bathroom light on closing the door so a little sliver peeks out. Just enough so we can still see each other but dark enough I'm not as self-conscious being naked and on display.

I watch as he grabs the bottom of his shirt lifting it up over his head dropping it to the floor. He slowly unzips his jeans and pushes them off his hips. His erection is begging to break free from his boxers. My excitement builds. He pulls his boxers off, his dick springs out proudly as he shoves them down.

He moves towards me. I push away my fear, struggling to remain calm. He takes my feet in his large hands and rubs, gently massaging them. He trails up to my ankles, calves…to my stomach. He leans in placing tiny kisses around my navel. I feel like I've been in a coma and he is bringing every cell back to life, a brand-new awakening I never knew existed.

Slithering up my body he engulfs me. He is so big that it is intimidating. He hovers over me, my hands still griped to the headboard. He nibbles my ear, his palms run over my breasts as he devours my neck. I groan as he starts his wonderful torturous game with my tits. My nipples turn rock hard, loving the tease. He kisses me slowly, his lips soft against mine.

He smells good. Manly. Mostly him with a hint of cologne. I moan into his mouth as he tweaks my nipple harder. He leans back and smiles at me, slowly drifting down until his head hovers over me. He pushes my legs apart, so he can see me. I let go of the headboard to stop him.

"Hands on the headboard, I will not hurt you I promise."

I stare up at the ceiling, reluctantly willing my arms to resume their position. I'm sure I will die of embarrassment having his face that close to me, it is so intimate. I jump when he licks me. One long lick right up my clit. I gaze down at him. His expression shows me how much he wants this. He does it again his eyes never leaving mine. I throw my head back into the pillow. What kind of heavenly torture is this?

He groans, his deep voice vibrates against me. Oh. My. God. He moves his hands to spread me, so he can devote every ounce of his tongue to my pleasure. He nibbles, licks and sucks. Bringing me to edge then tearing away just as something crests inside me. He kisses my thigh rubbing the stubble of his beard against my leg. He allows me to catch my breath before beginning again.

My legs quiver. I can't take much more, it is too good. "Fuck," I scream out.

"Feeling a little frustrated, baby? What do you need?"

I want to rip my hands off the headboard and grab his head, force him to take me where I need to go. I'm so close.

He runs his tongue up again and flicks it against that delicious spot, pausing waiting for me to answer. He looks at me with hooded eyes. "Tell me, Anna."

"Please," I say as my entire body vibrates with need.

"Please what?" His breath whispers against me as he speaks.

I'm so embarrassed. I know he will not give me what I want…what I need until I ask for it. "Please," I moan loudly as he lightly bites at my swollen clit. "Fuck, Dylan, please let me come."

With that he devours me. I erupt hard and fast as he holds my waist tightly to prevent my retreat as my body convulses. He brings me to the brink again and again with no reprieve. I close my eyes, drifting into the darkness where only my soul and his exists.

He crawls up me and positions himself at my entrance. My eyes fly open. He reaches up to move my arms from the headboard. "It's okay, you can let go now." He runs his thumb over my cheek and stares into my eyes.

I panic. I feel myself drifting to Sarah. He must be able to sense my fear. Sense I am slowly leaving him. He kisses me hard. I taste myself on his lips, bringing me back momentarily.

"Look at me, baby. Don't look away. Don't hide. It's okay I will go slow. It's you and me, no one else."

Gently he presses against me. I try to close my eyes, but he reminds me to keep them open, to stay focused on him. He slowly slides into me. He leans over placing small kisses on my temple, looking deep into my eyes. He presses as far as my body will allow and then takes my face in his hands. "It will be over soon, just a little pain and then it will get better."

Before I can ask him what he means by that, he pushes into me hard and fast ripping past my barrier, making me his. I cry out and bury my face into his neck. My nails drag across his back as I struggle to stay with him. He is so large he fills me completely.

He holds himself still, giving me time to adjust to the invasion. A surge of pride spurs through me as I lay there with him inside of me. He took me, claimed me, made me his. Oliver can never take this away from me.

He leans back and looks deep into my eyes. "You good, baby?"

"Yes, I'm okay." I smile up at him.

I see something pass across his face as he smiles down upon me. Slowly he draws back then thrusts in again. It hurts, and yet it is oh so amazing.

"Fuck, Anna, you are so fucking tight and wet for me."

I watch him braced over the top of me. The veins on his arms pop out along the muscle, showing the restraint he is taking with me. Will I be able to handle him once he releases the beast? I know that he is holding back, this is his gentle.

He picks up speed and reaches down between us to gently torture my clit, pounding into me. I climb…climbing…climbing, an orgasm slowly warms me moving up through my body till I fall. I hear him groan loudly above me as he pushes all the way inside. I feel him twitch deep, his head falls and rests under my chin. I never want this to end. I need to be his…forever.

We stay like this for a long time, the sweat from our bodies keeping us glued together, him still inside me. Tears force their way out of my eyes, my throat tightens. He glances up suddenly looking concerned.

"Shit, did I hurt you?" he says wiping tears away from my face.

"No, well a little but no. It's…" I stop, I don't know what to say. I'm so happy and yet so sad. I can't explain it.

"What is it? Talk to me, baby. Was it too much too soon?"

"No. I just don't want it to end."

He frowns. "Never, I'm not leaving, I understand why that is hard for you to believe but I won't. I'll show you."

He gets up to shut the light off then pulls me into our usual sleeping position. But tonight, I turn around in his arms and bury my face into his chest. I curl into him as closely as I can, I want to memorize everything about this moment, his smell, his warmth. He tugs me closer. He slides his arm under my head running his hand along the back of my hair as his other drapes across my hip. I revel in the lingering ghost of his touch everywhere on my body. The heavy pull of sleep tugs at me as I glide into oblivion.

Chapter Twenty

Dylan

I lie awake listening to her breathe. She is sleeping soundly. I love having her next to me. She surprised me today, something has changed in her. I shouldn't have taken advantage of that, but she was so willing. I'm screwed now. I can never let her go. I thought once I had a taste of her that maybe the notion would subside. It didn't. I want more, much more.

She seems to enjoy the little bits of pain I give her along with the pleasure. I have a darkness in me. I think it started with my need to punish someone. I couldn't hurt the man who killed my mother and took my sister, so I found willing partners. Turns out a lot of women appreciate the dark. I never thought I would find someone like Anna, she responds to my touch unlike anything I have ever experienced.

She only moved her arms away from that headboard once. I wasn't sure she would obey, but I see now she is a natural submissive. I chose not to bring out the cuffs or rope. I need her to know I am not tying her up to force her to do things against her will. I want her to realize what it is. It is about letting me find her limits, pushing her. I'll never take her where she doesn't wish to go.

My mind drifts to Liam. I wonder if he'll show up tomorrow. Part of me wants to see him, he is like a brother. I wonder what he will make of all this. Of us. Anna and I. Together. Could it be I finally found my match in her? I never thought I would be a one girl sort of guy. She has ruined me for other women. I only need her. When she is beneath me, letting me touch her, she is in tune to every movement I make, hyper aware of me. I love it. It makes me feel more powerful than I've ever known.

I let myself relax with her in my arms, looking forward to morning, I can't remember the last time I looked forward to a new day.

I wake up to loud banging. Someone is at the front door. Anna jumps and sits up clutching the blanket close to her. Fuck. Liam must be here already. I should have known, when he sets out to do something, nothing stops him.

"Shh, it's okay." I run my hands up and down her arms, my heart contracts as I see the fear in her eyes. "It's Liam, I sent him the address. An intruder wouldn't knock." She seems to accept this but still looks very nervous. "I'll be right back just sit tight."

She reaches out for me as I stand up and grips my forearm tightly. "Are you sure it's him?"

"I'm sure, baby." I grab my jeans from the floor and pull them up. The banging continues prompting her to jump again.

"Please be careful, Dylan."

I smile as I bend down to kiss her. My heart swells at her worry over me. “I will, I promise.”

I make my way downstairs and look through the peephole. Yep, it’s him. He looks like a drowned rat. I swing the door open wide.

“Bout fucking time, it’s pouring out here you asshole!” Liam says, coming in shaking himself like a dog.

“Fuck stop you’re getting water everywhere. Now who is the asshole?” I grin pulling my friend into a big hug patting him on the back hard. He looks tired, I pick up his bag. “Come on you can take one of the guest rooms down here.”

He follows me down the hall as I point out the bathroom. “There should be towels in there if you want to shower or just dry off.” I immediately feel better having my friend here, another person around to keep Anna safe. “There are a few leftovers in the fridge, are you hungry?”

“No, thanks, man. I just need to change and get some sleep. That is quite the drive up here.”

“Yes, it is. She did a good job finding this place.” I notice the expression on his face as I mention her. He is angry and while I don’t like it I get it. It will be fine once he talks to her. He’ll understand why she kept who she was from him. I pat him on the back as I walk out to leave him to his bed. “I’m just upstairs if you need me brother.”

When I get upstairs Anna is not where I left her. I flip on the light looking around. Where could she have gone? She must be up here. I check the bathroom. Nothing. I sigh as I rest my hand on the door handle to the closet. Fuck. I open it and spy her in the far corner curled into a ball. “Anna, it’s okay baby, it was just Liam.” She doesn’t look up. “Baby, you remember Liam, Agent Sharp?”

Slowly she peeks at me. She is so scared it rips me apart. I open my arms and urge her to come to me. "Come here, baby." She hesitates a second before crawling towards me. I pull her into my chest, placing her between my legs. "It's okay I should have told you to expect him. This is my fault."

Why didn't I give her a heads up? I feel bad for scaring her. She hid in the closet. Crap. I'm so stupid. "Do you want to go see him for yourself? Would that make you feel better?"

She shakes her head no but catches herself as she remembers my direction from earlier. "No, I believe you. I'm sorry I thought it would be him."

I almost joke again about intruders not knocking but I stop myself. It terrified her. I don't want to discredit that fear. "What has you so frightened?"

"He…he called me."

"What? Who called you?" I know I heard her right. Am I confused? Then I remember I left her phone charging in the living room before I went for supplies. I wanted her to be able to call out if she had an emergency.

"Oliver. It was an unknown number. I shouldn't have answered, but I didn't think it would be him. I thought it was Frank or Irene calling to make sure I made it to where I was going."

Her trembling intensifies. I pick her up and carry her back to bed covering us both up. I pull her in close. I wonder who Frank and Irene are. They are not my concern right now. Oliver fucking called her. How did he get her number?

"Talk to me, baby. He isn't here, it was only Liam. Tell me exactly what he said," I coax as I hold her tight.

"He wanted to know where I was. I lied and told him I was in Texas, but he knows I'm not there. He knew I was lying. He told me I made a lot of trouble for him but that it wouldn't stop him. He is sending Brian for me."

She jolts out of bed and runs for the bathroom. I run after her. She makes it to the toilet just in time to be sick. I kneel beside her pulling her hair away from her face. I rub her back feeling her muscles tense as she heaves again. My heart breaks into a thousand little shards. I can't imagine what it was like for her. They didn't break her, but it fucked her up. They broke Sophia. I should have gotten to her sooner, maybe she would still be alive.

I push it out of my mind. I can't help Sophia anymore. She is in a better place. But, Anna is here, flesh and blood in front of me. I'm not lying when I say I'll never leave her. I won't, she will see.

Sitting on her haunches she reaches out to flush the toilet. "I'm so sorry. I don't know what happened."

"It's okay, nothing to be ashamed of." I release her hair watching it fall across her bare back. I scold my dick for twitching. Bad timing. I stand to turn on the faucet and wet a washcloth. I hand it to her. She washes her face and hands it to me as she stands.

Once I get her settled into bed, I ask her if she remembers anything else about the conversation. She says she doesn't. I wait until she settles down into a restless sleep. I make my way downstairs and grab her phone looking for a tracking device. There isn't one. I don't know how he has her number. It pisses me off that he got to her here, this was supposed to be a safe space and that fucker ruined it.

Tomorrow I need to get my ass in gear and get the security in place. He is coming, she is right. We need to find him before he finds her. I don't want him anywhere near her.

Anna

I wake up in Dylan's arms. Ugh, I'm so embarrassed about my reaction to Liam showing up here. What a way to end the night after…my minds drifts to Dylan fucking me. I'm not a virgin anymore. I smile into his chest and inhale his scent, running my hand over his smooth muscles.

He stirs, murmuring my name into my hair. He brushes it away from my eyes gently pushing me back. "Good morning Sunshine." He growls as he smiles down at me.

"Good morning," I say shoving my face back into his chest to avoid looking into his eyes. "I'm sorry about last night."

"What? It was amazing, you were so hot with your hands raised above your head. My little submissive." He rolls me over in bed, hovering over the top of me.

"Um, that wasn't what I was talking about."

He laughs leaning in to kiss me. "No worries." He nuzzles up under my neck. "Where shall we begin today? Liam is probably still sleeping." He jumps up and goes into the bathroom. I hear him turn the faucet on in the large jacuzzi size bathtub.

The sound of the water takes me right back to my first conscious day at Oliver's. Nope, not happening. I get up and quickly gather clothes hoping to dress and be downstairs before he comes out.

"Where do you think you are going?"

I turn to face him with my clothes in hand. He is leaning up against the bathroom door, naked and looking sexy as hell.

"I was just leaving to make breakfast." I take a step back towards the bed.

He stalks towards me. "Anna, I know that's not true, you don't like to cook." He stops cocking his head to one side. "You wouldn't be trying to run away from me now would you?" He runs his gaze over my body, poised for the attack.

"I'm just worried about our guest," I say shakily.

"He is a big boy. The kitchen isn't hard to find."

He takes my clothes from me and sets them down on the bed then leads me into the bathroom. I stare at the tub. I can't do this. I have been afraid of large bodies of water since Sarah drowned but the bathtub fear is new. I don't think I can get in there. At one time I loved taking baths. I loved tossing in bath bombs or bubbles, sinking into the warm water. It used to relax me. Brian ruined that. I hear him click the lock on the door bringing me back from my thoughts.

"I can't do it, Dylan."

He moves around to stand in front of me. "Yes, you can. I told you I was going to help you. Remember, I mentioned that you would not always like it? Well, this is one of those times." He steps in and holds his hand out to me.

I stand there looking at the water. What if he pulls me under? I know that's illogical but none the less it is in my mind. It screams at me. Run. Get away.

"Can't we take a shower?" I plead to him.

"Nope. Come on, baby, it's just a bath. I even added bubbles for you. Would I have done that if I wanted to kill you in here?"

I giggle at this. He is right. My fear is of Brian not of the bathtub. I tentatively reach out to take his hand and he steadies me as I step into the tub. He pulls me into his arms hugging me for a few minutes before he sits down causing the water to splash up along the edge.

"Here sit down on my lap facing me," he says.

He tugs me down gently, so I am straddling him. When I lower myself down onto him his cock prompts me to scoot away. He grabs me around the waist and forces me to settle on his lap. Leaning against the tub he places his arms behind his head, letting me get used to the water, keeping his hands up where I can see them. We just met but I am thinking he knows me better than I know myself.

"See, this isn't so bad is it?" he drawls.

"No, I guess not," I say nervously wiggling on his lap.

"So, today's agenda will be setting up security and I would like you to talk to Liam. I told him who you are. I don't know if you remember him from when we were younger, but he also worked for your dad."

"My step-father," I correct.

He sits up and puts his arms around my waist. "No, your dad. I don't care what Oliver and William Ramirez told you. Manuel will always be your father. He loved you, he always talked about you and your mother."

"I don't remember Liam. My mother liked to keep me out of everyone's hair." I ignore his statement about my father. I'm not sure I believe he talked about me. I didn't spend much time with him.

"Liam and Sophia were dating when Oliver attacked the compound. Manuel had sent a few of us guys to a training camp in the states. We were all away when the attack came. He was going to marry her."

I watch as Dylan slips to another time. Guilt consumes me. I am to blame for all this, for Dylan's pain. I see it now, etched in the worry lines around his eyes. I drop my head as tears spill down my cheeks breaking bubbles as they find their way to the water.

"Hey, Anna, look at me. Stop, I can see you are blaming yourself. The only person responsible is Oliver."

I glance up at him. I can see he doesn't blame me. Will Liam? I don't really want to face him again, but I guess I have no choice he is here. No avoiding him now. Dylan reaches up and places his hand on the back of my head. I tense, my muscles locking in fear.

"Eyes, Anna," he snaps at me. "Look at me, it is just you and I."

He doesn't remove his hand as he pulls me close to him. He kisses me, roaming down, exploring my jaw line, nibbling his way up to my ear. His dick twitches against me as my arousal grows. He leans back and runs his hands over my stomach coming up to cup my breasts, he then places his arms behind his head again. Smugness appears on his face, content with my response.

"You have beautiful tits," he says smiling at me.

I stare down to watch the bubbles, heat rushes to my face.

"I also love the way you blush. I'm a little sad Liam is here. I want to keep you all to myself."

I fidget on his lap not sure if I like all this attention. My movement only makes his dick twitch more, I am making him hard. I should be ashamed of myself at how much my mind has been in the gutter since meeting Dylan.

"So, tell me about yourself," he says. I peer up blushing even more as I wonder if he is trying to slowly kill me by his seductive, torturous ways.

"What do you want to know?" I struggle to concentrate on our conversation, my thoughts keep wandering to what is going on down below the bubbles.

"What do you like to do? Besides read. I already get you like that. You worked in a bookstore and from the looks of it you brought half of it here with you."

I laugh temporarily distracted from my crotch. "I do like to read. Other than that, I'm boring."

"I don't think you're boring." He reaches out and runs his thumb over my nipple. "You were a victim of circumstance, too frightened to get out in the world and live, so you lived through your books. We will change that."

I close my eyes, processing what he is saying but his hands are directly influencing the rest of my body. He is becoming my master. I'm slowly losing control of myself handing it over to him bit by bit.

My eyes open as he speaks again. "What have you always wanted to do? One thing, anything, no matter how silly you think it is I want to know."

My inner bad girl rises out of the fucking tub coming from nowhere and words come tumbling out of my mouth before I can stop them. "Well, since getting in here all I have wanted to do is ride your cock." I cover my mouth as I realize what I have just said. What the fuck was that?

He appears as surprised as me. I scramble to make my retreat, but he grabs my hands sitting up straight pulling me in close to his chest. He whispers in my ear, "looks like we want the same thing. Who are we to stop ourselves?" He leans against the tub, his eyes dark swirling pools of desire.

I glance towards the bathroom door then back to him. He shakes his head. No way is he letting me off that easy. Why did I say that? What is wrong with me? He rocks his hips, his cock glides between my legs. I drop my head letting my hair cover my face. I can't think of anything else but this. I don't even remember what his initial question was. I guess it doesn't matter we have seemed to move on from that.

He takes my hands and places them on his chest. "Go ahead, I will give you this. Take advantage. One time I will let you be in control." He brushes the hair away from my face pulling it over my shoulder.

I scoot up a little looking to him for guidance. He reaches down between us and grabs himself, helping me find the right position. I lower myself so the tip of him is at my entrance. He moves his hands back up behind his head letting me be in complete control. I take him inch…by…glorious…inch.

I grip his chest watching as my nails create little half-moons along his tanned skin. I stare at him intently. His eyes are closed, each time I move down on him his jaw clenches. Once he is inside me I stop and just look at him. He opens his eyes slightly a smile spreads across his face. He is pleased, this warms me. Why am I suddenly wanting to see him happy, satisfied?

I tense around him. He closes his eyes again and groans, leaning his head back. I lean over to kiss him down his neck, licking him. His skin is salty and warm. I nuzzle him deliberately raising my hips stopping so that just the tip of him is inside me. Then slowly…so…very…slow…glide down.

He fists my hair and tightly pulls my head backwards. I should be frightened by the brutal way in which he is grabbing me...but I'm not. It only makes me clench down more tearing another load groan from him.

"Are you trying to fucking kill me?" he says through clenched teeth.

"Feeling a little frustrated, baby? What do you need?" I say throwing his words from last night back at him. "Tell me, Dylan."

"You minx." He flips me around. "All fours, sweetheart." He makes me place my hands up on the edge of tub and face away from him. He drags his hand over my backside. I'm slightly scared but mostly excited and oh so turned on.

The same time I hear it the exact moment the pain registers in my brain. He spanks me. I shriek in surprise. He rubs the sting before giving my ass another swat. Shit, it hurts but evidently my pussy didn't get the memo because it is begging for more.

He leans over me as his cock slides between my cheeks. He growls into my ear, "We need to establish a few more rules, Anna. I don't beg. You see that is your role." He reaches around and rolls my nipples between his finger and thumb.

I place my forehead down on the edge of the cool tub. "So, what do you want?"

This time I don't hesitate. "I need your cock, sir."

He moans loudly and bites my shoulder. "Fuck, Anna, how could you be any more perfect?"

Again, my inner bad girl peeks out to play. "If your cock was inside me that would be more perfect." I yelp as he pinches my nipple.

He obliges shoving himself deep inside compelling me to brace myself against the tub. He pounds into me harder, faster as he fists my hair and pulls me backwards forcing my head to the side. He leans around kissing me hard. His other hand finds my clit and rubs with furious intensity. I stumble into that wonderful dark oblivion, the world where only Anna and Dylan exist. He tells me to come and then he pushes me over the edge into the most intense amazing orgasm. He holds me close to him.

My back presses against his chest, he moans out my name as his seed fills me.

I lower myself into the water, turning around so we are facing each other. I feel satisfied yet slightly embarrassed by the way I was acting. Where did that all come from? I'm timid, shy…who was that girl? I look up and notice Dylan is watching me intently.

A large grin spreads across his face. "It's nice to finally meet you, Anna."

Chapter Twenty-One

Dylan

Holy crap what was that? I thought I would get her in the bath to help her over her fear. I expected something but not that. I need to talk to her before this goes any further. She needs to understand who I am. I don't want to end up hurting her. She is young and naïve. She likes it a little rough. I threw a lot at her in that short time and she took it like a queen. When she called me sir I about blew my load. It flowed naturally off her tongue with no request from me.

I stand pulling her up with me. "The water is getting cold and I am hungry."

I dry us both off, she is trying to process everything that just happened. We haven't even been together for a full week, yet I feel like I've known her forever. I can't imagine a world without her.

I need to focus and get the security in place. Then I can relax a little and delve into who Anna really is. She is my sleeping beauty. She has been asleep in the world, hiding, waiting for a monster for the last nine years. I understand why her mother did what she did. She hoped Anna would adapt and create a happy, carefree existence as Sarah.

That wasn't fair to her, they forced her to live someone else's life. She doesn't even know who Anna is. I will help her find herself. I discovered something today. She is feisty. She isn't the shy, quiet girl she assumed she was. This morning not only surprised me, it shocked her as well.

"Come on, baby, let's go get dressed and I'll make you breakfast. Do you want pancakes?"

She doesn't answer.

"Anna?"

"Why did you leave my phone in the living room? Did you forget to take it yesterday?"

I sit down and pull her with me to perch on my knee. "I think we got off to a rough start, I owe you an apology. I wasn't thinking properly. I was lost in my grief over Sophia and I wanted you to draw Oliver. I should not have shoved you in the trunk. I'm not kidnapping you. Don't get me wrong, I'm not letting you go but I'm not trying to keep you from the rest of the world…from life. I left your phone in case you had an emergency."

"I don't understand." She frowns.

"I don't quite understand myself, but we will figure it out together. Okay?"

She nods but then adds, "I'm nervous about talking to Liam."

I push her off my lap, lightly patting her bottom as she stands. "It will be all right. He is a good guy. We are all grieving the loss of Sophia, but it will all work out. You'll see. It smells like he found the kitchen."

We head downstairs to find Liam flipping pancakes on the stove. He turns and looks at us as we make our way over to him. "Bout time you guys got up."

Anna hides behind me. I reach around drawing her up beside me and motion for her to take a seat at the breakfast bar. "We've been awake for hours," I say winking at her. Her cheeks turn that pretty shade of pink I'm becoming accustomed to.

Liam snorts. I pour her and I each a cup of coffee and hand hers across. "What do you think, Anna, two men in your kitchen and we both can cook? Every girl's dream, am I right?"

She nods in agreement. I let this one slide she is very nervous.

I punch Liam's arm and nod towards her. He rolls his eyes. I realize he is purposely avoiding speaking to her to make her uncomfortable. He is trying to punish her for lying to him. I'm sure it bruised his pride that he didn't figure out who she was on his own but it's not fair to take it out on her. He knows this. He just needs a gentle reminder.

"Anna, would you like pancakes? I feel bad you had to put up with Dylan's shitty cooking but now you have a real chef in the house."

She giggles, the sound is music to my ears. "Yes, thank you." She reaches over and takes the plate that Liam is offering her. "Um, sorry about lying to you. I've been very confused and wasn't sure who I could trust. Anyway, I'm sorry I shouldn't have lied to you."

"It's okay, I understand that you were troubled the day we talked at the bookstore and after we found you." His voice trails, I hear the sadness in his words. Anna hears it too. She looks down at her plate, swiping a run-away tear.

I try to turn the conversation. "Hey, we will get this fucker. First things first, I'm going to leave you both to your breakfast. I'll go out and set up a perimeter around the property. Then we can get cameras and motion sensors up."

"I'll help," Liam says.

"No. You two stay here. I think you need to talk about things." I pour my coffee in a travel mug and head out leaving them to sit side by side both with their heads down. They'll find their way. I need to get out and set things up. Liam will take care of her.

Anna

When we came downstairs, and I spotted Liam it was unreal. He looks so different from the few times I met him. I'm used to seeing him in a suit and tie. This morning he was flipping pancakes in my kitchen in nothing but a pair of jeans and a t-shirt.

He isn't as tall as Dylan, but he stills towers over me. They both have a presence that speaks for itself, a very strong one. He has blond hair, blue eyes and a short beard. In his suit he has a professional demeanor, in jeans he looks like a very hot bad boy. I wish Dylan would not leave me alone with him. I don't know what to say to him. God, I'm the most awkward person on the planet.

"I'm sorry I should have told you who I was. I didn't consider it at the bookstore, I was so used to being Sarah. Then when you found us, I couldn't bring myself to tell you. Oliver made me be Anna, I didn't want to think about that."

He sets his fork down after finishing his last bite, he reaches over and places his hand over mine. "It's okay."

"I'm sorry about Sophia. I wanted to get her out of there. I wanted to help her," I sob. He pulls me into his arms and shakes, overcome by his own emotions.

"Shh, Anna, we all wish we could have helped her. I wanted to marry her you know. I had all these dreams of finding her, taking her away from there. Erasing all her bad memories to replace them with new ones."

I sob into his shirt. "She wasn't the Sophia I remembered. She cried every night. I couldn't do anything but hold her. Oliver let me stay with her although I think he was just setting us up, letting her and I get close again, so he could separate and torture us even more."

"I'm glad she had you at the end," he says.

"It was my fault. She had the pistol because of me." I hadn't admitted this to anyone. Liam deserves the truth.

He pulls back and stops me, placing a finger over my lips. "I know, Anna. I went over the scene and the evidence. I discovered you had killed that man. His gun holster was empty, it was obvious what had happened. The marks on your hand. Do not blame yourself, she would've done what she was going to at some point. I don't think getting out would have helped. She had been there too long." He sits back down. "Let's talk about something else, shall we? Like what is up with Dylan? What have you done to him?"

I must give him a confused look because he chuckles. "I'm not sure what you mean? He is the one who kidnapped, well whatever you want to call it, but he did it. I have done nothing to him." I flash back to my encounter with Dylan this morning in the bathroom and shift, so he can't see my cheeks heating.

He laughs again so hard he almost falls off the barstool. "You are kidding me right? You got that man all kinds of crazy. It's okay, I realize you probably don't see it, you're just getting to know him."

"Oh, I can see that he is crazy all right." I cross my arms across my chest, finding myself growing irritated with his flippant attitude about Dylan taking me.

He smiles, he is so handsome. It saddens me. I wish Sophia would have had a little more fight left in her. Liam was perfect for her. The guilt creeps back inside me. I get up to rinse off my plate and put it in the dishwasher, then I take Liam's doing the same for him. I sense his eyes on me, it makes me nervous.

"Don't feel guilty. Oliver is a piece of shit." He looks behind him as if to make sure that no one overhears our conversation. "Look, I want to ask you something." He runs his hand thru his hair looking anxious himself. "I need your help."

I listen to Liam's plan, my stomach slowly sinking, what he is saying makes perfect sense. He needs my aid to catch Oliver. Dylan recognized it too but now his obsession with me clouds his vision. When he finishes he says, "Anna, if you are not comfortable with this tell me. We will find another way."

I lean back on the counter and process everything he said. "No, I want to help. I'm tired of hiding. I want the monster dead."

He nods. "I'll do anything I can to keep you safe, but you understand how dangerous this is?"

"Yes, I do. He called me yesterday," I say.

"Oliver?"

"Yes. His right-hand man, Brian, must have looked at my number on my cell when he took me. It's weird. I don't understand why he did that, surely they didn't know that I would ever make it back to my phone."

"They are assholes like that, maybe they were going to call your phone while they had you to fuck with your parents. Sorry I mean the Madronos."

"Yes, I guess. So, what does this tracking device look like? You know once they take me they will strip me of all my clothing?" Liam grimaces at my words.

"It is injected under the skin. It is possible they will find and remove it, especially if they've learned you have been with us."

I don't know if I can do this. Can I let them take me again? He is right, even if they wait for someone to come it will be Brian and a few others. They could get them, but they wouldn't get Oliver. They need me to lead them to him.

"I have a backup plan. A tracker in a pill form, you swallow it. But, it only lasts as long you don't flush it away if you know what I mean," he says raising his eyebrows.

My nerves tingle on edge as I turn to look out the window, watching a little bluebird that stares back at me through the glass. He is tilting his head back and forth looking as confused as I feel.

"Anna, are you okay? This is too soon. Shit. Forget I said any of this."

"No, I want to help. So, I take the pill if I have time," I say.

"Yes, if they sneak up on you, then that won't work, we would need to rely on the tracker under your skin."

"Dylan will not go for any of this. Are you going to tell him?" I ask.

He sighs. "No, I'm going to tell him that we found Oliver and he is being transported to the states. He will want to see for himself. It will send him on a wild goose chase while we wait here."

He looks at me long and hard, trying to gauge my thoughts. He is struggling with what he is about to do. I'm struggling too. But, I refuse to hide any longer. I want to help him get his revenge. It's the least I can do.

"I've never lied to Dylan about anything," he says as he buries his face in his hands.

I walk over to him and place my hand on his, trying to support him like he had done for me. "It will all work out, Liam."

"I have no right to ask this of you." He shakes his head as if he is about to change his mind.

"You will tell him once they take me? He'll find me even if the trackers fail. He will." I hug myself, hoping that I am correct. Does Dylan care enough about me to come looking for me? He looked for Sophia, they found her too late. I am risking the same fate.

"Yes, I will tell him. He will hate both of us."

I laugh nervously. "Yes, yes, he will."

Liam takes me into the bedroom he is staying in and injects the tracker on the backside of my upper arm. He places a band-aid over it instructing me to remove it as soon as it stops bleeding so that Dylan doesn't see. He then gives me the pill form. I cradle it in my palm. It looks like a Tylenol capsule.

"Keep it where you can get to it quickly. Remember, if you flush it and then you change locations we won't be able to find you."

"Do you have any idea how close they are to finding me?" I ask.

"No. The last location we tracked them to was Belize. My theory is that he is sending his guys up through Mexico. It could be weeks, months, I wish I had an answer for you, Anna. You will know when I inform Dylan that the FBI has captured him."

He sits by me on the bed and puts his arm around me. "If you change your mind, please tell me."

I shake my head in understanding and lean over on his shoulder. I see why Sophia loved him. He is easy to be with. I see how much he hates asking me to do this but we both realize this needs to end. This is the only way.

"I'm going to go outside and help Dylan. Are you okay?"

"Yes, I'm fine. It will all fall into place won't it?"

He kisses my forehead before standing. "I think so, I wouldn't ask if I didn't expect this to work. It has to or else you and I will both be in a world of hurt."

I understand what he means by that. Dylan will kill him. He may murder him even if the plan works and I don't get hurt. Both these men are ruthless. Both will do what they need to do to protect and defend those they love. I shake my head at the silly thought, Dylan doesn't love me, he loves my body maybe but not me.

Chapter Twenty-Two

Dylan

As I'm finishing up with the security around the perimeter of the property Liam walks towards me. He smiles and waves that must mean it went well. I knew the two of them would get along. They just needed to feel each other out.

"Get everything all worked out?" I ask him.

"I see why you like her," he says.

"Don't get any ideas, she is mine," I joke and slug him in the arm.

"Dylan, are you sure about what you are doing with her? She has feelings for you. She's been through a lot. Do you really want to continue down this path? I don't want her to get hurt."

He flinches at his own words, what is that about? I pick up easily on people's reactions. He is keeping something from me. That's what has made me good at what I do. I watch everything, the way people shift their eyes, nervous twitches, their dialect. Every detail about a person gives me more information than what they say.

"I'm not going to hurt her. She sees the real me. I'm not hiding anything from her. I think we were destined to meet. I recognize I have had my share of ladies, Liam. But, I want her, only her."

"Okay man, she is young and vulnerable right now. I want to make sure you have good intentions."

I laugh at this. "Oh, I have good intentions." I wiggle my eyebrows.

He slugs me back and laughs, finally the mood is lightening. "What do you need help with?" he asks.

"Information. I don't want his men stepping foot into Colorado without me knowing. I do not want them coming anywhere near her. We need to cut them off before they find her," I say.

"So, if we get them what is your game plan for getting to Oliver? You know he won't risk coming to the states."

"I will make his men talk."

"We've tried that in the past. It's never worked, they are all loyal to him."

"They aren't loyal. He just scares them more than we ever have. That won't be the case this time. I will fillet their skin off inch by inch until they tell me where he is." My adrenaline spikes with just the image of torturing one of them.

Liam looks back up to the cabin, sullen, deep in thought. "They were in Belize a few days ago, that's all I know." He kicks at a rock on the ground.

"Hmm, well maybe he is filtering them up through Mexico. Isn't that how they got in when they came for her a few months ago?" Something sends off alarm bells in my brain. I watch him closely.

He continues his mini soccer game with the stone. He looks back at the house again. "Yeah, they have the drug cartels behind them. You know it's all in the family with these assholes."

"I think I will head inside to determine if all the cams are syncing up to my computer. No one is coming in or out without me knowing," I say.

When we approach the cabin, I notice that Anna has found a shady spot under a tree not far away. "I'm going to check on her." I point towards where she is sitting.

"Sure." He hesitates, he is nervous, reluctant to go inside. "I'm sure she is fine. She has a lot going on in her head."

"I know, but she doesn't have to do it alone anymore." I leave him on the porch and make my way over to her plopping down on the hard ground. "Hey, baby, how are you doing?"

She is leaning back against the trunk with a book face down in her lap, looking out over the mountains. It is a spectacular view. "I'm good," she says turning to me.

I pick up the novel thinking I will get to scold her for reading longer than an hour. But, I realize she hasn't made it past page one. I close it and put my arm around her hugging her tight. "What's going on in that pretty little head of yours?"

"Nothing, I'm just enjoying the sunshine." She turns away from me back to the mountain view.

"How did your talk with Liam go?" I watch her face closely to try and get a read on how it all really went.

She drops her head and looks to her lap, wringing her hands together. She seems uneasy, they both seem nervous. "It was good, he is very nice. I understand why Sophia liked him."

I brush her hair back and tuck it behind her ear. "You talked about Sophia?"

"Yes…there is something I need to tell you." She takes a deep breath and then hesitates before saying, "um, it was because of me that she had the gun."

I put my hand over hers to stop her from wringing her hands together. "I know, I read the file. She took her own life, how she got that gun doesn't matter."

"I dreamed we would be free, turns out neither of us would ever be."

"You are free, Anna, I told you I was not kidnapping you," I say.

"No, I'm not. I am hiding on this mountain waiting for Oliver to find me. It looks like freedom, but it doesn't feel like it."

When Anna told me she had something to tell me, I expected it would be whatever her and Liam seem to be keeping from me. I don't know what is going on. Could be that they are both just grieving. "Come on, baby, let's go in and you and I can whoop up dinner. Liam thinks he is a better cook than me. I need to show him up."

She laughs and smiles at me. She is so beautiful when she smiles. That and the sound of her laughter makes life so much sweeter. This girl has no idea what she is doing to me. I wish I could make her forget Oliver Wright.

Anna

Dylan pulls me up and hands me back my book. I tried to read. Usually I become so engrossed in a novel that the world could burn down around me, and I wouldn't notice. I can't get my mind to go there. I have so much going on I cannot keep it all straight. Dylan, Liam…Oliver. I almost slipped and told him about our plan. I can't tell him. He will stop us. I can't risk that. If there is a chance to be free of Oliver, then I need to take it.

I follow him up the steps into the cabin. Liam is sitting in front of a laptop at the kitchen table. As we walk in he tells us that the cameras are all working. We peer over his shoulder. Little boxes of video feeds from around the property light up the screen. Liam clicks on one and brings up a view of the road leading to the house zooming in on it. Dylan pats him on the back.

"Good deal." He reaches over and clicks a different image. "They all seem to work."

I glance at the images. I wonder if I will see Brian come for me. Will I be able to just sit here and wait, knowing he is right outside my front door? A shiver rips through me. Dylan notices, he catches everything about me. He hugs me to him and kisses me on my forehead. I like it when he does this. He touches me with such ease, it makes me feel safe in his arms. The prospect of him leaving and Brian coming terrifies me. I really don't know how I will go through with this plan.

"Anna and I will start dinner. I thought she should learn from a pro," Dylan says.

Liam looks back at us. "You are kidding me right. If you want her to learn to cook, why don't you let me handle this. I am the better chef and the better teacher." He throws me a wink and a smile.

"Hmph, no way, man. Quit trying to move in on my girl." Dylan pushes me towards the kitchen. "I would ask what you want us to make you but now you get whatever I decide."

I giggle, I can't help it. I love the camaraderie that these two have. I have never had a friendship as theirs. Although it seems more than that, they act more like brothers. I'm sad that Liam has to lie to Dylan. It is all my fault. Dylan had a plan, now I have clouded that vision. I always seem to cause problems for everyone.

He pushes me to the counter and sets a chopping board and knife in front of me. He grabs my chin to tip my face so that my eyes meet his. "I can trust you with this can't I?" He grins, I know that he is teasing me. I'm sure he knows we have moved past me wanting to hurt him. I want to do things to him but stabbing him has been crossed off my list.

He laughs and backs away from me opening the fridge. He tosses a few tomatoes at me. "Let's see how bout we start with a salad. I think you can handle that."

"A salad. I better be getting more than that. After I made pancakes and bacon this morning," Liam declares joining us in the kitchen. Dylan hands him a beer and pushes him. "Out, this is our kitchen tonight."

Liam laughs and goes out to the living room. He sits down on the couch and props his feet up on the coffee table. Dylan places a few more items in front of me. "Here you go, just chop all this up and toss it in the bowl. Then I'll show you how to make the dressing. What else should we have? Do you like lasagna?"

I shake my head yes. I'm about to correct myself and speak the word but before I do he presses me into the counter and wraps his arms tightly around my stomach. He bites my earlobe. "Words, baby." I peek up to see if Liam is noticing what is going on in the kitchen. He has picked up the remote and is flipping stations with his back to us.

I turn my head slightly to the side and whisper so that only Dylan can hear, "yes, sir." I bite my bottom lip and wait for his reaction. When I called him sir in the bathroom this morning, it seemed to drive him a little crazy.

He slips his hand under my shirt and finds my breast running his thumb over my nipple. I brace my arms on the counter as his other hand finds its way down the front of my shorts and dips inside my panties. "Anna, Anna, what am I going to do with you," he rumbles in my ear.

His finger slips inside me and I bite back a groan. This feels too naughty with Liam sitting on the couch just a few feet from us. He works his magic while his thumb presses firmly down on my clit. I lean my head on his chest.

Then he whispers for me to come…and I do. How did he do that? I struggle to keep the moan that is trying to escape trapped behind my lips. I tremble in his arms. Dylan holds me tightly against him, ensnaring me between his hard body and the counter.

After my post orgasm tremors stop he pulls away from me. I turn my head slightly and risk a glance at him. He smiles slowly and then sucks his finger into his mouth. "Mm, delicious," he says a little too loud.

Liam stands and comes out to the kitchen. "Hey, if there is any taste testing going on I don't want to be left out."

I turn back to my chopping duties. Dylan meanders to the sink to wash his hands.

"Try one, the tomatoes are tasty," he says. Liam reaches around me and grabs a chunk of tomato popping it into his mouth then heads to the fridge to grab another beer.

What am I doing? I had my first orgasm yesterday morning. Now I'm standing in the kitchen having one in mere minutes in front of an unsuspecting bystander. Anna, I scold myself, this is not right. Why does being bad feel so damn good? I think Dylan could just tell me to come without even touching me and I would. He has more control over my body than I do.

Throughout dinner, I sense Dylan's eyes on me. I don't dare look at him. I might self-combust if I do. He showed me how to make the lasagna, casually bumping into me the entire time. He is working me up, priming me for what is to come.

"So, Anna, you said you didn't get to leave the ranch often, before that I assume you were at the estate most of the time. If you could go anywhere where would it be?" Dylan says as he reaches over pouring me another glass of wine.

"I don't know. I haven't given it much thought." I take a drink, savoring the rich flavor as it runs down my throat. One glass would have been enough, but it helps relax me.

"Oh, come on now, surely there is somewhere or something you have always wanted to do or to see? You've read a lot so someplace in one of your books?" Dylan asks, trying his best to encourage me to open to them.

I stare into my wineglass. The liquid gives me courage. I can share a piece of myself with these two men. "Well, yes, I guess there are plenty of places I would like to visit. I just don't consider it much. The chances I will see anything besides this cabin and Oliver's new residence are slim."

Liam speaks up, "Anna, don't think like that. You are young, you will have lots of experiences."

I look at him. I see the empathy in his eyes. I don't want to think about Oliver, so I answer Dylan's question before this conversation gets too deep. Liam is about to spill our plan. He is feeling sorry for me. "I would like to visit an ocean. We flew over one, but it was night and I couldn't see anything."

"You amaze me." Dylan says looking at me admiringly.

"Why? Doesn't everyone want to go to the ocean at least once? I didn't think it was that special," I say confused by his response.

"With your fear of water, I am surprised that it is the one thing you would like to do."

I shrug my shoulders. "I didn't say I wanted to get in the ocean. I've been so close my whole life but never close enough. It is beautiful here though. The mountains are unbelievable. I can't complain."

Liam yawns into the back of his hand and stretches in his chair. "I'll do the clean-up since you guys did the cooking. I'm heading to bed early. I still have a little jet-lag." He looks at me like he doubts our plan. I shouldn't have said those things. He is feeling guilty it is written all over his face.

Dylan nods towards the room Liam has been occupying. "Turn in, we got this." He stands and gathers dishes from the table.

"Okay if you say so. I'm not going to argue, the beers did me in." He leans down and kisses me on the cheek. "Sweet dreams, Anna." He then punches Dylan in the arm before pulling him into a bro hug. "Good night, brother."

I watch him walk down the hall leaving Dylan and I alone. Dylan starts the water in the sink. I'm suddenly shy again. I realize what is next. I glance towards the stairs. He approaches me and brushes my hair to the side, nuzzling my neck.

"Anna, I want you to go upstairs and wait for me. I will finish cleaning up." He crouches down beside me and rubs his hand over my thigh. "Undress and be kneeling on the floor when I come up." He stands and kisses me on the top of my head. He grabs a few more dishes before going back to the sink.

Shit. What do I do? He wasn't asking, why does part of me like that. My stomach does that flip-flop thing again as I reflect on what he said. Each time I'm with him things seem to escalate. If I'm honest with myself it scares me a little. I chew on my bottom lip and look at the stairs willing my legs to move. Finally, I obey. I make my way up slowly.

I stand in the bedroom and wonder how much time I have before he comes up. What if he gets up here before I'm naked and kneeling what would he do? The bad girl wants to find out, but the good girl wants to please him. I hear the dishwasher turn on downstairs. I quickly close the door and pull my shirt over my head as I do.

I crouch down on the floor near the end of the bed. He said to kneel, what does he mean? Does he want me on all fours, head down or up? So many questions why didn't I get clarification? Adrenaline pumps through my veins and prompts my fight or flight response. Just as I consider locking myself in the bathroom I hear his footsteps come up the stairs. I kneel with my head lowered and sit my butt on my heels placing my hands on my knees in front of me.

It seems to take him forever to reach the top. My heart pounds. My mind races to the day that Sophia pulled me to the floor and the punk rocker came in. I tremble as I think back. The door opens, I'm almost expecting to look up and see Mr. Punk Rock. He is dead, Anna, Oliver killed him. Maybe this wasn't such a good idea. My excitement is slowly turning to fear. Why does this always happen?

I keep my eyes focused on the ground trying to get myself together. Dylan has watched me lose it more times than I care to admit. He stops in front of me. I stare at his boots. I repeat over and over to myself, this is Dylan, it is Dylan, not punk rocker, it is Dylan. He touches my head and runs his palm down the length of my hair.

"Anna, look at me," he says and squats down, cupping my face in his large hand.

I immediately breathe a little easier seeing him. He is studying me intensely. Relief washes through me. It's just him and I.

My body reacts to the fact I am naked, and he is fully clothed. Something about this whole scene is incredibly sexy. He continues to rub my cheek, gazing deep into my eyes.

"Anna, before we go any further we should talk." He sits down and leans his back against the foot of the bed, pulling me to sit between his legs. "I realize you are inexperienced. I do not want to scare you away from anything, so we will come up with a safe word. If while we are together, you need me to stop I want you to use your word and I will stop. I promise you I will stop no questions asked."

"Water," I say without even contemplating.

"Okay, baby. I know that you are afraid of water, we are going to work on that. But we can use that word. So, if you want me to stop or if you need a little more time, you will say water. Do you understand?"

I shake my head then stop myself. "Yes, I understand."

"Is there anything you absolutely don't want me to do or try with you? You are new to all of this. We will move slow but if there is something you know about right off the bat, we should talk about it."

He has his arms around me and rubs his hands over my stomach gently. I think about it. A few weeks ago, you wouldn't have gotten me to believe I would be taking showers with or kneeling for anyone on my own accord. My life has been flipped upside down over the last few months. Recently my mind has been consumed with Dylan.

"It's okay. If you can't think of anything that is fine, just promise me you will use your word if you need to. I will push you, Anna. You need to know this. All I ask is that you try to trust me. I won't take you farther than you can go but I will absolutely stop if you need."

He gives me a few more minutes to think.

"Um, there is one thing," I say.

"What is it? No judgement here. It's just you and me."

"Um, would it be okay if you never called me kitten?" I never want to hear that when I'm with Dylan. He can call me anything but that.

I am trusting him enough to try new things. I'm not sure I will like them all, but I want to try. If I don't like something he said he will stop. I don't want to say anything is off limits.

"Why? Kittens are cute and cuddly just like you." He tickles my sides making me laugh. I wiggle around in his arms.

"You can call me anything else. I don't like that pet name," I reply as I try to break free from him.

"All right then, no kitten calling. Anything else?" he asks hauling me to our original position.

"No, sir," I say trying to catch my breath.

When I call him sir or run from him, it always seems to cause an instantaneous response. I can sense the change. He becomes quiet. His hands halt over my stomach. He shifts slightly and plucks something out of his pocket. He reaches around me and covers my eyes with a blindfold.

I wasn't expecting this. I can't see anything. He ties the black material behind my head then draws me back into his embrace. He doesn't speak, we just sit there for a few minutes. He is giving me time to adjust.

I jump at the sound of his voice. "Up. I will help you." He gently scoots me back and tugs me to stand with him. He wraps something soft around my wrists. I realize he is tying them together. I try to pull away, but he halts my escape and tugs at the restraint. It is snug, but it does not hurt.

He walks me over to the wall and pushes my back up against it, raising my arms above my head. "Don't move, do you understand?"

"Yes," I reply shakily. Should I say my safe word? He told me to use it. I should just say it. No. I should wait, he isn't hurting me. If I could see then I would at least know what to expect. He drifts away from me. Where did he go? It seems like I have been standing here a long time. Just say the word and then this will stop.

"I wish you could see how incredibly beautiful you are," he says.

I relax at the sound of his voice. He is close. I shift my weight back and forth on each leg, my self-consciousness rears its ugly head. "Dylan…"

"Shh, it's okay, baby."

The heat of his body blankets me. He places his lips on mine and gently kisses me, demanding that I open to him. His warmth and scent calm me. I try to focus on keeping my hands above my head. He backs away. I twitch as he places a vibrating object just below my collarbone then drifts down over one breast, pausing over my nipple then the other.

I press into the wall, trying to remain standing. The vibration makes it nearly impossible to stay still. He moves it lower over my abdomen. I know where this is going. I try to steel myself for what is coming. He taps my foot with his instructing me to spread my legs farther apart for him.

The minute the vibrator meets my clit, I explode into an orgasm. He pushes himself close and holds it there. I lean into his chest, keeping my hands above me pressed to the wall. Fuck. Finally, he shuts it off and backs away from me. I rest my head back and struggle to catch my breath. My legs are jelly. I'm afraid of sliding down the surface unable to hold myself up.

A swish echoes through the air before the sting of a thousand licks dash across my stomach. What the fuck? The pain is easing as another lash strikes. Fire ignites my breasts. He is whipping me with something. It stings, it hurts…it turns the burner on between my legs

His hands are on my shoulders. "What is your word, Anna?"

What? Oh yes, my word. "Water."

"Good girl. Use it if you need to, baby." He kisses me hard and turns me around, letting me lower my arms in front of me, they tingle. I try to shake them to get the blood pumping again as a swoosh cuts through the air. The whip licks my ass.

"Ah, fuck," I groan.

My body is humming. I rest my head on the wall. Something about having Dylan behind me turns me on. He rubs his hand over my bottom. He brings the whip up again letting it lick lower. Whipping. Rubbing. Torturing. Worshiping. He finishes and drops it to the floor.

My legs tremble. He moves close and reaches around tweaking my nipples with both hands. I roll my head to the side pressing my cheek against the wall. Every nerve in my body is waiting, begging, pleading, dying for his attention. He turns me harshly and pushes my back to the wall. My excitement skyrockets as I sense his spike.

He pulls my arms up and wraps them around his neck then lifts me off the ground. I naturally wrap my legs around his waist as he lowers me down onto his throbbing cock. Oh. My. God. He is so fucking amazing. I love it when he is inside of me. I belong to him. Nothing else matters. He slides one arm under my ass and places his other over my neck possessively. He pounds into me gripping my throat tight.

"Anna, you are so fucking good," he moans into my ear.

I am helpless. Held up against the wall by Dylan's large body. My world is dark with the blindfold. Every part of me is on fire ignited by his touch. I climb higher each time he pushes into me.

"Dylan…yes, oh god yes."

I come so hard that I think I may have blacked out. The next thing I know is that I'm on the bed in a cloud of softness.

"Watch your eyes, baby, I'm going to take the blindfold off," he says.

He pulls it away. I blink up at him trying to adjust to the sudden burst of light. He smiles and sits me up, untying my wrists, rubbing his hands up and down my arms. He leaves me to go into the bathroom. I hear the water running in the bath. Unbelievably I'm not frightened.

My entire body is sated. I'm perfectly content lying here on the bed. I lift my head slightly to glance down at the red marks crisscrossing my breasts, stomach and thighs. I lay my head back down and stare at the ceiling confused. He marked my skin. I should be angry shouldn't I?

I look down again and run my finger along a welt. I smile. It doesn't hurt but it does burn a little. When Dylan controls the situation, I like it. I really like it. I don't understand. Maybe I don't need to. I'm more alive than I have ever been in my entire life.

I hear the water shut off. Dylan comes back and scoops me up in his arms carrying me like a sack of potatoes. He smacks my ass. Instantly, heat surges straight down my spine. A lightning bolt that threatens to ignite. He sets me down on my feet in the tub.

"Go slow, baby, it might sting," he says.

I slowly sink, my breath hitches as water licks at the little red welts.

"Lay back. Relax. You did so good tonight. I can't believe how brave you are with everything I throw at you," Dylan breathes, pushing me back in the tub. My hands fly up and grip the sides of the tub. It is my natural reaction to being forced backwards towards the water. "It's okay, I won't push you under, sweetheart."

I hesitantly let go of the side and force my hands to rest at my side.

Dylan sits by the edge running his fingers through the bubbles making tiny circles in the suds. He frowns, his mind seems to be somewhere else. I made him feel bad. I didn't mean to freak-out. Shit. I need to get the train back on the tracks.

"You aren't joining me?" I shyly look at him through my long lashes.

The trance breaks. He smiles.

"No. I think I've given you enough for one day. If I get in, I won't be able to keep my hands off you."

"You lied." I slap on a pout.

"What? No. How did I lie to you?" He looks at me with his scary serious expression.

"You said you would not kill me." I try giving him a sexy smile. I'm a little awkward. I've never tried to flirt with anyone. I've been sporting the tomboy vibe for a long time now.

It must work because he stands and gets into the tub pulling me to him.

"I said I wouldn't kill you. I didn't say I wouldn't try." A slow grin spreads across his face.

I laugh. "I guess I don't mind you trying as long as you don't succeed." He pulls me down, so I am laying on his chest, water laps up under my chin.

"But, I think you are trying to kill me as well, Anna Velasquez."

I smile into his chest. It is nice to hear my name. Especially when he says it, with his deep sexy voice.

"Dylan?"

"Yes, baby?" he replies.

"Do you think someday we can go home?"

Chapter Twenty-Three

Dylan

This girl. What am I going to do with her? She pulls at my heartstrings like nothing I have ever known. She is unbelievable. She rolls with life, taking everything in stride. When she asked me if someday we could go home, it took my breath away.

For one, she used the word *we*, I love that. Secondly, she wants to go home. Home…I have only been able to go back to the estate a handful of times. I want to. My plan was to take Sophia there to let her heal from all the trauma Oliver inflicted. Every time I go it is just too lonely. There are people there so lonely isn't the correct word, yet it is.

I hired a large staff to care for the grounds and buildings. Even after the attack many families eagerly applied to come and work for me. Life is not always easy in Mexico. Most were eager to make a decent, fair wage, have a place for their family to live and for their kids to get an education.

Anna's mother had a building designated as a school. She filled it with all the supplies and books needed for the children on the estate. I hired a few teachers to replace the ones we lost. I replaced the entire staff, but it's not the same. If I take Anna there she would fill that void. She is a Velasquez. Maybe she is, Oliver told her that Manuel is her father. I don't really care either way. She will always be Manuel and Annette Velasquez's daughter.

We can't go home right now. I wish we could. She broke my heart at dinner talking about only seeing this cabin and shit heads new residence. I can help her. We aren't just going to sit here and wait. We will live a little. She needs to make up for lost time. I want to show her she means more to me than she imagines. Yes, I love her body but…ah I don't know how to describe it. She grips at something deep inside me. I have never felt this way about anyone.

I pull her closer. She is sleeping soundly in my arms. I will let her sleep in today while I start on my surprise for her. She deserves excitement and happiness. We aren't going to wait for it to happen. I'll make it happen. I kiss her naked shoulder lightly and pull the blanket up over her tucking it in under her soft lithe body.

When I get downstairs, Liam is up sitting at the breakfast bar with his head in his hands, a cup of coffee in front of him. I open the cupboard to grab a mug and startle him. "Shit, man I didn't mean to scare you."

"You didn't scare me," he says grumpily.

I put my hands up. "Okay, okay, geez someone woke up on the wrong side of the bed. What are you doing up this early anyhow?" He looks terrible.

"Sorry, I shouldn't have snapped. I didn't sleep well." He gets up and pours himself another cup.

"I'm here if you need to talk, Liam." I grab an apple and a granola bar wanting something quick.

"I'm okay." He sits back down and watches me rush around the kitchen. "What's up, you're not making me breakfast?" he asks laughing.

"Actually, I was going to ask you if you could make sure that Anna eats and if you could keep an eye on her this morning. I need to take a quick trip into town."

"Sure, but there is no such thing as a quick trip to town out here," he says.

"I know, I hope to be back by early afternoon. I'm planning a big surprise for her. She broke my heart last night. I want to do something fun with her," I say as I sit down beside him gulping down my coffee.

He sighs. "She shattered mine too. Fucking bastards why does this world have to be so ugly."

"It doesn't. That is why I'm running to town. So, you are good with staying with her today?" I eye him suspiciously. I have a feeling he and Anna are up to something.

"Yes, I said I would. I suppose I should start breakfast for her. You know she'll be nervous that you left her alone with me." He stands and walks to the cupboard in search of ideas of what to prepare her.

"I trust you. She will learn to trust you too. Just keep an eye on her for me, make sure she doesn't lock herself away. If you don't keep her engaged, she retreats inside herself." I toss my trash and grab a travel mug getting my fill of coffee.

"We will be fine. You want to let me in on your little surprise?" he says as he cracks a few eggs into a bowl.

"Shit no, you are terrible at keeping secrets." I give him a bear hug from behind as he tries to reach around to punch me, both of us laughing.

"Shh, you'll wake your girl before you make your get-away," he teases. I dodge him and grab my cup to head out.

"Call me if anything comes up," I say as I close the door.

It's still dark out, perfect an early start to the day. I can't wait to surprise Anna. I'm going to give her the world.

Anna

I wake up to the sun peeking at me thru the curtains. I glance over at the empty bed. Dylan must be up already. What time is it? I grab my phone off the end stand, shit it is almost ten in the morning. Why did he let me sleep so late? I lay there and listen for any noise coming from downstairs, nothing. Hmm, he could be outside working on security.

I get up tugging on my jeans, a t-shirt and slip my feet into a pair of sneakers. In the bathroom I take a minute to reminisce over a few bathtub memories with Dylan. I'm looking forward to spending the day with him. I can't remember the last time I looked forward to anything. I stare at myself in the mirror, smiling, it's nice to see myself. Good morning, Anna, I say out loud. So many years wasted, pretending.

I pull my t-shirt up to study the marks that Dylan made last night. They are lighter today, in a day or two they will be completely gone. I don't consider this type of "play" typical but then my life has been anything but normal so what do I know. My parents and the Madronos didn't tie each other up, spank and whip each other. Or did they? What people do in the privacy of their bedroom is really no one else's business if they enjoy it, who is to judge.

I run the brush through my hair. I study myself again, ugh I'm such a tomboy. For the first time I wish I had something nice to put on or a touch of makeup. I know little about that sort of thing. I miss my mom. I wish she was alive, so I could ask her all the questions that are ping-ponging around in my brain. I guess Dylan could take me into town to shop, I giggle to myself shaking my head. I never dreamed I would want to impress someone let alone go shopping.

I jog down the stairs, Liam is sitting at the table looking over file folders. He looks up at me smiling. "Late night?" he smirks. I'm sure I turn a nice shade of pink. I ignore him as I step into the kitchen to grab a cup of coffee.

"Sorry, I didn't mean to be a smart ass. I made you breakfast it is in the warmer." He moves around me and opens the oven to pull out a plate with a hot pad. He sets it down on the counter and points to a chair instructing me to sit. Something seems off, my heartrate picks up.

"Thank you. Um where is Dylan?" I ask nervously and glance behind me.

"He had to run into town for a few errands, he said he would be back this afternoon," he says as he sits down at the table picking up a file to study its contents.

I turn and stare at my plate, the meal looks delicious, but I can't eat. Dylan is gone. Did Liam send him away? Does he have information that Brian is near? I swallow hard. I try to push down the panic. I think about the tracker pill that he gave me, should I get it? I hid it in the nightstand by my bed.

My throat tightens as I speculate about Dylan being gone. I don't want Brian to come for me. I can't go back. Stop, Anna, you must, it is the only way for Liam and Dylan to find him. If there is any hope of taking Oliver out I need to take the risk. I look at Liam. He doesn't seem as if he is on alert or anything so maybe Dylan did just go to town for errands.

"What's wrong, did I make you something you don't like? I can fix something different. You need to eat." He comes over to me.

I shake my head. I open my mouth to tell him that what he made was fine, but a sob escapes instead. I dart around him and head for the stairs. He catches me at the waist as soon as I reach the second step pulling me back against him tightly.

"Anna, it's okay, it's not time. I have gotten no word that anyone is in the states. Please don't cry." He rests his chin on top of my head.

I say nothing, I can't, fear has gripped its claws in me. I am certain that someone is coming for me today, he is lying. I want to hide.

"Anna, please. I promise you are safe. Dylan will return just calm down." He holds me as I break down, my crying only gets louder and uglier I am sure. One thing I am not is a pretty crier.

Liam drags us back and sits down on the steps. He keeps me prisoner in front of him on the step lower than his. "I always envisioned holding Sophia like this, letting her cry while I held her tight."

Does he think he is helping? He isn't. I don't want to think about Sophia and the hell she endured because of me. Wait. That is why I am doing this. This is why I am working with Liam, to get to Oliver. To take him out. Pull it together, Anna. You have no reason not to trust him.

I quit crying. He lets go of my arms and lets me wipe at my tears, keeping me protectively wrapped between his legs. "I've been thinking, we should tell Dylan."

"No!" I blurt turning to face him. "No, I'm sorry I…I don't know, I'm sorry. I'm okay. We can't tell Dylan he will stop us. You saw how I reacted when I assumed Brian was near, I thought this was it, that it was time. I can't live like this. I need Oliver to die." I plead with him and grab at his shirt.

He looks down at me. "Anna, I'm sorry I can't do this to Dylan. He is feeling something for you. We can't do it. We will come up with a different plan. We will talk to him, I can't do this to my friend, he is like a brother. He is all I have."

I listen to what he is saying, did he say Dylan has feelings for me? Now I'm even more confused than before. I let go of his shirt trying to scoot myself away from him. "No, you are not hiding. Dylan gave me specific instructions to see that you eat and that you don't run off to hide. So far we are zero for zero on those two things."

He tips my chin and gazes into my eyes for a minute. His are a gorgeous blue, they are hard but kind all in one. "Please, Liam," I plead.

He runs his thumb over my cheek. "No, Anna, we can't do this to him. We both need him too much."

I close my eyes to trap the tears. He is right. I do need Dylan, look at me I'm a basket case when he isn't around. If Liam wasn't here I would be up hiding under my covers or locked in the bathroom. "Okay. I'm scared. I don't know what to do."

"We will figure it out. It will all work out. Let Dylan and I worry about everything, you're not alone anymore." He smiles and my heart melts a little.

He is so kind, I wish he could have gotten his happily ever after with Sophia. He said I wasn't alone. It is a nice thought but eventually everyone leaves me. Liam and Dylan will too, it's just a matter of time. I stand up and back down the stairs running my hand over my hair. I try to pull myself together. Back to business, one foot in front of the other.

Liam leads me to my breakfast. "Eat, if Dylan finds you half-starved he will tan my hide." He kisses the top of my head, content with the fact I have come to my senses for the time being.

"How did you guys learn to cook so well?" I ask after swallowing a mouthful of eggs.

"Dylan's mom, she used to scold us saying if you eat, you cook, *and* you clean." He laughs at his memory sitting back in his chair. I smile too, picturing them as young boys helping Dylan and Sophia's mother in the kitchen.

He pushes his paperwork from him. "Hey how about we take a walk after you finish up? Dylan told me there is a stream nearby."

"Yes, it isn't too far away. That would be nice, thank you. I'm a little apprehensive to walk by myself," I say.

I clean my plate as he goes to his room to grab his shoes. I sit at the table in front of the laptop and stare at the boxes showing the feed from all the cameras Dylan installed. I run my fingers over the keys of the keyboard thinking about how all of this started. The tears threaten to return when I hear Liam clear his throat behind me.

"No more tears, seriously I can't take it. You are killing me." He smiles to lighten the mood. "I was just reading a story the other day that went viral over social media. It was about a large anonymous donation to the family of my hotel murder victim. I was thinking about it and wondered if you knew anything about that." He taps me under my chin winking at me.

I drop my shoulders. He is right, I can't keep doing this to myself. I didn't know what was waiting for me, that murderers and rapists were after me. I have tried making amends for my mistakes the best I can that is all I can do.

I take his hand as we walk outside, inhaling a big breath of fresh air. I need to stop looking behind me and look ahead. We walk together silently and stop to view the wildflowers. "Have you been to Colorado before," I ask him.

"No, first time for me too. I like it here, it is so different from the rest of the world, huh?"

"Yes, things move slower out here," I say as I pick up a daisy bringing it to my nose. "Dylan said nothing about going back to town. Did he have much to do there?"

"He didn't say. Relax, I'm not tricking you."

"I know." I sigh and drop the flower. "I guess I am just wondering why he didn't tell me that's all."

"Maybe it's a surprise," he teases as he picks up the daisy I dropped tucking it behind my ear.

I pull my shoulder up to my cheek. "I hate surprises."

"What? Everyone likes surprises." He pulls me towards the sound of the stream as it comes into view. Suddenly he turns to look at me. "Shit, I'm sorry, I can see why they might not be your cup of tea. Just don't listen to me, I'm an idiot."

I laugh. "No, I don't think you are an idiot. It's okay, I'm sure most people do." I make my way over to my favorite rock and climb up to sit down to look over the stream.

Liam climbs up beside me. "It is peaceful here, I like it," he says scanning the area.

"Me too." I pull my legs up and hug myself. I close my eyes listening to the sound of the stream and the birds, breathing in the fresh scent of pine.

He takes off his shoes and folds up the bottoms of his jeans. "Come on, let's explore."

"No, thank you. You go ahead, I'll watch from the sideline," I say.

He scrambles down off the rock. "Have it your way, but if you change your mind…" He jumps into the stream and makes a loud splash. It only comes up a little over his ankles. He stands there wiggling his eyebrows at me trying to entice me to join him.

I laugh. "Okay, okay you win." I pull my shoes off and cuff my jeans, going to the edge. He reaches his hand out to help steady me. The water is cold making me screech. Once I adjust, I watch it swirl around my ankles. The rocks are so smooth under my feet, the water has worn them down over many years.

Liam releases my hand and walks a little way down from me, reaching every so often to pick up different rocks, showing me his newfound treasures. I follow his lead as my eye catches something shiny. It is the ring that Oliver gave me. I tossed it in the other day. I hope it is not a bad omen that I stumbled across it in the stream. I kick a rock over the top of it. Not today Oliver, not today. Liam comes over and hands me a stone shaped like a heart. "Here you go, Anna, it's a sign."

"What does it mean?" I chuckle and turn it over in my palm noticing the still visible scar on my hand from the rope I used to kill Oliver's guard.

"It's a sign that love is in the air." We both look up as we hear a loud noise at the same time. "That sounds like a helicopter." He pulls me into his arms, and I tremble as we both stare at the sky. He notices my fear. "Hey, it's okay. I doubt someone sneaking up on us would do so in something so rude." I watch his face as he searches for the source of the commotion.

I see his reaction when he spots the chopper. He gazes down and smiles at me. "Anna, your surprise has arrived." He gives me a peck on the cheek and pulls me out of the stream. "We need to get up to the house, Dylan is back."

"Dylan? Dylan is in that helicopter? How do you know? I don't know, we should hang here," I say.

He tosses me my shoes. "I'm sure. Come on, if we make him wait he will be pissed."

I unroll my jeans and pull on my shoes. As soon as I get the last one on he drags me to the clearing.

"Dylan will be worried when we aren't at the cabin. I don't want him to worry," he says slowing down a little to let me catch my breath.

When we reach the clearance, there it is, a helicopter, a fucking helicopter. I pause and yank my hand out of Liam's grip. He stops a few feet ahead of me. "Don't be scared."

I watch as the blades slow down and come to a stop, then the door opens, Dylan jumps out. He looks out across the grass his gaze lasering in on me. I clutch the rock in my hand tightly. It's him, my pulse speeds up at the sight of him. I'm so happy to see him. When I am near him, my world stops spinning, he grounds me like nothing I have ever known.

I watch as he smiles and saunters towards me. Our eyes never break contact. I hear Liam stifle a laugh. "I guess I was right, love is in the air." He doubles over laughing at his own joke. He slaps Dylan on the back as he makes his way past him.

When Dylan reaches me, he picks me up in a hug lifting my feet off the ground and kisses my forehead. "Miss me, baby?"

I wrap my arms around his neck and cling to him…my rock.

Chapter Twenty-Four

Dylan

God my girl is beautiful. I could see the confusion on her face when I spotted her and Liam walking back to the cabin. Confused or concerned I'm not sure which but when I set her down on her feet, she punches me right square in the chest.

"What the fuck?" I say rubbing my hand over my chest.

"You can't just run off like that, Dylan. Why didn't you tell me you were leaving?" She crosses her arms across her rib cage, a pouty expression forms on her face.

I worried her. I forget that everyone she has ever known has abandoned her. I need to keep this in mind. She will forgive me once she sees where we are going.

I pull her into my embrace and pull out the charm. "I'm sorry, baby, you are right I should have told you, but I wanted it to be a surprise." She can't resist me. She lays her head down on my chest wrapping her arms around my waist.

"I was scared," she whispers and peeks up at me through those long lashes.

"Scared of what? Did you worry I wasn't coming back?"

She looks down to avoid my question. I tug on her hair gently to force her face up.

"Yes, and no. My head doesn't always think logically," she says.

I release her and run my hand down her back giving her a light squeeze. I forget how much she has been through sometimes. All I can do is reassure her. "You are stuck with me. I'm not going anywhere."

She grips me around the waist a little tighter. I glance down and catch her smile at my words.

"Dylan, did you fly that helicopter here or is there someone with you?"

I take her hand as we walk towards the cabin. "I flew it, one of my many talents," I say winking at her. She giggles at this and blushes. I am sure she recalls some of my more recent show of skills in the bedroom.

When we get to the porch, I turn her to face me. "Anna, I want you to go upstairs and pack a bag, enough for two or three days. I will be up to collect a few things myself. I need to talk to Liam for a minute. Understand?"

She shifts her weight from foot to foot and stares at the ground. I know she is hesitant to trust me especially since she has no idea where I am taking her or what is going on. I let her take all the time she needs as she mulls over her thoughts. Finally, she straightens her posture and lifts her head looking directly at me. "Yes, sir."

Fuck, I reach down to adjust myself, instant hard on hearing her call me that. She smiles shyly, she knows what this does to me. "Change of plans, go upstairs pack a few things. Then I want you to wait for me naked, kneeling, facing the long mirror in the bedroom."

She scurries away quickly leaving me to stand on the front porch with a raging hard on. Oh, the possibilities with this one. When I get inside Liam is sitting on the couch with a big shit eating grin on his face.

"She looks happy you're back." He laughs and props his feet up on the coffee table. "She seems to be in a hurry for something."

"Fuck you," I say plopping down beside him. "I'm going to take her away for a few days, do you want to go along, or hang out here?"

"I'll stay, I like it here. So, where are you traveling for your little rendezvous?"

"San Diego, I'm taking her to my beach house. She wants to see the ocean and I want to show her. We might spend tonight in town, so I can take her on a real date. I doubt she has ever been on one and she deserves it," I say.

"San Diego? Are you sure man that is awfully close to the border?"

"I know but nobody knows she is going there. How could they? I've chartered a private plane out of Denver to fly us straight there. I didn't want to waste time driving, hence the helicopter."

Liam laughs. "The full wow factor huh?"

"It worked didn't it?" I glance towards the stairs and wonder what kind of state Anna is in right now.

"She was worried while you were gone, I eventually got her to eat and then we went for a walk. She is sweet I can see why you like her."

I stand, I think I have given her plenty of time to imagine all the things I might do to her.

"Dylan, I need to talk to you about something."

"Can it wait until we get back?" I rub my hand over my jeans, my cock painfully begging for release.

He laughs again and shakes his head. "Yeah, man it can wait. Go get your girl."

Anna

I ran all the way upstairs. I love to poke at the beast in Dylan. It doesn't take much. His eyes noticeably dilate when I call him sir. He likes it, which scares me and excites me. All my earlier worries of the day have vanished, replaced with a surging burst of excitement. I am sure he has something wonderful planned. I don't know if I have ever been more eager for anything in my whole life.

I threw everything in a bag as quickly as I could, splashed cold water over my face and ran the brush through my hair to make it extra shinny. I kneel and look at myself in the full-length mirror. I can see the door to the bedroom behind me, I watch it patiently waiting for Dylan to enter.

I gaze at my reflection. Blushing, I realize I have never really looked at myself naked in the mirror. I look sexy. The red lash marks still visible on my body, my dark hair spilling down my back and around my shoulders. I guess I understand why he likes me to sit like this for him.

I study the blue eyes staring back at me in the mirror. I am sitting back on my heels. I part my legs slightly so that when he walks in, he will be able to not only see my backside, but all of me. I bite my bottom lip. I don't know, maybe I'm being too brazen.

I hear the door click. I peek up as he comes in. I take a deep breath to prepare myself for the onslaught that is Dylan. He steps in his eyes instantly glued to mine in the mirror. He runs his eyes down, a smile forming on his face. I lower my head suddenly embarrassed.

He crouches down behind me and reaches around grabbing my chin to force my face upward, compelling my eyes to meet his. "Don't be shy, you look sexy as hell," he whispers in my ear.

I offer him a small smile and watch as his other hand runs down along my side then dips between my legs, cupping me. I close my eyes enjoying the heat of his palm on me. He is so warm.

"Open your eyes, baby. Don't take them off me. Do you understand?"

"Yes, sir," I say breathlessly.

He pushes me over, so I am on all fours our eyes still locked. I watch as he pulls his belt out and unzips his pants. He pushes them down and rubs himself across my bottom.

"We are on a tight schedule today. So, I am going to take you hard and fast. Don't close your eyes, keep them on me."

He swats my ass as he thrusts all the way, only stopping when he can go no further. He reaches down and draws his finger along my clit trailing it through the moisture building there. He pauses over my ass and looks intently at me. "Hold still."

I am about to protest as his finger slips inside me. I hiss at the intrusion unable to move. His cock pulses as he gently coaxes me. He leans over my back and bites me lightly on the shoulder. "What's your safe word?"

Shit, I forgot I had one. I should have used it before he pushed inside my bottom but now that he's there it really isn't that bad. "Water," I say as I suck my bottom lip in between my teeth.

"Good girl." He tenderly strokes me. I push back against him wanting more. He doesn't disappoint as he slips in a second finger drawing a loud moan from somewhere deep inside me.

He smacks my ass again, making me tighten my muscles hard around his cock and fingers. He groans as he reaches over to pinch my clit lightly as he picks up his pace. "Anna, when I come I want you right behind me."

I shake my head yes, I can't speak, I can't move, all I can think about is how full I am. He is everywhere inside me, but mostly he is in my mind, filling the emptiness I have suffered for so long. He pumps harder and faster. I am building, needing to release. He told me to wait for him…oh god…I can't…I can't and then I hear him moan my name loudly as he shoves all the way inside me, his cock spasms deep…I close my eyes…falling…trusting…flying…unquestioning while Dylan holds me tight.

When I finally regain my senses, he is staring at me in the mirror. Our eyes lock. He rubs his hands down my back, over my ass, and looks at me with smoldering intensity. My legs tremble, he sits back and pulls me into his lap, kissing my temple. He never takes his eyes off me.

"That was beautiful," he whispers.

I break eye contact with him and coil into his chest curling up as close as I can get. In a matter of days Dylan is slowly shifting into my entire world. I am exposing myself to him, allowing him to take me in the most intimate of ways. I worry, am I letting him see too much of Anna? What must he think of me? Everything is happening too fast. He is suddenly my oxygen, if he leaves I may forget how to breathe.

He holds me for a long time running his hands up and down along my arms, my legs and over my back. "Anna, hey talk to me."

"I'm okay, I'm just shy I guess."

"I don't want you to feel that way around me. I want to see you, the real you. You make me happy, Anna. I like that you are trusting me." He tickles me making me squirm on his lap. "Ah, I better stop. You will make my dick hard again and then we will be late."

"Late for what? Where are you taking me?" I ask as I remember the helicopter still outside.

He pulls back and looks at me. "Oh no you don't, you will see, patience, Anna." He brushes his lips across mine. "In due time, all in due time."

He pulls me to my feet and swats my butt. "Wash off and meet me downstairs in ten." He tosses his things in a bag. I hurry and close the door behind me.

I don't know where we are going but I am giddy with excitement. I quickly throw my hair up and step into the shower to rinse myself off. I have never ridden in a helicopter before, my body is tingling, endorphins surging happily through my veins.

After I get dressed, I grab my cell off the end stand and glance at it hastily. My heart stops. A text from an unknown number…three words…*where are you?* Shit, I should tell Dylan and Liam. I hug the phone to my chest. I don't want to spoil Dylan's surprise. I have been putting off life hiding for the last nine years. I open the text and type Texas but then I delete that. Dylan might be taking me there. I'm not sure where we are traveling. I'm just not going to reply, I don't owe Oliver anything, let alone a response.

I delete the text from him and shove my phone in my back-pocket, hurrying downstairs. Dylan is waiting at the bottom of the stairs. He taps his finger on his watch giving me a stern look. I stop mid step to observe him. "Ten, Anna, ten, not fifteen." He clicks his tongue. "I will have to spank you for this little incident later."

I attempt to appear unaffected by his words. I brush past him and run my fingers lightly over his groin as I pass by. He growls behind me. I turn to give him the sweetest of smiles. "I'm sorry, sir, I shouldn't have been such a bad girl." I spin heading out the door bumping into Liam on the way out.

He grabs my arms to steady me. "Slow down lady, it's okay, where's the fire?"

Dylan comes out and laughs. "Yeah, baby, where's the fire." He winks at me slapping my butt and drags me away from Liam. "We will back in a few days, call me if anything comes up."

I turn to look at Liam as Dylan ushers me to the helicopter. He waves. "Have fun, don't worry you are in good hands."

I smile at him. He is right. I am in good hands.

Chapter Twenty-Five

Anna

I am so excited. We took the helicopter to Denver and then we hopped on another plane, a private jet. Evidently Dylan has made a life for himself, able to afford all of this. It was incredibly sexy watching him pilot the chopper. It was hard to peel my eyes away from him to scan the scenery below.

Once we landed he couldn't hide our destination from me any longer. We are in San Diego, palm trees, warm temperatures and the ocean. I realize that is why we are here. I haven't seen it yet, but I know. When he told me where we were I thought my chest would burst. I can't remember anyone ever doing something like this for me. He truly listened to me.

"Are you excited, baby?" Dylan's voice pulls me out of my thoughts.

"Yes, yes, I am," I say to him grinning from ear to ear.

"Good, we are almost to the hotel. Today will be a little different. I need you to trust me."

"Um, okay," I reply nervously.

He leans over and kisses me. "Don't worry, it's not what you think. I'm leaving you to get a few things set up for our mini getaway. You are going to go do some shopping and let me pamper you. One of my security guys will be your chaperone for the day. I don't want you to be afraid of him, okay? I trust him, you can too." He takes my hand in his, placing a kiss on my knuckles.

I breathe a sigh of relief. "How long will you be gone?"

"A couple of hours. My guy's name is Anthony. He also worked for your father, so I know he'll take good care of you. You listen to him. He knows where to go and when. Everything is set up, no thinking on your part. I mean it, just enjoy today. Meet me at the bar in the hotel at exactly six tonight…don't make me wait like earlier or you will earn double the punishment."

I turn to the window to hide my blush. I cross my legs to curb the fire he ignited with his threat. "Yes, sir." He leans over the seat and tugs the back of my hair forcefully, bringing his face up beside my ear.

"If we weren't on such a tight schedule today, I would take you up to that motel room and give you your punishment right now."

I lean into him as the car slows. We have arrived at our destination. He let's go of me and slides back to his seat. I turn to study him. There is an undercurrent of arousal swimming in his eyes. My door opens, and our driver politely reaches inside and offers me his hand.

The resort is amazing, there are hundreds of different colored flowers everywhere, they stand out against the stark white of the hotel. It is so beautiful. I wonder how near we are to the ocean. I am impatient now that I know we are so close.

I don't dare ask Dylan. He planned this trip all for me, I'm not going to question him. He is running the show. I'm a little surprised at how much I like that. I guess I am tired of hiding in my bed. I want to see the world. I have always been too afraid to do that. With him by my side I could try anything at least once, the possibilities seem endless when he is with me, I feel safe.

Dylan places his arm around my waist and ushers me inside. We stop at the desk and he checks in under a name that is not his. This would normally set off alarm bells but, he is taking every precaution to keep me safe. Oliver may have found out we are together. I don't know how, but I doubt nothing with him.

We walk by the restaurant. He steps inside the doorway and points over to the long bar towards the back of the facility. "I will wait for you there. At what time?"

"Six, sir." He tightens his grip around my waist. He loves it when I call him that. I like it too which is slightly confusing. It made me angry when I heard the girls at Oliver's having to say it to the men in charge there. I guess the difference is that I want to do it, no one forces me too. I love his reaction to the word. His eyes darken and his nostrils flare. It makes me instantly warm.

"Good girl." He kisses my temple and ushers us to the elevator.

We get to our room and I spot my bag sitting on the end of the bed. I search around for Dylan's. "Are you not staying here with me?" My anxiety spikes to new levels at the thought of sleeping here alone.

He pulls me into a hug and runs his hand down my hair, soothing me. "I told you to trust me. I'm just leaving for a few hours. You will sleep beside me tonight. We aren't staying here. This is a temporary stop for you to freshen up and change. I'm taking you on a real date."

I pull back and look up at him. "A what?"

"A date, silly." He thumps me lightly on the nose. "We started this relationship off with me shoving you in a trunk. I think the least I can do is be gentlemanly enough to take you on a date. Unless you don't want to?"

"I, I…yes, yes I would like to go out with you." Dylan surprises me, he is not the man I thought he was when he shoved me into the trunk. I guess that is what he is trying to show me. He wants me to understand him. He is hard, he is gentle, I enjoy both.

A knock interrupts the moment. Dylan peers through the peephole. He smiles before he swings the door open wide. "Anthony!" he bellows, giving the guy a bear hug, the same ease of interaction he has with Liam.

The man glances over his shoulder at me and winks. "So, this is Anna Velasquez." He pulls away from Dylan turning to face me. He wraps me in his arms and picks me up off my feet and then sets me back down. "I haven't seen you since you were nay high." He puts his hand out to show me how tall I was the last time he saw me. "You look good for being dead." He laughs.

Dylan senses my discomfort and comes to stand beside me. "Jesus, Anthony, give her a minute to get to know you.

"Ah, Anna and I will be best friends I can tell. Now, she and I have places to be, so if you don't mind." He grabs my hand and pulls me away from Dylan to head out the door. I glance back hesitantly at Dylan, he shrugs his shoulders and gives me a nod of encouragement, laughing lightly at his friend's brashness.

When we enter the elevator, he takes it down a notch. "Sorry, I come off a little high-strung. I knew Dylan would never let us leave if I didn't get the ball rolling."

I slide to the corner and wonder what the hell is going on. Does Dylan truly trust this guy? He is older than him by at least ten years. He is not as tall as Dylan more Liam's height. He is physically fit with short hair and wearing what looks like an expensive business suit. He is dangerously good looking. Anthony gets what he wants there is no doubt in my mind.

He eyes me. "So, I've made you leery of me. I'm sorry, I come off a bit strong. I'll try to tone myself down until you get used to me." He winks at me again.

I take a couple of deep breaths. If Dylan trusts this man then so can I. When the elevator stops he steps out to look around before he reaches in for me. Yes, I can tell that he is of the same breed as Dylan and Liam. He is taking this job seriously even if it doesn't seem so.

"Do you like to shop?" Anthony asks.

"No, not really. Where exactly does Dylan have you taking me?"

"Shopping and spa time. I may even get one of those massages while we are there." He pauses and moves his head from side to side as if checking his level of stiffness.

When we walk out he opens the door to a small black, race car looking vehicle parked right outside. I know nothing about cars but this one looks fast. Fast like him. I hesitantly slide into the passenger seat and watch as he rounds getting in beside me.

I freeze, I haven't been alone with anyone besides Dylan and Liam. I stare at the hotel thinking I should just get out and tell Dylan that this will not work and that I want to go back to the cabin. Anthony leans over me and reaches for my seat belt. I try to push myself back as far as possible, uncomfortable with him being in my space.

"Sorry, Anna. You are frightened, there is no need to be. We will knock off Dylan's list and I'll have you back here in no time. Besides, I wasn't lying, we are going to best of friends," he says as he clicks my seatbelt, securely locking me into place.

He gives me a smile as his foot pushes down on the accelerator forcing my head into the seat. We speed away, the hotel quickly disappears behind us. My nervousness is full force at how fast we are traveling through the busy San Diego streets. He seems unaffected by it all, this is just the normal pace of his life.

He shifts gears and weaves in and out of traffic. He knows what he is doing. He is confident in his abilities as a driver. An uncomfortable silence has crept into the vehicle. I can tell he feels bad about my obvious discomfort at the situation. He is a friend of Dylan's, so I should try to at least let him know I will not jump out of his car. He nonchalantly locked the door after he saw my hand grip the frame.

"So, Anthony, Dylan told me you worked security with him. Are you sure you are not really a NASCAR driver?" I tease.

He laughs and glances over at me. The tension eases from his face. "No, but I can't lie, when I was a kid it was what I wanted to be when I grew up."

"Well, I think you would be fantastic at it." I grip the door again as he turns a corner sharply.

He pulls up in front of a high-end clothing store. "First stop."

I peek up at the expensive-looking glass front. "Ugh, I'm not much of a shopper. Is there a shopping mall nearby?"

He looks at me and reaches out to brush a runaway lock of hair behind my ear. "Don't worry. We are only in need of a few things and I can help you out there. I have good taste."

He opens my door for me. The minute we are inside a tall leggy woman strolls over. "You must be Anna." She shakes my hand with her delicate cold one. "Mr. Lorenz called. We have been expecting you." She turns to head deeper into the store.

Anthony stops her. "I think we will be okay on our own. Just point us in the direction of your cocktail dresses and a dressing room. We'll let you know if we need any assistance."

She stares at him with her mouth open. "Mr. Lorenz made specific instructions…"

Anthony cuts her off with a wave of his hand. "We can go somewhere else." He turns to leave, but she rushes forward and grabs his arm.

"I apologize, I was just trying to follow the directions from Mr. Lorenz. The dresses are over there." She points to an area near the rear of the store. "A private dressing room is ready for her in the far back corner. I will leave you to shop. Please let me know if you need anything." She takes a step backward before retreating to the counter.

Anthony seizes my hand and drags me behind him. We reach the dresses. He sifts through the racks pulling several out, tossing them over his shoulder. He obviously knows what he likes. There is no hesitation in his movements.

After he finishes with his selections, he heads to the dressing room to hang them on a hook. He steps out and ushers me inside closing the door behind me. "I want to see all of them on you. I will be right outside waiting."

What the heck is it with the men in my life, oh so damn bossy. I smile as I look over the dresses he selected for me to try on. My smile turns into a frown. All of these are very, well very not me. What is me? I don't know but I am sure that all of these will look horrendous on me.

"Snap, snap. We have places to be," he scolds from outside the dressing room.

I grab the first one, a simple black spaghetti strapped number. I pull it on over my head slipping down into it. I gaze in the mirror. It fits me perfectly. How the hell did he pick out the correct size. I guess it doesn't look terrible on me, I turn back and forth looking at my reflection.

I hesitantly step out of the dressing room. Anthony is leisurely sitting on a white loveseat across from me. He runs his eyes up and down over me and makes a spin motion with his finger prompting me to turn around for him. He nods simply saying, "next".

Dress after dress we repeat the process until I come to a blue one that matches my eyes perfectly. It is an off the shoulders, with short little sleeves and an open back. I slip it on, the fabric clings close to me. It is form fitting and hugs my curves in all the right places. I turn to look over my shoulder blushing at the erotic woman in front of me. The back stops just above my tailbone. It is sexy with my hair trailing down, when I shift it furnishes a glimpse of my tanned skin.

I open the door a crack and decide at the last moment not to show him this one. He rushes forward gripping the side of the frame to stop me. "I want to see them *all*." He pulls it wide open. His gaze runs down my length, I hear the sharp intake of his breath.

I drop my eyes to the floor. This is what I have tried to avoid my whole life. This is not blending in. This will make me stand out in a crowd. "Perrrfect," he breathes out, stressing the center of the word.

I don't want this dress. It looks amazing on me, but I don't want it. It will draw too much attention. "I think I'll just go with the first one, the black one," I blurt.

"Absolutely not, this is the one. Dylan will be beside himself when he sees you in this," he says.

I think about it for a moment. I do like to make Dylan happy. I twist and peek in the mirror my eyes meeting Anthony's. "Are you sure it's not too much?"

"Too much what?" He smiles coyly at me.

"Too much, oh I don't know. Too much me?" I answer exasperated, struggling to find the right words.

"No. It is perfect, there is no such a thing as too much you. Why would you say that?"

"I don't like to draw attention to myself," I mumble.

"You are beautiful, Anna, you have been hidden too long. It is time to let people see you. This is you. It is stunning. I am going to wait around the bar just to watch my friend's reaction when he spots you."

"If you don't think it's too much." I peek up at him shyly, he nods back and forth. "Okay." I study the mirror and nod to myself. I can do this. Dylan put considerable effort in this trip. I want to look nice for him.

"Get changed, I will pick out shoes and a few other things while you do that. What are you about a size seven shoe?" I nod, he runs his eyes up and down me once more in quick assessment before he closes the door.

After we leave the clothing store our next stop is a day spa. Anthony informs me that Dylan has scheduled me to get a massage, nail, hair and makeup all done today. He kissed me on the cheek and told me he was going to indulge himself. Then he left me to the ladies of the spa for them to work their magic.

Everything about it was amazing and slightly uncomfortable at the same time. Everyone was so nice they made slow gentle movements making me wonder if Dylan told them to treat me with such delicacy. But, I am not accustomed to so much human touch and by the end of my time I was feeling exhausted.

Anthony finds me as the hairdresser finishes drying my hair. The products he used smell amazing. When the stylist turns me to investigate my reflection, I almost don't recognize the girl staring back at me. My eyes meet Anthony's in the mirror, he gives me a huge smile. I told the girls I do not wear makeup. They told me they would go light, and they did. It is a very natural look.

I see the resemblance to my mother. I wipe tears away embarrassed by my onset of emotion and not wanting to smear everyone's hard work.

The hair stylist politely leaves the room as Anthony swivels my chair turning me to face him. I swipe at a stray tear. "Let's get you back to Dylan, I think you could use some familiarity about now." The kindness in his voice tugs at me.

When we get to my room Anthony hangs the dress up and sets the other bags on the bed for me. He sits down beside them. "I could stay if you would like, maybe you would be more comfortable leaving the room after you are ready with someone to accompany you?"

Dylan, Liam and Anthony are all perceptive. They seem to know what I need before I do. "Thank you, Anthony. Really, thank you for everything but I think I can do this myself."

He stands and gives me a quick peck on the cheek. He checks his watch before walking out. "It is five thirty." He gives me a knowing wink and leaves me to stand in the room alone.

Shit, it is five thirty where did the day go. I rush around dumping out the bags. I stare at the skimpy little black lace strapless bra and panties that fall out. I smile, thankful that Anthony didn't make me pick these items out for myself. He definitely has good taste.

After I finish dressing, I slip into a pair of stiletto heels. I pause in front of the mirror to study my reflection, holy cow. I almost appear sophisticated. My hair spills across my back. This must be a dream. I am in San Diego, in the most amazing dress, about to meet Dylan.

I glance at the clock on the end stand. Five fifty-five, shit, no time, or… I smile wickedly at myself in the mirror. Maybe Anna Velasquez arrives when she damn well feels like it.

Dylan

It is a quarter after six and Anna still hasn't come down to the bar. I search around again and find Anthony tucked in a booth off to the side. He gives me a little nod. He has a smirk on his face. I walk over to him.

"Is your girl making you wait?" He smiles as I approach.

"Fuck you, what time did you take her back to the room?"

"Five thirty and all she had to do was get dressed. Are you sure she isn't making you wait?" he says casually, not concerned about her well-being in the slightest.

My voice rises slightly. "She wouldn't purposely make me wait." As the words leave my mouth, I wonder if what Anthony said could be true. I smile back at him. "You must know something I don't."

He holds up both of his hands. "No, no I don't. I did my job, took her shopping and to the spa. I have no inkling what could be holding her up." Then I see him look past my shoulder and his shit eating grin gets wider. He picks up his drink and swirls the brown liquid handing it to me. "Here I think you may need this."

I don't accept it and turn around slowly. "Fuck." Anna is standing at the bar, with her back to us. I leave Anthony chuckling in the background. As I approach her, she pivots to scan the room looking for me. She finds her target. She swallows hard, the movement ripples down her neck.

I stop a few steps in front of her, drinking her in with my eyes. I don't think I have ever seen anything as beautiful. She was late on purpose. Naughty, naughty Anna. I reach out and grab her by the throat, pulling her close. Her eyes dilate, a fire ignites in them with my forceful touch. "What time is it?"

Her tongue darts out to lick her top lip. She shudders against me. "I'm sorry, sir, I had trouble with my dress." She reaches up and removes my hand from her neck turning around wiggling her tight little ass. She forces my eyes to drop to a zipper running up the dress to her tailbone. "Could you help me?"

I grab her waist and draw her back into me, zipping it. I whisper into her ear, "we will not make it to dinner, if you keep playing this game."

She faces me with wide innocent eyes that tug me into the blue depths, drowning me. "What game, sir?" she says as she runs that delightful little tongue over her teeth.

I laugh. "Anna, Anna, Anna, you will not win."

"Won't I?" She turns away from me and stalks out of the bar. I follow like a dog on her heals, hearing Anthony roar at the scene we enacted for him. I don't care, I am caught up in Anna, I need to see what she will do next.

She makes her way into a stairwell. I lean my back up against the door as she backs up into the corner. Sliding into the shadow of the stairs, she gracefully slips into a kneel. The blue material of her dress climbs up her thighs as she glides into position. She parts her legs ever so slightly. A pair of black lace panties peek out at me.

I groan as I stalk over to her. She reaches up to unbuckle my pants, dragging the zipper down. My dick has been hard since the moment I laid eyes on her. I usually like to be in complete control but something about Anna makes me want to give in to her. She is controlling the situation while still being submissive. I don't think I have ever been so fucking turned on.

She reaches in and pulls my raging hard on out gently gliding her hands over me. Her little tongue darts out giving her bottom lip attention, attention that my dick is begging for. She hears its silent plea, focusing her eyes on mine, she ever so lightly runs her tongue down my length making me hiss in a breath. I place my palms on the wall above her to brace myself. Anna always seems to amaze me. Anyone could walk in at any moment. Confidence and trust are written on her face, she knows I will keep her safe, hidden behind me in the shadows. I love that she trusts me, I will never let her go, never.

She sucks me into her mouth until I feel the back of her throat, her hand wraps around the base of me and grips tightly. It will not take much. Seeing her in the bar with hair spilling down to her ass, her bare spine begging my hands to run down it. Ah fuck. Then the confident display of initiating this scene. Shit, she is so perfect for me.

She goes a little farther each time drawing me into her mouth. Her confidence builds with each stroke and flick of her tongue, my moans giving her encouragement along the way. Then she stops and pointedly locks her hands behind her back. She stares up at me with those beautiful blue eyes, so much trust. She is offering me what I need, allowing me to take charge, submitting fully.

I carefully place my hand on the back of her head while bracing myself with my other on the wall above her. She sits perfectly still as I rock my hips and slide into her hot little mouth going deeper. I pause myself inside her until I know she needs a breath then slowly pull out. It only takes minutes before I am coming, cursing myself that I should have warned her, not wanting to risk getting that amazing dress dirty. She accepts it and swallows not even blinking. She is something else, my girl, Anna, she is all mine.

I rest my head on my forearm for a second before pulling out of her mouth cupping her cheek. She leans into my hand sighing. "Anna, you are going to send me to an early grave." I stare down at her, she has her eyes closed looking perfectly content on her knees before me.

I pull her up to her feet and tuck myself back into my pants watching her closely. She is happy and relaxed. I am glad. She is amazing. She has come so far in such a short time. When we first met, I would never have dreamed that this is how it would be with her. "You've made us late." I scold her playfully swatting her on the behind.

When we walk out of the stairwell Anthony is waiting by the lobby doors. He smiles and holds the door open. I punch him in the shoulder as I pass by him. He knew I would flip when I saw her. Anthony is the epitome of fashion.

Chapter Twenty-Six

Anna

I almost lost my resolve when I saw Dylan in the bar. He looked angry at first, maybe I shouldn't have made him wait. He gave me that serious look where he tips his head down and looks intently at me. When he stopped a few feet in front of me, heat flooded between my legs. He is so incredibly hot.

I hadn't thought about what I would do after I came in late but as we spoke I could see how turned on he was. I wanted to do something for him, just for his pleasure. I wasn't sure I could go through with it but hearing the sounds he made as I took him into my mouth was all the encouragement I needed. I was in control, even when I locked my hands behind my back, I still felt like I was the one in charge. It was incredible, Dylan makes me feel safe, able let myself come out and play.

When we left the hotel, Anthony was enjoying seeing his friend all riled up. He whispered as he helped me into the car that the dress did the trick. I smiled at him and thanked him for his help. I like Anthony. He is right I can see us being good friends.

I have to remind Dylan to keep his eyes on the road as we drive. The dress is working too well. It all seems like a dream. We went to dinner, the entire time we were at the restaurant all eyes were on us. He didn't seem to notice. Always calm and cool. He notices everything about me, helping me when I seemed unsure about what to order.

After dinner he told me we were going to a club, he handed me a fake ID making me blush. I forget our age difference sometimes. He is not that much older than me but enough he can go places I cannot. "Dylan, are you enticing me into a life of crime?" I smirk at him as I watch the shadows play across his face as we drive under the streetlights.

He reaches over and grabs my hand. "Enticing yes, I will be definitely be doing some of that tonight." He gives me a heated smile. "I forget how young you are, but don't worry about the ID, my guys only make the best, no one will notice that it is not real."

"I'm not worried, I'm used to being someone I'm not," I say.

He flinches at my words and screeches the car to a stop on the side of the road. He grabs the back of my hair forcefully, turning me to look dead into his eyes. "I do not want you to pretend to be someone you are not."

I suck in a few calming breaths. Dylan's reaction catches me off guard. "I'm sorry. I didn't mean it like that. You are the only person in the last nine years who has encouraged me to be myself."

He looks intently at me slowly realizing that he overacted. He yanks me towards him hungrily and takes my mouth, dropping greedy kisses down along my neck and over my collarbone. He leans back in his seat and releases me from his grip. He runs his hand through his hair, trying to regain composure. "I'm sorry. I just want you to be yourself. You. Not Sarah, not Ramirez's daughter, not Annette's…just you, Anna. I demand the real you."

I don't know what to say, I can still feel his mouth on me, the brutal kisses he just thrust upon me still tingle across my skin. The air in the car has electrified. My pulse pounds in every part of my body. "I want you too."

He drums his thumbs on the steering wheel looking like he is having a tough time deciding where to go from here. "God, I wish I could take you home and ravage every inch of you. But, I promised you a real date." He pulls away from the curb and continues towards the club.

I'm humming at the image of the night to come. I want him to take me home too. But, I've never been to a club and the prospect of going has me excited. We pull up to a long line of people waiting outside. Dylan shifts into the lot across the street and hops out to open my door for me.

He tugs me out next to him. I peek up giving him a flirty smile. He is in a black suit and tie. He is sexy tonight. A wolf in sheep's clothing. He appears lethal towering over me.

As we cross the road, the people in line stare at us. I'm sure he gets this a lot. He is someone you can't take your eyes off. He seems not to care and makes his way directly to the front of the line. The bouncer notices him right away giving him a pat on the back.

"Long time no see, Dylan. What have you been up too?" The big burly bouncer then spots me on his arm and looks down at me with a knowing smile. "Never mind, I can see what you have been up to."

Dylan looks down at me squeezing me close to him. "This is Anna."

"Anna, very nice to meet you," he says as he unlocks the gate allowing us to pass by him.

When the door opens, the music comes flooding out, the beat taunts those still standing in line. The club is dimly lit and crowded. Dylan pushes his way through like he owns the place bee-lining to a booth, letting me slide in first. I glance out at the dance floor. It is full of people lost in the melody, bodies grinding and rubbing against each other.

A cute girl in a leather tank top and boy cut shorts comes to the table. She yells down at us asking what we want. Dylan places our order. She bends over and shakes her tits in front of him, looking like she would love to lean in and devour him. An unfamiliar feeling works its way up from the pit of my soul. Am I jealous? Oh yes, yes I am. The thought of Dylan touching anyone but me makes my stomach hurt.

He doesn't seem to notice her much. He leans down and speaks directly into my ear, so I can hear him. "So, what do you think? Do you want to dance?"

I shake my head no and look back at the crowd gathered on the floor. I'm suddenly overwhelmed by it all. The realization I was jealous of our waitress compounds everything. The music is too loud, there are too many people, I want to throat punch the bitch…breathe, Anna, breathe, I tell myself. "I think I will find the restroom," I say.

He looks at me. "Are you feeling okay?"

"Yes, I just need to freshen up," I reply trying to keep it together.

He points to a hallway where the restrooms are and kisses me on the forehead. "I'll wait for the drinks," he says.

What if I come back to discover leather girl drooling over my man? My man? Shit. The day sneaks up on me fast, it's all too much, too much human contact, too many people, too much everything. I scurry trying not to bump into anyone which is near impossible in the crowd. Just as I get to the entrance of the hallway a hand wraps around my arm and pulls me into the darkness of the club.

My first thought is that Dylan has followed me. But, when the person twirls me, pushing me against the wall, I realize that it is defiantly not Dylan.

"Hey, sexy thang, I haven't seen you here before," a man's voice breathes down over me. I can smell the alcohol on his breath mixed with his way too strong cologne.

I push on his chest trying to push away from him. "I'm here with someone," I say pushing harder on him. He doesn't budge, he looks down at me with a hungry expression in his eye. I coil up inside. I try to see around him, but he is blocking my view of everything, the entire club behind him.

"Don't worry sweet thang, we can leave out the back door. Your boyfriend probably won't even miss you. There is a lot of fresh ass here tonight," he says as he licks my cheek.

He fucking licked the side of my face.

I push harder, trying to fight the tears. "Please just let me go. I need to use the restroom, I'll be right back I promise," I plead with him.

He puts one palm on the wall behind me and presses me into it, his other hand grabs my thigh slowly roaming up. I tremble. No, this cannot be happening. I shut my eyes tight. Then I detect a whoosh of air as the heat of his body leaves mine.

I open my eyes to see that Dylan has his forearm locked around the idiot's neck pulling him from me a few feet. The man's face turns red as he presses his arm into his throat. Dylan stares at me, seeing my tears he pushes the man away from him, and punches him square in the face. I hear the man's nose crunch as his fist makes contact.

He falls onto the floor. Dylan leans over him and continues to pummel him. A few men try to hold Dylan back, to no avail. He is going to kill him…I rush over and place myself behind the man's head forcing Dylan to look at me. He stops. He grabs me and pushes us through the crowd out a door to the side. The cool night air assaults me.

He walks me calmly to his car and opens it for me. The minute I get in, I turn towards my window staring at the club. What just happened? I can't look at him, he is so angry. I have never seen him like this. When I thought he looked lethal tonight, I guess I was right.

"I'm sorry," he says as he starts the car.

I round on him. "You are sorry? What for?" I ask my tone coming out harsher than I intended.

"I'm sorry I ruined your first date," he replies looking down at the steering wheel.

"You ruined nothing, that man did, he did, I did, I ruined it…" I cry. He reaches for me, but I stop him. "I ruined it. I was running away." I see the shock on his face. "No, I mean I wasn't running away from *you*, but I was trying to get away." My words rush out in a flurry.

"I'm sorry I should have told you. The day was catching up with me, the people, the waitress made me jealous, the noise. I was running to the bathroom to get away from it all. I shouldn't have left your side. I'm sorry."

"The waitress made you jealous?" he says giving me a dopy lopsided grin.

After everything I said that is what he heard. Ugh, why did I tell him? "Yes." I can't deny it. I have gotten used to having Dylan all to myself. When someone else showed interest in him it forced the green-eyed monster out.

"I couldn't even tell you what the waitress looks like. You have ruined me, I only have eyes for you," he starts the car and pulls away.

I wipe at my tears and turn to face the window. We drive for a short time. Dylan pulls into a driveway hitting a button on his visor, the garage opens. Inside is a black SUV similar to the one he bought in Colorado. We pull in and the door closes behind us. Dylan shuts off the car. We sit in awkward silence for a moment.

"I would have killed him if you wouldn't have stopped me," he says.

"I know," I whisper.

"I made tonight a complete mess. I just wanted you to have everything you missed out on, a first date, dresses, dinner, clubs…" his voice trails off.

"I know it didn't end like we both expected but I want you to know I appreciate all that you planned. It was sweet Dylan, really. I love how much you put into tonight. I have had no one invest so much into me…ever. I'm sorry, I am just not a normal girl."

"I don't want a normal girl, I need you, Anna. I'm sorry I should have kept it simple. I wanted to show you how much I…how much I care about you," his words tumble out.

I understand how hard it was for him to admit that he cares about me. This I understand. It's tough to allow others to see the real, raw you. "I care about you too, that is why I didn't let you kill that man in front of all of those people." I giggle. "I'm sorry." I giggle more trying to stop myself. "He deserved it."

Dylan smiles at me. "You know the night is not over. Someone was a very bad girl. Punishments shouldn't linger until the next day. How many times did you make me wait for you today?"

I press my legs together an instantaneous fire ignites between them. "Um, twice…but…"

"No buts, your dress being unzipped was no excuse." Dylan gets out of the car and comes around opening mine for me. "But, first I have a surprise for you."

I am in awe as he leads me through a door to a large bright white kitchen. It opens to a living room with comfy looking couches and lounge chairs that face wide floor to ceiling windows. I make my way to the living area and peek through the glass catching the moon cast a silver thread of light through the water…the ocean.

I squeal with delight and wrap my arms around Dylan's neck. He lifts me up off my feet and I wrap my legs around his waist placing furious little kisses all over his face. His laugh vibrates through my entire body as he walks us through the living room, sliding open a glass door. Once on the deck outside he sets me back down on my feet.

The sound, it is so much louder than I imagined it would be. I inhale the salty air, a light mist caressing my face. I close my eyes and breathe it all in, trying to memorize every detail. It is powerful. I gaze up at him. "Thank you, thank you, thank you!"

"Anything for you baby, I should have brought you here first. I'm sorry."

I shake my head at him to halt his apology. "No, tonight was perfect. I got to see your…your deadly side. Please don't feel bad, it was perfect in its imperfection." I glance back at the ocean.

"You know I would never hurt you?" he says in all seriousness.

"I know." I chew on my bottom lip. "I'm not scared of you, Dylan, you will always try to keep me safe."

He tugs my lip out from between my teeth. "Always." He leans down and kisses me hard. He slaps my ass as he pushes me towards the beach. "You are itching to get down there, go ahead."

I kick off my heals and leap off the deck, skipping the stairs entirely, running. He is close behind me. I stop as soon as my toes hit water, I take a deep breath. He wraps his arms around my waist. "It's beautiful," I breathe out.

"Sorry it is dark, but tomorrow we will spend the entire day out here just you and I." He rocks us back and forth as the waves lap at my feet.

"I can't wait." I say leaning my head into his chest. The evening's events slowly retreat from my mind. After some time passes, he nibbles at my ear and his large hands make small circles across my belly. I sense the mood between us changing.

"Anna, don't think I have forgotten your punishment." His nose nudges through my hair, breathing me in. A tight bud of excitement builds inside me as thoughts of what he might do run through my head.

He draws me away from the water back into the house. We head into the bathroom and he slowly turns me to unzip my dress. "You are gorgeous in this but even more so out," he says letting it puddle at my feet. I shiver as the cool air touches my skin.

He reaches into the shower and I notice blood on his hands. "Are you hurt?" I ask frantically turning his palms over, looking for any cuts.

"Shh, baby, it's not my blood. I'm fine." He pulls away from me and pushes me into the shower. The warm water pours over me instantly relaxing every muscle in my body. He washes me head to toe, making me squirm under his touch.

I return the favor. I try to slide to my knees wanting to taste him again, but he halts my movements and pulls me up to my feet harshly. "You ran the show earlier, not this time. Get out of the shower, do not dry off, go directly to the bed and drop to all fours. Do you understand?"

I glance up at him nodding and whisper, "yes, sir."

I practically run to the other room leaving little puddles along the way. I stop at the foot of the bed contemplating on how I'm about to get it all wet. He clears his throat behind me, compelling me to jump quickly getting into position.

I watch as he walks to the head of the bed pulling at a strap attached to the top of the bedframe with a cuff on it. He secures it around my wrist doing the same to my other side and my ankles. I'm very vulnerable, strapped to the bed, naked, wet, ass up. He runs his hand along my back making me moan as I try to lean into his touch.

"What is your safe word, Anna?"

"Water," I breathe out, writhing against my maestro's hand.

"You will use it if you need to do you understand?"

"Yes, sir."

"You know, not telling me how you were feeling in the club made it harder for me to keep you safe. You will not do that again will you?"

He is right, I should have told him what was going on. He could have taken me outside to get air or something. "I'm sorry, I'm just used to handling things on my own."

"Not anymore," Dylan says as he runs his fingers down over my backside, lightly touching my clit then running them up slowly.

"Yes, sir. I will tell you from now on," I pant. I am having a hard time focusing on the conversation.

"How are you feeling now?" he asks.

Shit, I don't know how to respond.

"Anna, I expect an answer." He runs his hand down and pushes two fingers deep inside me.

"Mm, I don't know excited…hot." He drags his fingers out quickly, then pushes slowly back in. Why is he making me talk? I can't communicate not while he is… "Oh my god, please."

"Please what?" he chides.

"Please give me more." I try to push against his torturous hand, but my bindings are holding me in place, not giving me room to move.

He pulls away forcing me to groan loudly with his denial.

"Punishment first. I'm going to give you ten spankings. Five for the first time you made me wait and five for the second. I should add another five for not telling me what you were experiencing at the club, but I'll let that one go…this time."

The bed shifts from his weight. He moves behind me, reaching under, I feel a pinch on my nipple that causes me to cry out, and then again on my other side. I peer down to see little clamps on each side with a chain connecting them hanging between my breasts. I close my eyes, adjusting to the sensation they deliver. All my senses become heightened.

He tugs at the chain lightly then slides his other hand down to my clit to resume his attention to the tiny bud. "You are so wet for me. You like this don't you?"

"Ah, fuck." I bury my head into the pillow and lift my ass high for him, his tongue glides across my little bud and then it's gone. "Dylan…"

The first smack on my bottom stings making me stifle a cry into the pillow. One after another he spanks alternating cheeks. He stops for a few seconds in between smacks to rub my clit and bring me to the edge only to stop and deliver a blow to my ass. "How many are we at?"

Shit was I supposed to be counting? I don't know, I don't know!

He tugs at the chain between my breasts and leans over to brush my hair to one side, biting me lightly on my shoulder. "Since you can't seem to remember, we start again."

I cry out as he delivers a series of four strikes in a row. "How many, Anna?"

"Four, sir," I say through gritted teeth.

"Good girl." He stops for a second and rubs my ass. Cool liquid glides between my cheeks as he slips a finger inside. I look over my shoulder spying something in his hand. He slides out and presses the cold object against me driving me to pull away from him.

"Shh, you will like this, I promise, relax." He pushes it slowly, leaving it there as he resumes my punishment. Every smack on my ass makes it push deep inside me.

I remind myself to count as he rubs little circles over my clit. Five, six, oh my god this is so good, what is wrong with me, seven, more rubbing, his mouth, shit I am going to come, eight…."Sir, I need to come," my words rush out.

"No," he growls and leans over grabbing my hair pulling my head towards him, only fueling the fire. "You will wait unit your punishment is over, then you can come as many times as you like. Now where are we?"

"Nine, sir, please…" nine, ten…Dylan pushes deep inside me and curls his finger to hit my g-spot. I explode into the most intense orgasm, screaming out his name. I clamp down on the plug in my ass and his fingers that still push against my most delicate area. His other hand holds me tightly around the waist.

He pulls the plug out but keeps his fingers stilled deep inside, his thumb circles my clit as he quickly brings me back to the edge. I hear myself speak incoherent words as I buck against the binds, still so sensitive from the explosive orgasm.

The head of his cock rubs against my ass, no, too much, too much. I briefly think about saying my safe word, but he rips another orgasm from my body. At that moment he pushes inside me. More non-sense words and phrases tumble out of my mouth. I am floating in darkness, noticing every place that Dylan is touching and filling me. He presses deep drawing a moan from my lips.

"Anna, you feel so good, you are doing so well. Ahh, god you were made for me, only me." He glides in and out faster and harder leaning over he reaches around to rub me bringing me closer to the threshold. His other hand suddenly removes one of the nipple clamps.

"Fuck" … the pain… "Ah, Dylan, I can't, I can't." Slowly I tip over the edge as he eliminates the other clamp. I cry out, coming hard at the same time. He plunges deep, filling me, pulsing inside me, seemingly in rhythm with the beating of my heart.

He releases my bonds and pulls me into his lap as he leans against the headboard. He runs his hand through my hair, the other one runs along my hip. I lay my head against his chest and listen to the drum of his heartbeat. Slowly both of us come down from our high.

"That was, was amazing," I breathe out.

He chuckles. "I'm glad, I got something right today."

I sit up and look at him. "Dylan, you got everything right. No one has put as much thought into making me happy as you have."

He brushes the hair out of my eyes and tucks it behind my ear. "So, you are happy?"

I tuck myself back up under his chin suddenly shy. "Yes, I am happy. But…"

"No, buts, if you are happy you are happy. Enjoy the moment, we can't worry about all the what if's, we are here together now." He hugs me tightly. After several minutes he gently pushes me off his lap. "Come, we need to shower and change the sheets…someone got them all wet."

Dylan

When I saw Anna pinned up against the wall by that asshole I saw red. When I pulled the idiot off her and tears were streaming down her face that was it, he was dead. Then I glanced up and she was standing there. She didn't look frightened, she looked worried. Not worried for the man bleeding on the ground, but for me, she looked worried for me.

Other than my guys no one has ever been concerned about me, not since my mother and sister anyhow. I pulled her out of there, guilty for ruining the night. I want to give her everything. I need to protect her, if I could pack her in bubble wrap and keep her with me always I would.

I run my hand down her long locks as she sleeps next to me. Her naked body is pressed against mine. She is perfect, her ass is red, my handprints are on her skin. I should talk to her about all of this…us…it confuses her. She didn't get a vanilla relationship. She went right from innocence to my dark desires. She responds on every level. I saw it in her eyes. She questions her body's reaction to the pain. It turns her on and that puzzles her.

A light flashes in the room, ugh my phone. I slowly pull my arm out from under her and grab it heading into the bathroom. It is Liam. "This better be good it is three in the morning."

"They have been spotted at the border," he says, cutting to the chase.

"Fuck," I say gripping my hair in one hand. This is happening and at some point we will have to face the situation head on. No amount of ignoring it will make it go away. Oliver wants Anna, and he is coming for her.

"I'm headed to Denver now. My plane is scheduled to arrive there at three in the afternoon. Can you pick me up? If not I'll grab a rental."

"No, I'll come and get you. We need to talk. I would rather do it away from Anna. I'll have Anthony stay with her."

"See you shortly brother. I'll call as soon as I land."

I hang up wanting to throw the phone at the door. Damn it, why did I bring her here? We should have stayed in Colorado. They can't know we are here, but we are so close to the fuckers, too close. I don't like it.

I crawl into bed making Anna stir. She sits up and looks at me sleepily. "What's wrong, Dylan?"

I cradle her against me. "Nothing, baby, shh go back to sleep, it's not time to get up yet."

She murmurs happily against me and wiggles. I growl in her ear, "You are being a naughty girl again aren't you?"

"I don't know what you mean," she purrs and presses that little ass against me making me instantly hard. This girl…

Chapter Twenty-Seven

Anna

Dylan sleeps as I trail my hand over him. I lay my head back on his chest and listen to his breathing. He seemed upset in the middle of the night. He had been in the bathroom with his phone. He doesn't think I noticed, but I did. Someone called him, a call at that time of the night cannot be good. I shiver against him as I think about what it was about. Doom is lurking around the corner. It is the same feeling I had the day Liam visited the bookstore.

Dylan always perceptive of me, even in his sleep, rubs his hands over me as he wakes. "You cold, baby?" He pulls the covers up over the both of us.

I shake my head against him not wanting him to see my fear. "No, but I am hungry. I will make breakfast." I straddle him to get out of bed. He rolls me over onto my back and holds himself over the top of me.

He kisses me with greedy passion. "I'm hungry too," he says, smiling down at me. "But, you don't know how to cook. So, I guess you will have to wait for me to give you instructions and I'm not ready to get up yet."

I stare up at him, an excited tension bubbles inside me. He pushes my legs apart with his knee and reaches down to tease me. His mouth roams over my collarbone, down to my breasts, sucking in a tender nipple. He groans against my skin sending a flood to my core.

He pushes in slowly, bringing his head up to kiss me softly. I reach up and run my hands through his hair, then along his back pulling him down closer. His lets his weight settle fully on top of me.

He consumes me. He is becoming my everything. The source of my pleasure, my pain, my safety, he is mine. He plunges deep inside making me gasp, he whispers into my ear to come for him and I do. He follows right behind, our bodies mingled together, giving at the same time taking whatever we need from each other. It is heavenly bliss. We lay there panting, his weight still on me. I think back to the days I hid in my room and buried my nose in a book…this is so much better.

He lifts off me and throws me a devilish smile. I don't know if I will ever get enough of him. I'm not sure how all this happened but I am glad it did. If Oliver never would have taken me Dylan wouldn't be here right now. With every burden comes a blessing and every blessing a burden. I would take a million burdens for this time with him.

"Okay now we can go make breakfast." He gets up and tosses one of his t-shirts to me. "I want you to wear this, and *only* this until we finish eating." He tips his head looking at me with smoldering dark eyes.

I smile shyly at him. I don't know why his demands turn me on, but they do. I try not to question it. I've had no other relationships, so I have no preconceived ideas of what this should be. It feels good. He likes it, I like it and at this point that is all that matters. Time is valuable, I'm not going to waste it by questioning my obvious sexual tastes.

We barely make it through breakfast without going at it on the table. He made me sit on his lap while we ate. He had to scold me for wiggling too much. I left a wet spot on his leg which he laughed about while we cleaned up. "Later, baby, I promise," he says, and I give him the poutiest face I can garner but it doesn't work.

"You want to get out to the beach don't you?" he teases.

"The beach! Yes!" I say excitedly. Dylan has kept me busy all morning causing me to put where we were on the back burner.

I pull on the bright yellow bikini I purchased the day before while shopping with Anthony. When I come out of the bathroom, he pounces off the bed in front of me forcing me to squeal. I dodge him and run through the house giggling, making it out to the deck before he catches me.

"Later, baby, I promise," I taunt him with his own words. I wiggle in his grip. He picks me up off my feet and pretends to haul me back inside. But, before we get to the door, he turns around carrying me down to the water.

"You are a little devil you know," he says in my ear.

He sets me down. I focus my attention to the site before me. "It is so beautiful here. Did you rent this place?"

"No, it's mine. Now we have a beach house and a cabin," he suggests staring down at me.

My heart swells at his words, *we*. I can only hope for that to be true, for it to last. I look back at the waves rolling in. "Dylan, thank you, for everything. I guess I'll forgive you for locking me in my trunk now."

He laughs and pulls me down to the ground with him. It is a beautiful sunny day. The sand is warm. He wraps an arm around me. "A lot of bad things happened to get us to this point. I don't regret taking you, I do regret the trunk." He places a kiss at my temple.

I let out a sigh. "I am glad you found me." I snuggle into him and watch the waves.

It was a perfect day on the coast, Dylan even coaxed me into the water. I was hesitant to get in, no, that would be an understatement, terrified a more appropriate word. He walked in slow and held me tight. He is so strong, he stood so his body took the brunt of the waves. Standing in his arms in the ocean's turmoil I stared back at the calm of the beach. I realized he has been my anchor. He has kept me grounded the last few weeks, during the storm of finding myself. I hope he never leaves me.

I flip over to my stomach and peek at him. He is flipping burgers at the grill. The sun catches the copper highlights in his dark hair. He must sense my eyes on him, he glances up grinning ear to ear. "The burgers are almost done."

I brush the sand off me then gather my blanket, book, headphones and cell so I can join him on the deck. I notice I have a message. I turn so that my back is to Dylan and stare down at the screen. Oliver sent me a photo. Do I open it? What if he has found me? I click it. The phone swirls as the image loads. Is it a picture of me? I look around slowly to see if anyone is watching me? There are other people on the beach, but no one is paying any attention.

The image appears. No! Staring back at me is Frank with a gag in his mouth tied to a chair in what appears to be a warehouse. A second picture comes through of Irene, also tied and gagged. I recognize the background. She is at the bookstore. My heart pounds and my ears start to ring. My world tilts off its axis.

I glance behind me. Dylan must have gone back inside. Tears bang at the door screaming to be let out. More people are hurting because of me! Sweet Frank and Irene. No, no, no, no. I study the photos again, pain stabs at my chest and then another message pings at my heart.

Maybe this will help jog your memory. I wouldn't waste time. Your friends are hungry and tired. Tell me where you are. As soon as Brian calls me saying he is with you, I will let Frank go and he can make his way back to his dear wife.

My mind shorts out. What do I do? I know he can see I opened the pictures. He knows I am holding my phone. He knows, he knows! I am still tied to him even though we are more than likely thousands of miles apart.

I can't let anything happen to Frank or Irene. They are the epitome of what I have always wanted. It breaks my heart to think how worried they must be about each other.

I hate him. I hate him!

I take a few deep breaths. I can't tell him I am here. I don't want them coming here, this place is good, I won't let him ruin that. Hold it together. You have the tracker. You have the pill. I need to think for a few minutes. I walk up the beach as Dylan comes back out with plates.

I keep my voice as level as I can and hug him from behind. "I'm going to change quick before we eat."

"Hey, I forgot to mention this earlier, but Liam got bored at the cabin, so he is going to join us. I'm picking him up at the airport after we finish lunch. Anthony will come and stay with you this afternoon while I'm doing that, he said he might run a little late. Will you be okay by yourself for a few until he gets here?" He turns and sets the plates on the patio table.

This is my chance. My spirit is sinking even as I hear the words fall out of my mouth. "Sure, I'll be fine, I have a book and the beach, what more could a girl ask for?"

I slide open the door and gaze back at Dylan. My heart is breaking in half. How can I leave him? I must, I can't let Irene and Frank suffer. I just can't. I make my way numbly to the bathroom and sit on the edge of the bathtub reading the message from Oliver.

I text my reply.

I am being followed, but I will try to get away. I am in San Diego. I will sneak to Bailey's coffee shop near Ocean Beach Pier at two o'clock when they switch shifts.

I had to tell him I was being followed. I don't know how long it will take Oliver's men to get here. If Anthony comes to look for me and they spot him, Frank and Irene are as good as dead. I stand up to change out of my suit. I stare at my phone on the counter terrified for the reply. Oliver may as well have his hands wrapped around my neck. I feel the tightness in my throat. Stop, Anna, you can't cry now.

Perfect. You better hope you are alone, if someone is there when my guys show up you know what happens to your friends. See you soon, kitten.

Chapter Twenty-Eight

Anna

I peer at the roman numerals on the large clock of the coffee shop. It is almost two. I take several deep breaths. There are only a few patrons in the cute little brick building, a few lady's chit chatting in the corner. Everyone else has their noses in either an electronic devise or a newspaper. Now, to wait. I hate waiting. I've done so much of it in my life, except today I know what awaits. I shiver as I think about seeing Oliver again. I have no choice, Irene and Frank need me to do this.

I left soon after Dylan headed to the airport to pick up Liam. He knew something was wrong. He struggled to leave me. I tried my hardest to convince him that everything was fine. I played on the fact I was nervous about Liam's surprise visit. He has information, more than likely it is that Oliver's men have reached the border. Unfortunately, I know how true that is.

I quickly packed my things which I left at Dylan's house along with my phone. He will search through my messages. I did not delete the ones about Frank and Irene. I hope that the guys check on them and make sure they are okay. I wrote a note to Anthony to tell him I went for a walk on the beach hopefully giving me more time. I'm not sure how long I'll wait for Oliver's men.

I pull the tracking pill out of my pocket and glance at the clock once more. Two O'clock, I wash it down with my French vanilla coffee and think back to Liam's words. I stare out the window sifting through the crowd in search of the bad guys. Only unaware families. I watch a couple with a young girl sit on a bench across the street. They are laughing as they try to help her with a dripping ice cream cone. It's scenes like this that make me miss my parents.

Someone sits down beside me. I don't look away from the happy little family. If I keep my eyes on them, maybe the nightmare that just arrived in the seat next to me will disappear.

An arm slides behind me and rests on the back of my chair. A familiar voice assaults my ears, forcing my gaze elsewhere, not wanting to taint their fairy tale life. "Anna, it's so nice that you could meet up with me today," the devil's right-hand man says in my ear.

I look down at my hands in my lap. It is happening. I want to scream, to alert the coffee shop that I am about to be abducted *again.* There is not one doubt in my mind that if I succumb to my thoughts, everyone in this building will be dead in a matter of minutes.

Instead, I focus on the fact that this time someone will miss me, they will come for me. Dylan will come for me. I need to be strong. "I wouldn't have missed this for the world." I seethe.

Brian chuckles, then he taps his fingers on the table for a second. "Why don't we take a walk, it's such a lovely day." He stands and reaches his hand out to help me.

I don't accept the offer and stand on my own. I wait for him to lead the way to hell. He doesn't protest and strolls to the exit, I notice he winks at the girl behind the counter as he walks by. She gives him a flirty smile. Oh, honey if you only knew. I toss my cup in the trash as he holds the door open for me. Last chance, I could stand my ground, why even think about it, foolish, it can't happen.

As soon as we are outside, he puts his arm around me and leads me behind the building to a dark car. He scans the area before we enter the alley, satisfied that I came alone he proceeds. He opens the door, before getting in I peek at the man driving but he doesn't even turn his head to acknowledge us. Brian's hand pushes at the small of my back gently ushering me in.

I slide in all the way to the far side and press myself up against the door. That damn uncontrollable shaking devours my body. Brian gets in beside me, taking up double the space that my tiny frame does. I stare out the window, silently hoping that Anthony might be nearby. Please find me I repeat over and over in my head.

Brian reaches over and places a strong hand on my shoulder, I detect a pinch on my neck and a quick heaviness follows then swallows me into the darkness. It's happening, please find me…please find…please…please and then nothing, wonderful nothing.

Dylan

I felt bad leaving Anna, I could tell that she sensed danger. I could almost smell her fear. She knows Liam flying in has nothing to do with being bored and everything to do with her safety. Hopefully, Anthony got there soon after I left. Liam's plane was right on time. I am eager to get back to her. Spending five minutes away from her is torture, anything longer than that is excruciating.

"Thanks for the ride man," Liam says relaxing into the seat as we pull onto the freeway.

"No problem, it gives us a chance to talk without Anna overhearing. She is nervous enough with your arrival, she isn't stupid she knows something is up." My phone vibrates in my pocket. I pull it out with one hand on the wheel. "It's Anthony," I say as I hit the button to answer.

"Anthony, hey wait a minute I will put you on speaker, I'm on the freeway." I drop the cell on the console. "What's up? Did you make it to the house? How is Anna?" There is a long pause, shit I sit up straighter, Liam and I exchange nervous glances.

"She's not here, but before you freak out, she left me a note saying she was going for a walk."

My heart sinks. She wouldn't leave, especially knowing Anthony was on his way. Something is wrong, very wrong. "Go check her things, now!" I yell a little too gruffly, my foot gets heavy on the accelerator.

"Okay, Dylan, calm down, man."

He sighs on the other end. "Her bag is packed and setting here on the bed. I see nothing lying around, all her stuff is gathered."

"Is her phone in there?" I say through gritted teeth.

"Yes, it's here," Anthony says.

"Go through her messages, if that fuck messaged her I will rip his throat out."

Another long sigh. "You should pull over before I read this shit to you."

"FUCK!" My foot slams down. Liam reaches out to brace himself as I weave in and out of traffic. I need to get there. I need to find her!

"Dylan, slow down, man. If we get in an accident, we will be in no shape to help her. Slow. The. Fuck. Down!" he screams at me.

I let off the accelerator a touch, I can't breathe my vision is closing in on me. I can't lose Anna. The blue-eyed, dark-haired girl has my heart, she has it, and I can't live without it. My throat tightens at the thought of never seeing her again.

"Pull over Dylan, I will drive," Liam insists.

I reluctantly park and numbly switch places with him. I hear Anthony still on the line, it sounds like he is outside, the wind is whistling through the receiver. "Is he out from behind the wheel Liam?" Anthony asks.

"Yeah, go ahead. How bad is it?" Liam replies.

"He sent her pictures of an older couple both gagged and tied up, from what I can gather they are friends of hers. She told him she was being watched but she said she might be able to get away and would be at Bailey's coffee at two. I'm headed there now."

Both Liam and I glance at our watches, fuck. Why didn't she tell me? Her friends? She never talked about having any friends. I guess there is a lot I don't know about her yet. *Yet,* will I get the chance to know her better? I close my eyes, fighting a wave of nausea.

The one thing I do know is the amount of guilt she feels for everyone that had been hurt at Oliver's hands. She blames herself. This is more than likely no different, remorse made her keep this to herself. She wouldn't let anyone else suffer, she acted alone. I didn't want her to have to do that anymore. I was there and so was my team, she should have told me. We could have figured it out together. Does she still not trust me?

"Anthony, call us back as soon as you get there, we are on the way." Liam says. He looks at me intently and reaches in his pocket, pulling out his cell and handing it to me.

"You are going to kill me," he takes a deep breath but continues, "I put a tracking device in her. Pull up the app on my phone, we can see where she is."

"You what?" I roar not believing what I am hearing. "How did you put a tracking device IN her?"

"We were going to tell you, but then you left on this trip…"

"Shut up, where is the fucking app?" I scroll through all the icons on his cell trying to find it. I already know what he is going to say, I recognized those two were up to something, this explains it. I should be mad right now, but I am just thankful that we can track her. Liam reaches over clicking one. There are two dots on the map, one is near the beach, but the other is moving, it is almost to the border. Shit, shit, shit. "Why are there two fucking dots?" I ask confused.

"I injected one under her skin on the backside of her arm. The other is a pill tracker, I instructed her to swallow it if she had time."

I should throttle him. He was going to use her. I guess I was going to use her too, hence the whole trunk incident. "Would you have gone through with it?" I ask him, I need to know.

"No. I would have told you. I didn't want to spoil your trip. She was a fucking mess when you left her alone with me. She freaked, there was no way I was going to offer her up on a silver platter to that asshole after seeing how scared she was." We both look at each other, each envisioning how afraid she must be at this moment. "We both agreed to tell you, both of us realized we couldn't lie to you."

"But she did! She knew he was coming when I left to pick you up. I saw it on her face, but I thought it was just her concern over you showing up. I guess she didn't lie, but she kept it from me." I put my head in my hands, wishing she would have trusted me.

"Dylan, you heard Anthony, Oliver has her friends. You know how guilty she feels about Sophia, about everyone." He shakes his head as if trying to shake the memories away to focus on the here and now. "Enough, let's just concentrate on saving her. Where the fuck are the trackers showing?"

"One near the beach not moving the other is heading for the border. They are close, too fucking close to crossing. We will never get there in time." I pull at my hair. I had been so wrapped up in Anna and how good we were together that I completely let my guard down. I shouldn't have left her, if he hurts her…

"Okay, we head to the border. We make a few calls to the guys and have them meet us there with supplies, they are close, they have been waiting to hear from one of us. Anthony will check out Bailey's confirming that she isn't there and then he can fly out and catch up somewhere along the way. Text him anything you need from the house." Liam sits up straight letting his training take over his emotions.

I'm glad he is here. I watch the little dot head further away from me. I shouldn't have been so harsh on him during our search for Sophia. Now I realize exactly how he felt. My world is spinning apart without her. Please hold on Anna. Oh, how many times I whispered those same sentiments to Sophia and where did she end up, six feet in the ground.

Liam grabs the front of my shirt hard pulling me from my anxieties. "Dylan, stop. You need to focus, time is everything. It is our only advantage. She needs you."

Chapter Twenty-Nine

Anna

If I thought waking up the first time Oliver Wright abducted me was frightening, it was nothing compared to the second. Some of it familiar, the headache, the cold, the initial confusion, the thirst, the hunger, the nakedness. This time I'm in complete darkness, at first I thought I had lost my vision, maybe I have. I still cannot see anything. I'm too scared to move, I woke up lying on the hard ground. I crawled my way over to a cement wall and here I sit, alone, my only companion my fear.

I don't know how long I have been here. The only memories I have are of getting into the dark-colored car in the alley and a foggy recollection of being in a desert. I remember waking up to someone pulling my hair screaming at me about not throwing up in his car. My knees feel like they are scraped, they hurt so the memory must be real. I was drug out of the vehicle and dropped to the rocky, dusty ground. The only thing I saw was dirt and some treeless mountains in the distance as I heaved.

I run my hand over my knees welcoming the burn that accompanies the touch, at least I know I am alive. I reach behind my arm. They took the tracker out. I don't recall that thankfully, but I can feel the cut they made to get it out. The other one I assume is lying out in the desert somewhere. Fuck, I remember trying to swallow down the nausea but the drugs, movement of the car and my fear had their own plans of evicting my lunch. Unfortunately, the tracker came up with it.

How are they going to find me now? Maybe they were following, maybe Liam knew where they were taking me. Maybe, maybe, maybe. I got away once, I'll do it again, I will. I close my eyes, the darkness behind my eyes easier to accept than the darkness surrounding me. I force myself somewhere else, the beach, yes the beach with Dylan. The warm sand, the sun, yes that is it. You are better already.

Hours, maybe days go by as I sit here in the dark trying to focus my mind on good memories, all with Dylan. Occasionally, it wanders to Frank and Irene. I wonder if Oliver let Frank go so he could get back to her. I hope they are okay, I'm sure the guys sent someone to check on them.

I drift to sleep which is wonderful, the only escape to my cruel reality. After a few times I fight it because each time I wake it is in a panic. Is there enough air in here? Is anyone ever coming? Just as I am certain they have left me in here to die the lock clicks.

The light, oh my god, my head splits in two by the brilliance that bleeds in from the doorway. I must be dead. This is the bright light people talk about. Then a shadow appears. A man is blocking out the brightness, standing within the frame of the door. I hear a loud groan and realize it is coming from me.

"Sounds like you're not happy to see me. What is up with that? I thought you would wait prettily on your knees for me." He crouches down in front of me and brushes the hair out of my eyes, running his hands over me, he accesses my current state of well-being.

"Fuck. You," I growl as my head screams to shut up.

"How bout you say, it's so nice to see you again, Brian. Then I'll take you down to use the bathroom, shower and eat." He is hunched down waiting for my answer.

My skull screams, I roll my forehead up against the cool cement wall to seek relief for the insistent pounding.

"Come on." He gently tugs at my arm pulling me, steading me by my elbows, patiently watching for me to gain some semblance of balance.

He leads me down a hallway with high windows all streaming in too much sunlight. I try to pull back to the safety of my dark hole. He grabs my arm tighter and hauls me along. We walk into a locker room style open area with several shower stalls. We make our way over to a toilet, then he turns and walks away, moving out of my line of vision. I quickly relieve myself and as soon as I flush he is by my side once again. At least he gave me a little privacy.

He pushes me towards a shower stall and turns it on, shoving me under the spray of water. He points to a bottle in the stall's corner containing soap. He leans his arm on the cement block wall and stands there. Okay, he is not going to give me any privacy for this part. I wash off quickly, my head throbs as I lean over to rinse my lower half.

When I stand back up, I glance at him, his features appear almost sad. The sadness etched on his face surprises me. Soon enough the hardened bully returns. "Come on let's see if we can keep food in you, Sam wasn't too happy you tossed your cookies in his car." He laughs as he shuts off the water and hands me a towel.

Once I'm finished, he hands me a sun dress. I slip it over my head shimming it down, thank god Oliver is letting me wear clothes. We head down the hallway, then he opens a door at the end of it leading outside. The warm sultry air blankets me as we leave behind the cool building. I shield my eyes from the sunlight trying to discover where we are.

There are several buildings, with guards all dressed in black carrying large rifles. We make our way towards a house with a spacious courtyard surrounded on three sides by the walls of the home. There are bright red flowers and different tropical looking plants surrounding the patio. An elaborate fountain at the end.

There is a small table set up with several silver platters of breakfast foods and a large pitcher of orange juice. He pulls out a chair for me that faces the fountain, the main entrance to the house behind me. There are three place settings. I silently groan, hopefully Oliver doesn't have any surprise guests joining us like last time.

I stare at the condensation built up on the pitcher. Little droplets of water slowly build up then slide down the pitcher. My mouth is so dry, I am tempted to lean over and lick the side of the glass. I jump when Oliver's voice is behind me and sit up taller in my chair.

"Kitten, I am so glad to see you arrived safely," he says as he places a kiss to the top of my head.

Brian starts to leave but Oliver motions for him to take the seat next to me. He sets a file folder down on the table and takes the chair across from me, blocking my view of the fountain. I keep my eyes focused on the empty plate in front of me.

Even though the air is warm and humid outside, I'm chilled. Are we in Belize? Liam said they thought he was in Belize, please let that be where we are. It could make the search for me easier if there is one.

"Go ahead you two, we are all old friends here. Brian why don't you help Anna with her plate?" I peek at Brian as he reaches for my plate. I search his face for answers, something seems wrong. I can tell that he senses it too.

He fills my plate and sets it down in front of me. He then pours me a glass of juice. I take it from him bringing it to my lips drinking it all down in one shot. Thankful for the sugary liquid, I enjoy the surge of energy it provides. He takes it back and fills it again.

He loads his own plate all the while Oliver sits with his elbows on the arms of his chair. His fingers are steepled in front of him and resting on his mouth. I peer up at him. He gives me that angelic smile of his. I hate him.

"Eat, eat, you must be famished from your journey. It was so convenient of you to be in San Diego. Almost as if you were waiting for me to pluck you out of the states."

Oliver doesn't eat, he sits and watches Brian and me. I slow my chewing wondering if he has poisoned the meal. I glance at Brian. He is eating away not looking up from his food. I peek at Oliver again. He smiles, reading my mind.

"It's not poisoned, Anna, I have too much planned to kill you," he says.

Brian stops and stares at the both of us and tosses his napkin onto the table, leaning back in his chair. I sense a power struggle brewing. Oliver looks unaffected, he turns his attention to me. "So, we have plenty to discuss. Where should we start? First off good news for you, you no longer have to marry me."

He slides the folder over and opens it, placing a pen on top of the stack of papers. "Since your father is dead, I don't see any reason for us to get married, plus I am not into sloppy seconds."

What the fuck did he say? Sloppy seconds! I set my fork down and clear my throat. "Great, I'm sure you know, I was not that enthused with the prospect of becoming a sex traffickers' wife." I glare at him across the table. He looks at me like I slapped him. Good, I hate him, I am tired of his fucking game. Brian bristles beside me, he silently tells me to shut my mouth.

"Sign the papers, my attorneys have everything ready all you need to do is sign your father's inheritance over. Then you will not have to worry about any of it any longer."

"Did you let Frank and Irene go?" I ask.

"Yes, the minute Brian called me, he should be home safe with his loving wife. I do not need to hurt an elderly couple," he says with an incredulous tone.

Wow, he acts like he has morals. I don't know if I believe him. But, one thing he has never done is lie.

"I will gladly sign. I do not want his fucking money." I grab the papers and sign on each sheet that is flagged for my attention. I slam the folder shut when I am finished sliding it back across the table.

He stares at me for a long moment, neither of us takes our eyes off each other. "Good, now on to the second matter. You have caused me a great deal of difficulty over the information you supplied to the FBI. Would you like to share with me how you remembered all the names and locations you spewed to them?"

I don't even flinch. "Your gift."

"What do you mean my *gift*? Don't play games with me, kitten," he says through gritted teeth.

Good, I am getting to him. I should stop but I can't, I hate him. My scorn and fear are begging to come out and scratch his beautiful exterior.

"You told me once I was a talented writer, the FBI thought so too," I say giving him my prettiest smile. I languish in my dig at him as I see him ponder my words. Slowly it dawns on him what I had done.

"Hmph, aren't you a smart little kitten? Well, that answers that. Now the last thing to discuss is what to do with you. I hear you have been fraternizing with my enemy."

My tough exterior crumbles. He knows about Dylan. This upsets me. I don't want Oliver in my head messing with my thoughts about Dylan, tainting them. "I don't know what you mean."

Oliver slams his fist down on the table making the plates and silverware clank together loudly. I jump and push my chair back looking for a place to run and hide. Oliver stops me and grabs my throat tightly. Brian sighs to the side of me, but he doesn't move.

"Please, please just let me go. You got what you wanted I signed the papers. Let. Me. Go!" I scream at him gasping for air as his fingers grip harshly and his nails dig into the skin on my neck.

He pushes me forward roughly. Then returns to his seat, I watch him through the hair covering my face. He forces each of his muscles to relax. As soon as he gathers his composure, he fills his plate and motions both Brian and I to finish our meal.

We eat in silence. I force each bite down, my teeth chatter so loudly that I am sure they both can hear, neither looks at me. He is not letting me go. I don't understand. He got what he wanted. I signed his damn papers. You were stupid for giving the FBI all that information, stupid. But I had to save as many girls as I could, I needed to make amends for all the terrible things Oliver had done to the people I love.

"Brian, don't you think Anna looks similar to that girl you have been pining over, what is her name?" Oliver finishes his breakfast and motions for the attendant who has been quietly standing by to clear the dishes from the table.

Brian straightens in his chair. "Yes, I guess there are similarities."

The server pushes the cart away, Oliver waits to speak as the cart rattles against the tiles of the courtyard. Once the sound fades, he speaks up again, "Brian, I have a wonderful idea why don't you take Anna? I know she will never replace your little infatuation, but I would bet she has potential if Dylan Lorenz took her to his bed."

My mouth drops open. I am speechless on so many levels. Did he offer me to Brian, and he spoke Dylan's name? "Fuck you," I scream at him.

Oliver places his hand out to silence me. "Anna, this is a conversation you are not a part of. What you want, what you think, what you need is no longer your concern."

Brian seems confused. "Sir, no disrespect but I thought we had an agreement that if I found her for you, you would bring back Addison. That was the deal, and I found Anna not once but twice."

"Actually, you found her once. The second time she told me where she was and all you had to do was retrieve her." Oliver looks over at me and winks.

"At a risk. Going across that border was a risk, one I was willing to take to get Addison back." I can visibly see he is trying to keep himself in check. He knows who he is dealing with, for some reason Oliver seems to enjoy chiding him.

"Hmm, yes you are correct. But, you should thank me. Anna is exquisite, and she still has spirit left in her. I have heard Addison, is that her name? Anyhow, I heard she is nothing more than an empty-headed little sex slave these days." Oliver's words glide out of his mouth slaying Brian in his seat.

Brian's face turns bright red. He grips the arms of the chair so tightly that I think they will break in half. I slide myself back in mine feeling like I am just a supporting character in the story that unfolds in front of me. "Boss, you promised me Addy."

"Yes, and you promised me your loyalty. Did you think I wouldn't question why you had Anna's phone number? Why, Brian? Why would you stop in the middle of a kidnapping to look at your victim's cell and memorize the number?"

Brian drops his head, defeat deflating his earlier anger. "Boss, I, I…"

"You were going to contact the people she was with weren't you?" Oliver accuses.

My head bounces back and forth between them, is the crack forming between them a benefit or a detriment to me? I don't know, but I am interested in Oliver's question myself.

"Yes, I'm sorry boss, she looks so much like Addy. I felt bad for her, for her family, I felt bad for taking her." He looks up now and stares at Oliver pleading with him. "I didn't do it. I never once called the number."

"But, the thought entered your mind none the less." Oliver turns to me. "Brian has been with me for many years, Anna. You and Addison seem to be a weakness for him. Brian, tell me how long has it been since you trained her?"

"Thirteen months." Brian's doesn't look up his head sullenly in his hands.

"Thirteen months, I thought the little infatuation would subside. Then you came along and got him thinking about her again. So, it is decided then. You now belong to Brian. You will help him forget about her. You can do that for me can't you, kitten?"

I stare at him. "No." I shake my head. "No, I gave you what you wanted just let me go. I will disappear, you will never have to deal with me ever again."

Oliver laughs loudly. "You act like you have a choice in this matter, kitten. You think I am giving you back to Dylan? You belong to him now." He tips his head towards Brian. "Don't worry he will teach you some manners among other things. Won't you, Brian?"

"Yes, sir," Brian says still not looking up.

"Good, I know this has been a tense morning for all. I am looking forward to seeing Anna after you deliver her first punishment for all the problems she has caused us. I will see you both at supper tonight. Don't worry, Anna, I'll make sure we dine inside, in the *soft* chairs."

What the fuck just happened? I can't wrap my head around anything. I sit quietly and watch Brian, waiting. When he sits up, I jump in my chair. He doesn't look angry. He looks almost sorry.

"Come on." He holds his hand out for me to take. He leads me to my cell. Instead of locking me inside he follows me in and shuts the door behind him. I drop to the ground scurrying away from him over to my wall, feeling my way, surrounded by nothing but blackness.

He pulls me into his arms and sits with his back up against the wall. I don't fight him. It would do no good. At least I am still dressed. I can't control the shaking, even wrapped in the warmth of his arms.

"I wish I wouldn't have found you," he whispers in my ear.

I hear the anguish in his voice. I don't speak, I just listen.

"I thought he would let me have her if I found you for him, he promised me. I never wanted to keep any of them until her. He is right you know? You look a lot like her. She is quiet, not a spitfire like you." He laughs and runs his palm down my hair the other lightly rubbing the side of my hip.

"I should have known he wouldn't bring her back for me. I should have taken her and left. Walked away from this shit, but no, fuck no, I stayed, I allowed Oliver to have his hand up my ass, my fucking puppet master." His voice cracks as he pulls me close to him.

I don't feel sorry for him. He chose this life. But, I can tell he is emotional, so a small part of his heart might have thawed when he met this girl, Addison.

"He will make me hurt you, Anna."

I tremble at his words. I heard Oliver myself but to hear Brian say it makes it seem so much worse. I need to try and reach that little thawed out part of his heart. It is my only chance. I have no idea when Dylan will find me if ever. "You don't have to," I whisper to the dark.

"He is expecting to see the marks on you at supper, you heard him."

"Um, Brian, I can help you find her," I breathe out shakily, not knowing what to expect from him. He is the man who drugs and tortures me. I know I cannot trust him but what choice do I have.

He stills not saying anything, so I continue, "Dylan and his team could help you find her."

He laughs at this. "Why would they help me? I don't think you know what you are talking about, doll, I appreciate your concern but…"

I sit up and turn towards him so my breath whispers across his face. I can't see him, but I need him to listen to what I have to say. "They will help because that is what they do, they save girls like your Addy. If you could just call them, tell them where we are, they will come. I will make them find her. I promise. They won't do it for you, but they will for me…for her."

He laughs again, but he doesn't dismiss what I am saying. "And you happen to have their number on you?"

Shit, I didn't think about that, wait the FBI. "I know you will not like this, but if you could call the FBI and ask to speak to Agent Liam Sharp."

"No, Anna." He dumps me to the cold ground. I see a sliver of light. He pauses before leaving and looks back at me shaking his head. He closes the door and the lock clicks.

I tried, I tried. The tears flow for the first time since I received Oliver's message while on the beach. I cry myself to sleep exhausted by the morning's events.

Dylan

We lost them. I lean over and pick up the tracker on the desert ground. I stare at the mountains. Where are you, Anna?

Liam puts his hand on my shoulder. "We will find her."

"How many times did we say that with Sophia?" I look up to see him flinch. "Sorry," I say as I place a fist in my hair, pulling until I can feel the pain.

"No, you are right," Liam says, His phone rings cutting our conversation short. He turns away from me to answer it.

I stare at the tracker in my hand. Liam slugs me in the chest to get my attention, pointing towards his phone, he covers the receiver and whispers, "it's the bureau, they say there is a man named Brian who wants to talk to me about a case."

I stand slowly, Brian, Anna told me a Brian had tortured her, shoving her into a bathtub of water, could it be? I watch Liam's face intently and look for clues as to what is being said on the other end.

"Yes, this is Agent Sharp." Liam says poking a finger in his other ear. He looks up at me and nods.

"Motherfucker," I say as we both jog back to the car.

Chapter Thirty

Anna

Brian woke me up out of a dream. I was with Dylan. He was leaning over me smiling with that sexy smile of his. We were on the beach lying in the warm sand. I was safely tucked under him. Now I am awake, in a fresh new kind of hell.

My arms are secured above my head. I can only take the pressure off my wrists by standing on my tiptoes. He didn't speak when he came for me. He pulled me up, drug me by my arm to this room, made me remove the dress and strung me up.

He is behind me. I listen to him breathe. The only thing I see is the cement wall in front of me. I can do this. Oliver expects him to punish me. I assume that he will whip me. Dylan whipped me back at the cabin, it wasn't so bad.

"I'm sorry," Brian says as I feel him move close. "I will try to do this, so it doesn't leave any permanent scars."

The marks Dylan gave me only lasted a few days and then faded. Why would he say that? Then he strikes, and I know. The slice of pain running through my backside steals my breath away. My legs cave out from under me, straining my shoulders, my wrists. I feel a trickle of blood run down my ass tickling down my leg.

"I'm giving you twenty, he will expect no less. I'm sorry." I hear the anguish in his voice.

A monster or a man I am not sure, he could stop this couldn't he? I tried to help him. I would have asked Dylan to find Brian's girl, I would have, I wasn't lying.

I scream as the whip slices into me again, and again, and again.

I try not to think of Dylan, this is nothing like the whipping I received from him, I realized that after the first strike. I let my mind go, far away from what is happening, away from Oliver, Brian and even Dylan. My friend is there, she is always there for me, always waiting.

"Anna, look I caught him." I peer into her small hands. A tiny little toad jumps out making us squeal and giggle. She grabs my hand and pulls me to the beach. "I got a new one," she says. She holds up a bright blue bucket with a white handle. We sit down packing sand inside of it. She smiles at me and I tell her thank you for being my friend.

The cold brings me back to reality. Brian is pushing me into a shower. How did we get here? I try to escape the freezing water, but he pushes me under the spray so that it cascades down my back.

"Anna, it will help ease the pain, just for a bit, okay?" Brian says holding me by my arms under the stream.

My teeth chatter, it's so cold. I glance down to see blood wash down my legs the drain swallowing it. My entire backside throbs. My heartbeat is rolling over each welt, keeping time with each beat of my pulse.

After what feels like hours Brian shuts off the water and carefully pats me dry. He applies something sticky to the lash marks, making me hiss at the initial contact. Whatever it is, it eases the sting after a few moments. He hands me a clean dress and helps slip it over my head. My shoulders scream in protest as I lift my arms for him.

"It's time for supper." He lifts my chin and forces my eyes to meet his, I don't see the bully Brian, I see a man who is tired. "Whatever happens tonight you need to hold on. I will try to protect you the best I can. Just don't lose hope, okay?"

"I don't want to go back to the house," I say. My entire body hurts, I cannot face Oliver.

He leans over and places his forehead against mine. "We have to, we do not have a choice."

I sense he wants to say something else, but he doesn't. After a few moments he gently takes my hand. We head to the main house. The sky is turning a brilliant shade of pink. As we walk I wonder where Dylan is at, is it night or day in his world? I would like to think he is close, please be close. We stop in a room that Brian tells me is his.

It is nice but there is nothing personal in here that would show me something, give me an idea of who this man is, his interests. He orders me to sit on the bed, he goes into an adjoining room and comes out handing me a glass of water and two white pills.

"It's just Tylenol with a little codeine, it will help with the pain. Don't tell Oliver that I gave these to you," he says as he crouches down in front of me. "Don't provoke him tonight. He is furious at the both of us." He runs his hand through his shaggy brown hair.

I nod my understanding. "Thank you."

"Don't…don't thank me. I have done nothing good for you," he declares, I sense the remorse in his voice as he stands to take the glass from me setting it on the nightstand. "Let's go."

Oliver is in the dining room when we enter, he looks up as he pours himself a drink. "Ah, the happy couple. Come in, supper will be served in a few minutes. Drink?" He doesn't wait for either of us to answer and turns two glasses over.

I stare at the table, four place settings, I glance at Brian. He also notices, and a wariness settles along his features. Oliver turns to watch us as he pours. "Go ahead you can sit, take the seats at the end. I have a business associate joining."

Brian pulls out a chair for me, then sits down next to me. Oliver sets the drinks in front of us and makes his way to the other end. I pick up my drink trying to down it in one gulp. Brian reaches out and takes the glass from me shaking his head. I guess he doesn't want me mixing too much alcohol with the painkillers he gave me. I don't care. I need any escape I can find.

A butler comes in heralding the arrival of Oliver's guest. A man walks past us, Oliver shakes his hand and then motions for him to take the seat beside him. "Derrick, so glad you could make it, how was your flight?"

"Good, good." The older man says and looks down the table at Brian and I, his gaze settles on me.

The guy is as tall as Oliver, with silver gray eyes. The look he gives me is a true predator stare. He has short hair and a short-clipped beard, both speckled with white. Oliver fills a glass for his associate, then beckons me over to him with his finger.

I freeze in my seat. Brian squeezes my leg under the table.

"Come here, Anna. Show Derrick and I the lovely lash marks that Brian made this afternoon. I watched the video feed, he worked you up nicely."

I don't move. I stare at Brian. He leans over and pushes my chair back urging me to stand and obey. I gaze down at the other two, they are patiently waiting for me. I swear the newcomer hasn't taken his eyes off me since they landed there. I inch my way over to Oliver, when I get within arm's length, he grabs me. He pulls me to his other side, so that I stand between him and Derrick.

Oliver lifts the back of my dress, my bare bottom on display. I place my hands firmly on the table, fear of my legs giving out beneath me. Derrick leans behind me and runs his large hand over my ass, igniting the pain over the broken welts.

Tears claw at the corner of my eyes. I focus my gaze on Brian. He has a bored expression plastered on his face, but I see the simmer of anger, of nervousness simmer below the surface.

"Very nice." Derrick nods his approval. He dips his fingers lower than necessary before removing them, reaching for his drink.

Oliver slaps my ass, pulling a yelp from me. "You can return to your seat, Anna."

Servers appear, a meal fit for a king arrives and everyone eats. I pick over the plate that Brian filled for me. I am not hungry. A numbness looms over me. My mind does not want to be here right now.

My head is somewhere else, I am uninterested in the small talk that Oliver and Derrick are having. The servers come back and clear the table bringing out dessert for each of us. Brian pushes mine closer silently urging me to eat something. I stare at it, then I catch my name from the other end of the table.

They are both looking at me. I glance at Brian. Did I miss something? His nostrils flare slightly and his muscles tense.

"Anna, did you hear me?" Oliver asks.

"No, I'm sorry," I say.

"We were just wondering if you remembered feeding the FBI the information on an auction I was having in Columbia. Do you remember, kitten?"

I don't answer. My heartrate picks up, a cold sweat tickles along my skin. I shake my head no. He wants me to speak but I can't.

"Hmm, I guess without your little book of poetry in front of you, it might be tough for you to recall. Well anyhow, Derrick was supposed to purchase one of my best girls. Do you know where that girl is now, Anna?"

I shake my head no again, trying not look at the man next to him.

"The problem is, we don't know either. Derrick here was looking forward to spending time with her. You ruined that didn't you? Brian worked very hard to train this one just right for Derrick. Do you remember, Brian?"

I jump as Brian's voice rumbles beside me. "Yes, sir."

"Derrick has unique…*tastes.* It took a long time to find a girl who could adequately meet them." Oliver's statement glides down the table, filling me with fear. "We need to figure out how to make amends to him for his loss, he waited patiently and now, well she has vanished. Do you have any idea how we could make it up to him?"

I shake my head again, pressing my palms into the arms of my chair wanting to push myself up and run.

Oliver leans back and looks up at the ceiling as if he is running ideas through his mind. "Derrick, do you have any suggestions?"

"I will take her." He nods his head down the table at me. "I've seen that she can handle a punishment, I would like to see how she performs in *other* ways." I visibly see the lust in the man's eyes, he is slowly trying to sink his claws into me.

"You gave me to Brian," I say in a rush. Who would have thought I would choose Brian, the man who drowned me in a bathtub.

"I did, didn't I?" Oliver steeples his hands in front of him, thinking. "Brian, you don't mind do you? I think Anna would be a great fit for Derrick."

"No, she is mine," Brian says flatly.

I glance between the two. I notice a guard has suddenly made an appearance, standing a few feet behind Brian.

"Brian, you know me. How about we forget about the whole phone number incident and you give Anna to Derrick? Then you and I will make a call and Addison can be on a plane back to you within the hour."

I look at Brian, tears spill down my cheeks. He will choose her. I am nothing to him. I will be given to the man staring holes in me at the end of the table. I watch as Brian works his jaw back and forth.

"I appreciate your offer boss, but I am keeping Anna," he says.

I let out the breath I had been holding and peek back at Oliver. I don't know what Derrick's tastes are but thankfully Brian stepped in, I won't be finding out.

Oliver reclines in his chair looking like a cat that just ate the canary. "I thought you might say that. But, unfortunately Derrick either wants Anna for himself or he wants her dead," he shrugs his shoulders as if he is no longer in control.

The guard behind Brian steps forward. Brian pulls me to my feet beside him. He turns to look back at Oliver. The guard slowly raises his gun, my eyes lock on his. Shit, I am going to die. If Dylan comes he will find me, dead. What if they burry me in an unmarked grave, Dylan will never find me.

Tears stream down my face. Brian and Oliver are talking but it sounds muffled, blackness encroaches on the edge of my vision. I'm not ready to die. I was just beginning to live. I try to picture Dylan in my mind, I will never know what we could have been.

The gun goes off, I swear I see the bullet leave the weapon. Brian jumps in front of me and knocks us both to the ground. He falls on top of me, gazing at me as he whispers so that only I can hear, "don't give up, they are coming."

Blood trickles out the corner of his mouth and his eyes still on me, lifeless. I scream frantically trying to push him off me, no, no not again. The guard pulls Brian off me and points his gun at me again, aiming for my head.

"Stop," Oliver orders.

The guard lowers his gun and takes a step back.

"She is all yours," Oliver says. He gets up and walks out of the dining room, without a backwards glance.

Derrick crouches down beside me. He looks at Brian then back at me. "We stay here tonight. We leave first thing in the morning. Obey me and I can make you happy. Don't obey…well I guess eventually you will, how long that takes is entirely up to you."

I close my eyes, willing myself somewhere else, the smell of blood holds me hostage. Derrick tries to pull me to my feet, realizing that I am a lost cause he picks me up and tosses me over his shoulder.

He walks down the hall into the guest room he is staying in. He dumps me without ceremony on the bed. I leap up and run to the door. His fists connects with the side of my face as I dart by and I topple to the floor. He kicks me in the side of my ribs and grabs my hair as I struggle to pull air into my lungs.

I grasp for his hands as he drags me back to the bed by a fistful of hair. He reaches into the nightstand drawer with one hand, his other presses forcefully on my chest, holding me down. The clang of handcuffs ring in my ears as he places them through the iron bars on the bed clicking them too tightly to each of my wrists.

I close my eyes. He squeezes my cheeks painfully. My teeth cut into my cheek. "Open your eyes you little bitch. You will keep your eyes open while I fuck you. Let's see how tight of a slut you are."

I scream for Brian. He is not coming. He is dead. Everyone dies because of me. It would have been better if the bullet would have found me. Brian should have chosen Addison, why did he save me, why?

A loud rip drags me from my thoughts. I glance down to see Derrick rip my dress and then drop the scraps to the floor. He runs his hands over me smiling. "This may be a better deal than I thought," he snarls.

He pushes my legs apart with his knee, bruising my thighs. I close my eyes again, but he smacks me hard. "Keep them open. If I tell you again, you won't like it." He unbuttons his dress pants and pushes them down off his hips, settling his weight on me. I fight the urge to vomit, thankful that I didn't eat anything earlier.

"Anna." Sarah's familiar voice calls out to me. I can't close my eyes to go to her, he won't let me. "Anna." I focus on the light in the ceiling. "Listen, Anna. I'm here. It won't be long. Brian said they are coming for you. Hold on, please hold on." I listen to her voice as I try to block out the grunts and moans falling over me.

Dylan

This could be a trap. It's not every day that an abductor calls an FBI agent and gives an exact location of his victim. He said he had his reasons. It is a risk but one we will take. Anna risked her life to save her elderly friends. One of our guys went to Texas to check on them, they are both shook up but otherwise okay.

I watch in the dark, hidden by the trees. It looks like Oliver is lying low, there are only a handful of guards, the rest of the people appear to be cleaning or wait staff. A limo arrived with a man accompanied by his driver. Maybe twenty people total, we have a team of ten, so this should go smoothly. Luckily no girls are here that eliminates that element.

Waiting for the house to quiet down and lights to go out has been sheer torture. We don't even know if she is inside. I sense that she is. A few hours ago, we saw two guards drag what appeared to be a body bag outside. I can see it now, they left it beside one of the cement buildings. I'm trying not to focus on that little fact. The way they struggled with it has me optimistic that it was not her.

Liam is in charge. His head is clear, mine not so much. I need to see her, to feel her. I also need to rip out Oliver's throat. I'm hoping for both outcomes tonight. I watch Liam. He is crouched down a few feet in front of me. He turns to give me the signal. Go time, a part of me has missed the adrenaline-fueled missions, I wish this one didn't involve the girl I have fallen in love with.

Chapter Thirty-one

Anna

Every inch of my body hurts but it is nothing compared to the humiliation, the defeat I feel. My mother tried to save me from this. The fear I saw on her face the day I left… well I understand it now. I should have just kept living as Sarah but then I would have never met Dylan.

Dylan. I loved every minute with him, even when he was difficult…I secretly liked his difficult. But now, now everything has changed. I don't know if I'll ever be able to look into his eyes again. This man…Derrick, is taking me away. We are leaving in the morning. He will end up killing me, I hope sooner than later.

He doesn't have a soul. He is cut from the same cloth as Oliver. He spent the last several hours, hurting me, humiliating me. He finally unlocked the cuffs. They were so tight I was sure my hands would lose circulation and fall off.

He is showering now. He ordered me not to leave the room.

I want to go see if Brian is dead, his eyes said he was, but I didn't check his pulse. He risked his life for me.

I'm tired, so tired.

Derrick is cruel. I don't want to see what he is like when I disobey. He seemed satisfied when he went to shower. I can never keep a man like him happy, his tastes, I am sure are much darker than what I saw tonight.

I left the bed, wanting to get away from it. I'm watching the bathroom door, waiting. I crawled to a corner behind a chair. I'm not really hiding from him. He will see me when he comes out. I need to keep him in front of me. I needed off the bed. I thought I heard a commotion outside but now it is quiet again.

The door to the bedroom clicks open, I wrap myself into a little ball. I watch as a dark figure moves inside the room, then another. They must be guards, they have guns, maybe Oliver sent them to finish the job. I try to stifle a sniffle. One guard hears me and turns finding me. I tuck my head down to my knees if he is going to kill me I don't want him to be the last thing I see.

Someone touches my head lightly. I look up as the guard in front of me rips off the stocking cap that covers his face. It's Liam. I should be happy. I should jump for joy. But, I'm trapped in fear. Derrick is still in the bathroom.

I can't speak, I'm too tired.

The other man pulls up his cap, it's Anthony. They came for me. It's too late. I'm drained.

Liam whispers, "is there someone in the other room?"

I point to the bathroom door and give him a slight nod. I tuck my face back down in the safety of my legs.

I don't want them getting hurt, everyone around me gets hurt.

"It's okay. Anthony will get them. You and I will stay right here, you are safe now."

Anthony and Liam are here. Is Dylan here? I hear myself groan. I don't want him to see me like this. I can't see him. He will know what happened. He won't want me. I don't want me. I wish the ground would swallow me whole. Maybe I could go back to being Sarah, to her life, that would be easier.

The bathroom door opens, Derrick curses, there are sounds of a scuffle and then silence. Liam speaks. I peek up. He is talking into something. "All clear in the west wing."

Another voice comes across, "east wing clear." Then I hear Dylan…he is here. "South is clear…has anyone found her?"

Liam looks at me, I shake my head no. I don't want to see him, not now, not like this. I try to jump up to go into the bathroom. He stops me. "I have her, Dylan, she is okay. Deal with Oliver and the others. I will get her out of here."

Silence.

Then after many seconds pass Dylan responds, relief infiltrating his voice, "tell her I love her."

I settle back onto the floor, no, no, no. He said he loves me. He can't love me. Not now. Tears stream down my face as I stare at the bed. Memories of what happened slice me to the bone.

Liam's eyes follow mine, the handcuffs still hooked around the frame, blood smearing the sheets. His gaze then settles on me. I lift my eyes to him. I can't speak but I scream to him inside my head, I need to get away, Dylan can't see me.

Liam pulls his gear and shirt off. He gently leans forward and urges me to release my legs, so he can slide his shirt over my arms. I let him. "It will be okay, we got them, they cannot hurt you anymore."

I pull my knees back up to my chest. Anthony comes in and crouches down beside us. I watch their exchanged glances. "Everything is secure, let's get her out of here. She needs medical help," Liam says.

I reach out and grab Liam's arm shaking my head furiously. I want no one touching me or looking at me. I wish I could go to my dark cell. He sighs. "Anna, it will be okay. Dylan is here. We are all here for you, sweetheart."

I shake uncontrollably, Anthony stands up to get a blanket off the bed. Liam stops him, pointing to another chair on the far side of the room with one draped across it. "That one," he says.

Anthony nods in understanding coming over with the blanket and covering me.

"Bring a car up to the front, I will carry Anna out," Liam says.

Anthony hops up and is gone in seconds. "I'm going to pick you up okay?" In slow movements he reaches out and scoops me up.

As we enter the hallway, I hear a man yell, screaming out in pain. It is Oliver. I push at Liam's chest to get him to release me. "No, Anna, I'm not letting you go in there. You don't need to see that."

I press harder, finally he sets me on my feet. I pull the blanket around myself tightly. I need to see. I need to know he will die. If I don't, I think the man will haunt my dreams forever. I would always look over my shoulder wondering if he was dead.

"Anna," Liam says urging me to follow him outside. I can't. My focus is on the screams coming down the hall. I must see. I can't explain it. I need to see with my own eyes.

I run, Liam follows me and grabs me around the waist just as I turn the corner to see Dylan leaning over Oliver. Oliver is lying on the ground a bloody mess. Derrick is sprawled out a few feet away with a bullet hole in his head. It appears he got off easy. If Dylan knew what he had done, I don't think he would have been so lucky.

"Dylan," Liam yells, letting him know I am in the room…watching.

Dylan stands and turns his eyes connect with mine. I can only imagine what I look like. My face hurts, everything aches. He glares down at Oliver. I see his jaw working back and forth, his demeanor as deadly as I have ever seen on any man. His eyes come up to meet mine again. He tilts his head, his focus intent on me. He is waiting for my response. Liam is still holding me tightly around my waist. He whispers in my ear, "you don't have to watch."

I swallow hard. I know but I need to. Oliver screams out, "Anna, kitten, please tell them to stop. I never hurt you, you know I never hurt you." I think to myself how pathetic he sounds but he isn't lying, he never physically hurt me, he let others do it…now...I will do the same.

Dylan is still looking at me his brows drawn together, a wolf waiting to tear into his prey. How long has he waited for this…I nod my head once. Dylan turns to Oliver, reaches down and digs his fingers into Oliver's throat. Tearing, ripping, pulling gurgling sounds from his helpless body. Oliver goes limp and his head drops to the side, lifeless eyes stare out. Dylan stands to his full height and howls, blood dripping from his hand. He has waited so long for this moment, to kill the man who killed his mother, his sister and so many others.

I look away, my legs crumble beneath me. Liam picks me up and carries me out into the night air. I gaze at the stars as he walks to the vehicle. Oliver is gone, the monster that has haunted me all these years is dead. I am free of him. It is too late. I am now a prisoner inside my body. I am tired, too tired. I want to sleep. Now I understand why Sophia was not eager to run with me.

Liam sets me carefully in the backseat of a black four-wheel drive. "Anna, Anthony will stay with you. You are safe. I am going to go inside for a few minutes, I will be right back."

Dylan

I look down at Oliver, his throat is ripped to shreds. The smell of blood, gunpowder, fear and death surrounds me. I looked over my shoulder in time to see Anna crumble and Liam swiftly scoop her up. Maybe I shouldn't have done that in front of her. But, I saw something in her eyes that told me she wanted to watch, needed to. I hope I made the right decision. Is she going to think I am a monster?

The way I killed Oliver was raw, primal.

"Dylan, we need to talk," Liam says as he kicks Oliver's dead body for good measure.

I turn to look at him, slowly coming down from the adrenaline high I had been on. "Where is she?" I head towards the door.

Liam presses his palm into my chest to stop me. "Wait, I want to show you something."

I study him, whatever it is it's not good. Concern is written all over his face. I follow him down the hall and into a bedroom. He runs his hand through his hair, sighing. "We found her in here."

I take in the room, broken glass on the floor, a lamp tipped over, then my gaze lands on the bed. I stare at the bloody sheets and the handcuffs hanging open around the headboard. I saw the bruise on her face, the swollen lip, the haunt in her eyes…we were too late. I fall to my knees. I want to murder Oliver all over again.

"She will need you, man. I wanted you to see what we are dealing with before you go out there to her. I found her sitting in the corner," Liam says pointing to where they had found her. "The other guy, the one you shot, he was in here with her. He was in the bathroom."

I picture her curled up, hiding from that asshole. Fuck, I wish I would have known he had hurt her. I would have made his death slower, more painful. My Anna, he touched *my* Anna. I yell out frustrated that there is not a damn thing I can do about it now.

Liam places a hand on my shoulder. "Get this shit out now, Dylan, then when you are ready, we will be waiting in the car. She needs medical attention. I think she may be in shock, so get it together quick." He turns to leave but stops at the door. "If you aren't out there in fifteen, I'm taking her to the closest hospital."

I stare at the sheets. Fuck. I need to get out there to her. I need her in my arms. How am I going to help her? I have saved so many girls. We find them and return them to their families. That is where it always ends for me. I don't know what to do *after*. Liam is right, first off I need to just make sure she is physically okay. She didn't look well.

I pull my phone out to make a few calls. I'm taking my girl home. I'm not taking her to a hospital in an unfamiliar country, she has been through enough. She needs to be home, if I admit it to myself I need to be there too. She is alive, I can do this, I love her and nothing else matters.

I stop on the way-out and grab one of my guys, Mark. He is a medic. I trust him. We are all trained in basic medical, but Mark stayed, learning more than the rest of us. He is smart.

"Hey, Dylan, everything is secure. The guys are pulling all the computers, files, anything we might use to take down any others. I can handle this why don't you head out."

"Actually, I need your help. Liam told me Anna is in bad shape. They hurt her…" my voice breaks as I speak. How did I let this happen?

Mark gives me a strange look. I am sure my emotion to the situation is foreign to him. "Dylan, hey man it's okay. I'll just go tell the others and meet you outside. Do you want to take her to the hospital?"

"No, I'm taking her home. A plane is waiting as we speak," I say wearily. He nods and turns to find the others to let them know our plans.

I steel myself at the front door. When I leave this house, I need to be one hundred percent focused on Anna and Anna alone. I will help her, I will love her, and I will never let her go ever again.

Anthony is standing by the SUV leaning inside. Anna is sitting with her legs curled up into her chest, her head buried. Liam is beside her not touching her, his hand rests protectively on the back of the seat.

Anthony spots me and comes over before I reach the vehicle. "Where are we going, Dylan?"

"To the airport, we are going home," I say. He gives me a small smile and pats me on the arm.

I walk over to the open door. "Baby?"

She doesn't look at me, but she leans her tightly wrapped body into mine. I wrap my arms around her and pull her into my chest, resting my head on top of hers. I glance at Anthony. He looks concerned. "Baby, everything will be okay. Our friend Mark is going to ride with us, he is medically trained. He will make sure you are okay to fly. If you are, then we are flying home. If he thinks you need to be in a hospital, then we will find one close by."

She feverishly shakes her head no at the mention of the hospital but doesn't look up.

Liam speaks to her and reaches out to touch her back tenderly. "Anna, if Mark says you are healthy enough we will go home but we have to do what he thinks is best. No one will leave you. We are all here."

She makes no movement or protest this time. I push her lightly to the center to get in beside her, keeping her tucked into my chest. Liam stays in the other seat next to her until Mark runs out with his medical bag. He lets Mark have his seat and moves to the front with Anthony.

"Anna, Mark is here now. We are going to drive to the airport, but we need to let him look so we can get an idea of how you are doing," I say in quiet gentle tones.

She doesn't move. My heart is breaking off in chunks as I sit here with her. I glance around wanting to burn the entire place to the ground, erase all of it. I run my hand down her hair, unable to control the tears that stream down my face.

Chapter Thirty-Two

Anna

I sense Dylan's pity as he sits next to me. I want them to all leave me alone. The last thing I need is pity. I want nothing but to be alone. I can't look at him. Liam told him, I hear it in his voice, feel it in his movements. He wants Mark to examine me. I don't want anyone to touch me. I could fight them but I'm tired. Maybe I will let Mark do his thing, then we can go home. I'm not sure what he means by that, back to Colorado, to San Diego? It doesn't matter. I need to go somewhere where I can be by myself.

Mark gently places his hand on my arm. "Anna, I'm going to take your blood pressure and inspect any wounds you have. Can you tell me where you are hurt?"

He sounds nice. They are all nice, nothing like the dead men inside the house. I try to speak, to make words come out but I can't. I shake my head no as I peek out at him from the cocoon I made for myself between my knees and chest.

He smiles at me. "It's okay if you don't want to talk right now." He pulls his blood pressure cuff out of a bag. "I'm just going to pull your arm out a little," he says.

I keep my head turned towards him. I can't face Dylan. Dylan lets go of me but keeps a hand on my back. The car is moving now, Anthony is driving, but it is not his usual fast pace throw you around sort of driving. I can tell he is taking extra caution, turning corners at a slow speed. No one makes a move to buckle me in.

Mark reaches out and gently pushes the blanket off me. I notice him glance down at my bloody, tore up wrist. He wraps the cuff around my upper arm placing the stethoscope over my beating pulse.

For the first time since they arrived I realize how lucky I am to be alive. Last night at supper I thought I had hit the end of the road. Do I want to be alive? I ponder the question as I focus on the warmth of Dylan's hand on my back. Yes, I think so. I just don't know how at this moment.

Mark rips the cuff off. "Very good, it's a little high, but that is to be expected. Your face and your wrists are hurt. I am just going to look you over quick to make sure nothing else needs immediate attention. If not, we can get on the plane."

I sit up and wince. I want this over with, I need to leave this place. I still don't know where we are. He takes my hand and flips my wrist over, then the other one doing the same. He runs his fingers lightly over my cheekbone. "Can you point to where you are hurting?"

I let my feet slowly fall to the floor. Dropping my eyes to my lap, I uncurl myself, a deep stiffness has set into my bones. I hold the blanket around me still but open it slightly to point to my ribs and then gesture towards my back.

He cautiously reaches out and places his hand under the blanket to feel my ribs making me suck in a breath when he hits a tender spot. "I'm sorry, you have bruised, possibly fractured ribs. As long as you're not having any difficulty breathing I think it's safe to get on the plane." He looks over my shoulder, speaking more to Dylan than myself. "But, you will tell me if you have problems, won't you?"

I shake my head yes, anything to not have to go to a hospital. He smiles at me again and says, "good girl." This warms me. It is silly, but reality is coming into focus. I'm not with the bad guys anymore. I am in a car with the good guys, they will not let anyone hurt me. "Sit up a little, I want to take a peek at your back, I'm guessing it is bruised."

I hesitate, if I allow him to look Dylan will also see.

Mark leans down and captures my eyes with his. I silently plead with him. "Okay, enough for now." He pats me on the leg. "I think she is good to fly. I'll keep a close eye on her."

Dylan breathes a sigh of relief, as he pulls me gently to him. I pull my legs up to my chest and curl into him. He came for me. He said he would never leave me. He knows what happened, and he still hasn't left me. He is taking me home. I don't know where that is but if he stays with me…I may just survive.

We reach the airport. A small private plane waits for us on the runway. We are in Belize I find out. They say it won't take long to get home. I'm tired but they aren't letting me sleep. Mark thinks I have a slight concussion. I'm sure I do, Derrick's fist hit me so hard my head snapped, pinching a nerve in my neck, the pain still radiates through me.

I keep my eyes lowered not wanting to look at anyone. Once we are in the plane Dylan kneels to help buckle me in for takeoff. I try to turn away from him. He doesn't let me. He places both hands on either side of my face and holds me tightly, forcing my eyes to his. "You are mine. Nothing and I mean nothing changes that, Anna Velasquez. I'm never letting you go, never."

His words should frighten me, he is being demanding Dylan again, but they comfort me more than anything. More than being away from the house of terror, more than Oliver being dead, more than even being held in his arms. He is claiming me. I am still his.

He doesn't seem to expect a response from me which is good because I cannot find enough energy to speak. He buckles in beside me. I stare out the window, flying away from my nightmare once again. This time it will not come looking for me, he is gone. Relief suddenly engulfs me. I collapse in my seat from exhaustion.

I wake up to an awful smell, shit. I push at the hands in front of me. It's Mark, he is crouched down holding something under my nose. He smiles when I focus my eyes on him. "Good girl, you are awake. You scared us for a minute."

He looks around at the guys. "She is okay."

I glance at the other three. They are white as ghosts. I smile, to have someone worry over me is nice even though I'm not sure what to do with it right now. They are all here. They came for me. They didn't leave me.

"And a smile to boot," Mark says.

Dylan leans over and kisses my temple. "We are here, baby, let's get you home."

I keep my eyes focused on the road in front of us, the sun is up, I see where "home" is. We are going to my parent's estate in Mexico. Everything looks familiar, yet it doesn't. My nerves are getting the best of me. Everyone in the vehicle is grows anxious the closer we get.

Liam keeps turning to peek at me, Anthony's eyes check on me through the rear-view mirror and then there is Mark and Dylan in the back. I'm sandwiched between two mother hens. Why is he taking me here? I remembered I had asked him if we could go home when we were in Colorado, but I didn't mean like this, not like this.

We pull up to the wrought-iron fence and the gate magically opens. I turn and look at Dylan, so many questions but I cannot find any words. He looks down at me. "We are home, baby."

I watch as we continue down the long tree-lined driveway until we arrive at the circle in front of the main house…my house. I want to run up the stairs into my mother's arms. She isn't here though. Dylan squeezes me gently as if reading my mind.

Anthony speaks up, being his usual self. "Damn it's good to be home!"

I forget that this is not only my home, we all grew up here. All because of the kind heart of Manuel Velasquez. So many things to deal with, so many memories flood my brain, it is all just too much.

"We need to get Anna inside, so I can make sure she is okay. Then she needs to rest. I want to take her to the infirmary first to capture an image of her ribs," Mark says.

"I'll visit Mrs. Cortez and see that she has everything ready for us," Anthony adds as he jumps out and takes the steps two at a time.

Liam mumbles a few choice curse words as he glides over to the driver's seat. "I'll pull us around, fucking Anthony, he is just worried about getting to the food first, he knows Mrs. Cortez will have a feast prepared."

I smile again and tuck myself in close to Dylan. I love these guys. I am so happy they didn't abandon me, if they hadn't come I would be in hell. I shiver as I think of Derrick.

We pull up in front of the infirmary building. A gray-haired older gentleman comes down the stairs. Liam gets out first and goes to the man, giving him a big bear hug.

"That is Liam's father, Luis, he is a doctor. I called for him to meet us here," Dylan says.

I glance at Mark, he sees my discomfort and quickly adds, "he is a psychiatrist."

I stare at Dylan and shake my head no. I'm not talking to him, I'm not. I turn in my seat to look back to the house. I wonder if I can make it there before anyone catches me.

Dylan turns my face towards him. "Anna, you don't have to talk to him, I want him here for when you are ready. You have been through a lot. You will need to get it out at some point."

Mark opens his door letting the warm air in, he motions for me to go to him. He takes my hand and leads me up to the front of the building. Liam and his father stop talking as we pass. Liam doesn't introduce me, thankfully. I follow as Mark leads, Dylan is close behind, his booted footsteps fall heavy.

He guides me into an exam room and instructs me to sit up on the table. An exam room, I can't hold it in any longer. The tears start, I can't stop them. I want to go to my room, shower and crawl into bed. Dylan rushes towards me but Mark stops him. "Why don't you wait outside."

"No, no one is touching her without me being here," he says with finality.

He pushes Mark away and comes to stand in front of me, pulling me into his arms, rocking me until my hiccupping sobs subside. Once I quiet down, he stares into my eyes, he is struggling. "Anna, let Mark do what he needs to do." He kisses me on the forehead and steps back, leaning against the wall on the other side of the room. Tough love, I hate it.

Mark had been busy getting everything set up while I was crying. He waits for me. "No hurry, we will take as long as you need," he says as he passes me a tissue.

I pathetically wipe my face and blow my nose. He seems satisfied I am ready. "First, I want to get that x-ray to make sure your ribs aren't broken." He hands me a gown and turns to Dylan. Bring her down as soon as she changes.

He leaves, shutting the door. Dylan picks up the gown and holds it open for me. I let the blanket fall and pull Liam's shirt over my head. I push my arms into it and tuck it behind me. Dylan leans around to tie the back. I stop him. He doesn't argue and allows me to hold it together.

Once we finish with the x-ray, Mark returns and clips the images in front of a light on the wall for his examination. "Well, I see a hairline fracture on the left side. It will be sore but will heal. Everything else looks good." He clicks the light off making the images go black. "Can you tell me how that happened?" he asks as he turns to face me.

I shake my head no in response.

"Anna, you haven't spoken since we found you, can you speak?"

My voice would be hoarse if I spoke. I screamed and screamed while Derrick had me. My throat feels like sandpaper. I could talk, I just don't want to.

"Hmm." He places a thermometer in my mouth, feeling my forehead as he does. "She isn't in shock. She may just not be ready to talk," Mark says looking over his shoulder at Dylan.

I turn my head to stare out the window. I can see the top of a tree. I watch a squirrel run along a branch until I can't spot him any longer. When I return my gaze to him he pulls out the thermometer.

He makes swift work of cleaning my wrists and the cuts on my face causing me to hiss. I lie down, and he presses gently on my abdomen, making quick assessments with his hands. "Okay, let's have a look at your back. You can stand, roll to one side or on your stomach. Whatever causes you the least amount of pain."

He walks over to a cabinet and pulls out two syringes, filling them from little vials. I squirm on the table, but I don't do as he asks, I don't want to follow his direction. I peek over at Dylan still leaning against the wall with his arms folded across his chest. I glance at Mark nervously.

"This is an antibiotic, and this one is for pain." He holds each of them up for my inspection. He brushes an alcohol pad over my arm, then quickly injects both. "The pain killer should help relax you. I know you are tired. We are almost done."

"Can you roll over to your side?" He gently urges me over, I grimace more at the thought of Dylan seeing my back than the injury, both excruciating. The pain medicine tingles through my veins and gives me a little more courage than I had before. "Good girl," he says.

Dylan moves close as Mark pushes my gown aside.

Dead silence.

Mark begins to wash the wounds across my backside. I bite my lip and struggle to not make a sound, so they don't discover how much pain I am in. I am thankful for the painkiller.

I hear the door open and close. Mark's hands are still on me. Dylan walked out, he left me. Sadness envelopes me. I turn my head to hide my face in the pillow.

"He isn't leaving you. He just needs a minute. He is feeling guilty for not getting to you sooner," Mark says above me.

When I don't respond he continues, "I am sorry that you had to go through this." He pulls the gown closed and helps me back up to a sitting position. He pushes the hair out of my face and looks at me seriously. "Did they hurt you anywhere else? I think they did. But, if they didn't I won't check, I won't put you through that."

My eyes flit to the door. I understand what he is getting at. Derrick did hurt me. I don't want to face that. I want to forget.

"Would you like to wait until Dylan comes back? Anna, I need to make sure you are okay," he says.

I don't want Dylan in here for this. He couldn't handle seeing the lash marks on my back, how would he handle this? I lie down on the table and focus on the light above me. Then I slowly close my eyes. Mark rattles the tray towards my feet. He understands my silent answer to his question.

"Anna, where are you?" Sarah calls. I push my way through the fog to my friend. She runs up the beach and hugs me tightly against her. "It's okay, I told you they were coming."

Dylan

It's been three weeks since finding Anna. She still hasn't spoken a single word, except for when she is sleeping. Then the nightmares take over. She screams, often it's her safe word, over and over. I saw the video of Brian, whipping her. If the guy wasn't already dead, I would whip him until every inch of him was covered, then I would let him bleed out.

He kept apologizing to her. Never once did he lighten up or hesitate. She screamed her safe word seventeen times, I counted. She was so out of it I think the word just came to her, she wanted it to stop, not knowing how to make it end. There was no way to stop him. He wasn't going to until he was done. Twenty bloodletting lashes over her backside. I flex my fists as I reach for my glass and down it, slamming it on the table.

I put Anna in a guest room, not sure if she could handle being in the master bedroom or her old pink room. I wasn't certain she would want me to stay with her but the first night she clung to me, giving me the answer, I had wished for.

I felt awful walking out of that exam room after seeing her back. She didn't need to see or hear my grief. Liam took my place by her side until I cooled off. It was for the best, after I left she let Mark exam her further, my brave, brave girl. They hurt her. Mark says she will heal. Her bruises and the lash marks have almost faded. I can still spot where every wound on her body was, but to someone who didn't know where to look they might miss them.

The guys are all here for a meeting of the minds. I am so thankful for my brothers. It has been good to be home.

"So, what are we going to do?" Anthony speaks up first, not shy in the slightest.

"I don't know," I reply exasperated. "She follows our directions. She gets up every morning, eats but then it's back to that damn bed."

Liam drums his fingers on the table, appearing like he wants to say something.

"What is it, Liam?" I ask.

"Ah, I don't know, Dylan." He runs his hands through his hair and gazes over at his dad. He nods in encouragement to his son. "We have all been tiptoeing around her for the last three weeks, which is fine, she needed to rest. But, she is pretty healed up right now from my understanding?" He looks at Mark.

"Yes, she has improved nicely. I don't think she will have any permanent scarring, except a little on the inside of her wrists."

"That is great news. But anyhow, my point is maybe us tiptoeing isn't doing her any favors. Forgive me for being so blunt here, Dylan, but Anna seemed to respond to your more, how should I say, dominant side," Liam says. He leans back in his chair and takes a long sip of his drink looking at me like he is hoping I don't get up and punch him.

I watch as all the guys tense, waiting for my response. They know I will kill anyone that ever hurts her again. But, what he is saying makes sense. I glance at Luis. "So, I assume you both have already discussed this?" I say with my glass in hand pointing my finger between the two.

"Yes, I haven't been able to get her to respond. She listens politely but only nods or looks away if I ask her questions. She needs to talk, Dylan. The longer she lets herself drift the harder it will be for her to function in the real world," Luis says.

I lean back in my chair and lock my fingers together behind my head. "I don't know if I can push her, I'm afraid she will break."

"She is strong she will not break," Liam says. "I caught her watching you yesterday. I went to her room for a visit. I was talking to her, but she wasn't there with me. She wasn't off in the sky either. Her eyes were intent on you. You were by her window planting flowers. Do you remember?"

I nod my head at him. I had taken the afternoon to plant the brightest flowers I could find outside of her bedroom window. She spent hours looking out. I wanted something cheerful for her to stare at. I even added little birdhouses to the mix. I looked up once and caught her staring at me. She gave me a shy smile before she turned away.

"She is in there. She isn't as far gone as we all think. She is right on the other side of her silence. I watched her lick her lips when you took your shirt off." Liam laughs as he relays the events for all of us.

"I had to leave, I felt like I was a third wheel. But, that wouldn't be the first time, would it?" He snickers. He isn't stupid, he knew what was going on in the kitchen at the cabin. I made Anna come while he was watching tv.

"Fuck you," I say as I chuckle. It's good to laugh. I haven't done that in a while. I think about it for a minute, yes, I have let Anna have her peace long enough. The beast has been at bay, if Liam thinks Anna is ready, then I can pull up anchor.

"Okay, but you pricks can't go around behind my back giving in to her. We all have to be on the same page, you will all follow my lead." I point to each one of my friends, they all nod in agreement.

"Good, it is settled. Now let's all have another drink. I think I am going to need it," I say. I am going to push her. I can't wait until she finds the courage to come back out and play.

Chapter Thirty-Three

Anna

After breakfast I walk back to my room. Dining room, bedroom, eat, sleep…my new life. I go down for meals but that is as far as I venture. I spend my days talking to Sarah in my head. It helps keep everything else out. The guys have been very nice, they come and visit me, and they don't expect me to talk. Sometimes I listen to what they are saying but most of the time I'm with Sarah.

I turn down the hall, my door is closed. Mrs. Cortez must have accidently shut it after she came in to tidy up this morning. She is a chubby woman with a hearty laugh. She bustles around each day speaking half Spanish half English sentences. When the guys upset her, the words literally fly out of her mouth. I don't understand what she is saying but I like it. She always puts them in their place and it usually ends with them kissing her on the cheek.

I get to my door, it's locked. I glance around, this is a big house, but this is the room I have been sleeping in. My sanctuary. I jiggle the handle again, it's fucking locked. I slide to the floor. What do I do now? I could find Mrs. Cortez and ask her to unlock it, that is if I was speaking.

My silence is probably to the point of ridiculous, but I don't want to talk. If I do, it will make it all real and pull me back to reality. They will ask me questions about what happened. If I speak I will cry, I don't want to cry. I have this fear of not being able to stop.

I sit there waiting outside the door, reaching up to shake it a few more times, like doing it more than once will magically unlock it. Fuck.

Speak of the devil, here comes Mrs. Cortez now. I wave to her and point to my doorknob hoping she will understand my plight.

"Oh, mija, dear, I am sorry, but Mr. Lorenz told me to lock your door and not to unlock it until he tells me to," she says.

I stand there with my mouth hanging open, he what? I place my hands together as if in prayer, pleading with her.

"I'm sorry, mija, Mr. Lorenz is the boss. It is such a beautiful day why don't you get some fresh air." She pats my arm as she scoots off.

Why, why would he tell her to lock my door? I stand there waiting for an answer that doesn't come. Is he angry at me for something? Fuck him, this is my house. I will give him a piece of my mind. I walk down the hall and go straight for my father's office.

I pause outside and press my ear to the wood. I can hear him and Liam talking. I shove the door open without thinking and push inside. I stop with my hands on my hips. Shit, I'm not speaking, fuck, now what? I didn't think past the stomping in part.

Dylan leans back in his chair and places his feet up on the desk in front of him. Liam quickly retreats to the far side of the room.

"Anna, it's nice to see you outside of your suite," Dylan purrs.

I stomp my foot, hoping he can read my body language…fuck you.

"What can I do for you?" He laughs lightly and smiles at me.

What the fuck, where is nice Dylan? The guy who has been giving me my space all the while tending to my every need. I walk over to his desk and hold out my hand out for the keys.

He takes my hand and turns it over placing a kiss on the top. He tilts his head and throws me that smoldering serious look of his.

Flip-flop.

I pull my arm away acting like he just stung me. He smiles and settles back in his chair.

I stalk away, slamming the door behind me. What was that? What should I do? I stand in the hallway and glance each direction not knowing which way to turn. I slump down to the floor, shit.

The door opens and Liam slides down the wall and sits next to me. He tugs something out of his pocket, pulls my hand over to his lap, pries open my fingers and places the object in my palm. He closes my fist around it then stands to walk away.

I peer down and open my hand slowly. It is the heart-shaped rock from the stream at the cabin. The one Liam found the day that Dylan whisked me to San Diego. I run my thumb over it. He said it was a sign that love was in the air. Then magically the helicopter with Dylan in it appeared. I smile remembering how the irony made Liam laugh.

Is this his way of reminding me that Dylan loves me? He says it all the time, he whispers it in the dark at night when I wake up from my nightmares. Or is it a reminder that I am alive and more good times could happen…if I let them.

I get up and walk down the hall to my room, my old room. Of course, this door wouldn't be locked. I push it open. Everything is exactly as I left it. I cover my mouth with the back of my hand to stifle a sob. I reach in and close it. Can't hide here, maybe I will go outside.

It is a cool morning. Mrs. Cortez is right. It is a beautiful day. I make my way up the hill to my favorite spot on the whole estate, you can see almost everything from there. As I climb I watch the tire swing sway from the tree. When I reach the top of the hill, I nudge the swing gently, Sophia used to push me on it.

From here I can see the main house, a few storage buildings, the lake where Sarah drowned and the little cemetery. I sit down in the grass by the swing and listen to the leaves bristle in the tree above me. Mrs. Cortez was right. This was what I needed.

My mother always used to shoo me outside, she would say Anna go out and let the wind blow the stink off you. I remember once asking her if I really stunk, and she laughed and told me she meant I had been inside for too long. Yes, I need fresh air, I had probably been inside long enough.

I catch Dylan and Liam walk down by the lake with their fishing poles. Dylan looks up at me several times. I smile, he is checking up on me, they might have planned to fish today but I doubt it. He is always near.

Could it be time to move forward? I want to. I have been thinking about Brian and Addison. I need to help her. I can't imagine where she is at. It can't be a good place. The thought of her being with a man like Oliver or Derrick makes my stomach hurt. If I wish to find her that means I will have to talk to the guys about it. Which also means I will have to be honest with them about what happened to me. Am I ready for that?

I haven't followed my motto as of late. One foot in front of the other hasn't seemed possible. Maybe it's time, Dylan has proved he isn't going anywhere. Today was his way of letting me know he thinks it is time…he pushed me.

When he gave me that look this morning it made my stomach do a somersault, that hasn't happened in a long while. I feel it again just thinking about him, that bit of coiled excitement in the pit of my tummy.

This is the perfect place for a new beginning, a chance to say goodbye to the past, to bury the hurt and to make a fresh start. I survived. I don't have to hide anymore. I glance over to where the cemetery lies. It is bigger than when I was little, it also has a new black wrought-iron fence surrounding it. One foot in front of the other, time to put the pieces of my soul back together, to find myself yet again.

I walk down the hill towards the cemetery. I laugh as I notice Liam and Dylan crane their necks to watch me. I love them. I run my hand over the cold iron of the fence and stare at the stones cradled within. I push down on the latch to release the door and step inside, closing it behind me. I used to come here to visit my grandparents with my father, Manuel. They once were the only people I knew here. Now I look around and spot many familiar names.

Oliver did this, I don't regret once what Dylan did to him. He deserved it. I walk over to where my grandparents are buried. I see a larger stone beside theirs, as I approach the name on it stands out, it's mine. I wander over to it and run my hand over the letters. Off to the side of my stone is a joint one for my parents. I swallow down the lump in my throat.

I sit on my grave, Sarah's grave. I should speak to Dylan about getting it changed for her. She deserves her own stone. I need to give her back her name. It is time for me to let her go…to grant her peace.

There are wilted flowers lying on a cement box in front of the grave tied together with a ribbon. I study it. It looks like someone could open the box. I lean over and pick up the flowers laying them off to the side in the grass. The top of the box has a silver plate engraved with the words *Letters to Anna.*

It is filled with personal messages, I shouldn't read them, but they are addressed to me aren't they? I lift off the heavy lid and set it down beside the flowers, peeking in. There are many letters inside, I can tell some are older than others, some have yellowed with time. A more recent looking one is on top. I pluck it out, it is addressed to Sarah. I consider the flowers. This one is from the Madronos. I fold it up and place it off to the side. They would visit their daughter, it makes sense. I'm happy that they visited her here.

I pull out a few more. I sift through them. Most are from my mom. I read a few. They all tell me about her life, her dreams for me, none indicating that I am alive and not buried here. I guess anyone could have opened it, Oliver could have opened it, I shudder at the thought. I spot one from Sophia, Sophia's mother and then I find one in the bottom from my dad.

I draw it out and unfold it. I read it several times. He knew he was not my father, the confession in black and white. Oliver and William did not lie, but what they didn't know was that Manuel had adopted me at birth, it says so in the letter. My heart swells, Manuel was my father, not by blood but he was by all other ways.

Manuel wrote of his love for my mother and me. It describes how he fell in love with me and my blue eyes the minute they placed me in his arms. He told me how he was sorry for not spending enough time with me. How he worked hard to look out for me. How important it was to him to save lives, my mother included. His work was paramount to him, it made a significant impact and Dylan and the others continue his legacy to this day.

I wish I would have known all this before, but I was young, my parents thought they needed to protect me. Unfortunately, I know all too well why they did what they did. They tried but the ugliness of the world finally caught up. I put Sarah's letter back in the box and tuck the other letters under my leg. I am keeping them. They are mine after all.

A peace settles over me. The wind whistles in the trees, birds sing. I am alive. I am alive I repeat over and over. I allow my mind to think about all that has happened. I wouldn't change it, it all brought me back here. Here with Dylan and the others.

If my mother hadn't hidden me away where would I be? Oliver would have come either way. If I would have been here when the attack came, he would have taken me at eleven years of age. I stop myself. I can't think beyond that. It wouldn't have been good.

I stand and gather my letters. I must start somewhere. I can't do it alone…I don't have to do it alone. I walk to the house stopping near the lake to wave at Liam and Dylan, giving them a small smile to let them know I am okay. I see Dylan's shoulders drop as he relaxes. He smiles back.

Liam's father, Luis, has parked himself outside my window on a bench each morning with a novel, sometimes a newspaper. I appreciate he does this in hope that I will come and talk to him. Today he will get his wish.

Luis smiles warmly at me as I approach. He folds the corner of his page down and closes his book, patting the seat beside him. I accept the offer, looking over at the window to my room, my locked one. No more hiding, Dylan is making sure of that.

He looks so much like Liam. When he grins his eyes crinkle in the corners, he is kind. He told me at lunch one day he had worked with some of the girls that my dad rescued. Most of them went home, a few had no family and nowhere to go so my father took them in until they got on their feet. He also said he helped my mother after they freed her.

Suddenly, I feel a little uncomfortable. I don't know where to start, what I really want to say. I hand him the letter from my father. He takes it, quietly reading it to himself. "Manuel loved you very much, Anna. Did you doubt this?" he asks.

I shake my head yes still not able to form any words.

"He did, he loved you and your mother more than anything. He was a hard worker, he never stopped. It consumed him almost to a fault, but he saved a lot of lives." He stares at me, trying to get a read on my thoughts.

"Do you want to talk about what happened to you?" he asks gently.

I shake my head yes. I need to try. It will make it real, but it will also get it out. If I don't, it will eat me alive. "Yes," I whisper peering down at my lap.

He places his hand over mine. "That was the first step, it will only get easier from here on out, I promise. What you say to me stops here, I will share none of what you say unless you ask me to."

I shake my head in acknowledgement, then let the floodgates open. I talk, I cry, I scream, I even get sick to my stomach, but Luis doesn't leave my side. He listens as I tell him every ugly thing they did.

I did it. It is out. I had locked all that shit inside for so long I didn't realize how heavy it had all been. It weighed me down so much I couldn't even speak.

Mrs. Cortez comes out from the house. "Luis, Anna, I brought you lunch, it is over here on the patio. The others have all eaten, I thought since it was such a nice day you would like to eat out here." She points to courtyard, then backs away, quickly leaving.

Luis looks at me. "What do you think? Hungry?"

"Yes, I'm sorry I kept you so long, you almost missed lunch," I say.

He stands and offers me his arm. "Oh, we wouldn't have missed anything, Mrs. Cortez would have made sure of that."

Dylan

It seems Liam's suggestion of pushing Anna is paying off. Locking her room was the hardest thing I have ever had to do. I have killed men, but locking that door, that was tough. I knew it would force her to face things, dark things. I almost gave in. But when she barged into my office, I realized I had made the right decision. The spark in her eye was back. She stood there and stomped that little foot of hers, oh how I have missed her.

I couldn't help but follow her. I didn't think she would hurt herself or run away but I had to make sure. I watched as her dark hair blew in the wind reminding me of the days my sister would push her on the tire swing. She is finding her peace, unfortunately some of that she must do for herself. I tried going to her when she went to the cemetery, but Liam stopped me. He was right she needed time to herself. She knew I was close by.

When she left there and walked to the house she made a point to walk by the lake, giving us a smile. For the first time since we came home, I knew she would be okay. She is finding her way. Once she passed I quickly gathered up our fishing gear to follow. How will I ever be able to be away from her? Eventually I will have to go back to work, it is a part of me. I don't think I can shut it off. We saved her but there are so many more, more than anyone can imagine, it is endless.

When Liam and I get to the house, we find her sitting on the lawn with Luis and she is talking. I watch her lips move. I'm overwhelmed with relief. She tucks her hair behind her ear, she always does this when she is feeling shy. My girl is talking, I should have locked her door sooner. No, she needed time. Now is her chance to heal. Liam pats me on the back as we head back in, she is in good hands, Luis will take care of her.

When I get inside, I unlock her room and go in and peek out through the curtains. She is crying, my heart breaks. Torment is splayed across her face. I turn away and walk out, I can't fix it, I can only be here for her.

Mrs. Cortez informs me she will take lunch out to the patio for them when they don't arrive for the noon meal. I look at my watch. They have been out there a long time. Is that a good sign or a bad one?

"Stop, Dylan," Liam says tossing an olive at me, hitting me in the head.

"Stop what?" I say grouchily.

"You know, she will be fine. You did the right thing today," he says about to toss another olive at me but pauses when I give him my death glare.

Anthony picks up where Liam leaves off and pelts me with an olive in my neck.

I fling it back so hard it splats on Anthony's forehead. Mrs. Cortez walks in at the exact moment. A long tirade of Spanish comes flying out. She smacks my hand lightly and removes all our plates, meal over I guess.

We laugh and haul ourselves down to my office to discuss business. We have been diving into the material we found at Oliver's. A treasure trove of information to a dark world. After we finish, I pour each of us a glass of scotch and recline in my chair, thinking to myself that I should go in search of Anna.

Someone knocks on the door. Anthony gets up and pulls it open, he peeks at me from behind the door, throwing me his shit-eating grin. He steps aside and Anna walks in. She stands there for a second taking us all in. She doesn't move. She tucks her hair behind her ear, I want to go to her, but I am glued to my chair. She is nervous, this is a big moment for her and every man in this room knows it.

"I…well I…I want to say thank you all for saving me and for staying with me." Her eyes shine with unshed tears. The guys all make comments about no thanks needed, they love her, it was nothing, all shifting nervously.

She holds up her hand to stop them and turns to look directly at me. "I have one more thing to ask. I need your help again."

We all glance at each other, not sure what she needs but all of us know whatever it is we will give it to her, on a silver fucking plater. She has us wrapped around her little finger.

She continues, "I need help finding a girl, all I know is that her name is Addison, and that Oliver was keeping her somewhere. Brian trained her…" She stops and wipes at a tear that was threating to slip over her cheek. "He trained her, and I think he fell in love with her. Anyhow, I want to find her. I would like to read through the information you guys took from Oliver's to see if I can find any clues to where she may be."

I stare at all the files on my desk, the flip drives all of it from Oliver's…all of it ugly. I don't know if she knows what she is asking. "Why?" I ask, I need to understand.

"He saved me, he tried to protect me from Oliver." I start to argue with her, I saw the fucking tape of him whipping her. She holds up her hand to stop me. "Listen, I am not naïve, I know what he did." She swallows hard but continues, "Oliver was going to kill me, his guard had a weapon pointed at my head. Brian jumped in front of me and took a bullet that was meant for me. He told me you were coming before he died, it was the only thing I held on to while…"

We all sit in silence not sure what to say. Someone fired a gun at Anna, how close was I to losing her? It all makes sense now, the phone call Liam received from Brian. He called us to spare her, but he also recognized how good she was and that if she lived he would also be saving this other girl.

"Okay," I hear myself answer, not needing to hear another thing.

"Okay?" she asks hesitantly.

"Yes, I said you were a part of my team when we were in Colorado and I meant it. You killed one of the assholes with your bare hands. You provided valuable information to the FBI. You are one of us," I declare as I go to her, I need her in my arms.

The guys all agree as I pull her into my embrace. Anna is back, the strongest woman I know, and she is mine, all mine.

Chapter Thirty-Four

Anna

Luis encouraged me to talk to the others. I am so glad I did. I want to pursue my dad's dream. I am Anna Velasquez. I will show the world that the monsters did not break me. They empowered me. I will continue my father's legacy with Dylan and the rest of the guys.

We are going to start by finding Addison. I want to find her for Brian. Monster's aren't always what they seem. I thought Dylan was a monster at first too, a drop dead gorgeous one but none the less that was my initial judgement. Maybe Brian wasn't all monster either. I will never know. Oliver looked like an angel, but I quickly learned who he turned out to be.

I have felt so much better these past few days. I even visited my old room, I imagined having a daughter of my own someday. It's good to be home. I see why my father loved his men and his employees. I love everyone here. I am happy to call them my family. Then there is Dylan, I love him, I can't imagine life without him.

I went to Mark today for a checkup. He gave me the all clear. I turn my wrist over, just a small scar on the inside are all that remains of my ordeal. That and the scar you can't see, the one in my mind. I'm getting past it, slowly, each day better than the previous.

I feel almost bad for snooping through Dylan's things, but I am looking for something. Something I think will help me get over these last few hurdles. I miss being with Dylan. He snuggles me every night, but he is reluctant to do much more than that. He thinks I'll break, I won't. I need him to see that. This is the only way I know how.

I take a deep breath as I saunter into his office. The guys are all in their usual spots sipping their drinks. They need this time to decompress. They deal with a lot of shit on a day-to-day basis. This is their time to joke around and give each other gruff.

I stroll in and Anthony jumps up to get me a drink, I politely decline. "Sorry guys, I'm heading to bed early tonight. I wanted to tell Dylan goodnight." I step over to him and lean in to kiss him, reaching behind me to pull the cuffs I found in his dresser out of my pocket. I place them on the desk while he is distracted by my lips. Then, I "accidently" bump into his glass, knocking it to the floor.

I quickly bend over to clean it up. "I'm sorry, Dylan, I'm such a bad girl." I peek up at him as he notices the cuffs. I set the glass in front of him, then turn to walk out, ignoring the catcalls from behind me.

Oh, how I love these guys. I hoped that if I did it in their presence, they would encourage him. He is afraid, but I need this, he needs it too. I have seen the beast prowling in the shadows of his eyes.

I go into our room and undress, kneeling by the foot of the bed. I need him to erase the bad memories, to replace them with good ones. I want him to be rough with me as crazy as that sounds. I crave it.

I don't wait long before the door opens. Dylan walks in and our eyes latch on to one another. As soon as the lock clicks, excitement bubbles inside me. He holds the cuffs up in front of him, dangling them off a finger. I lick my lips. I am so damn hungry for him to touch me that even the fear of the cuffs cannot stop the wetness from building between my thighs.

"It seems someone has been a bad girl." He walks towards me and stops so that his crotch is directly in line with my face. I can see that he is excited by the bulge in his pants. I wiggle on the floor itching for his touch.

He runs his hand over my hair. I lean into it. I have missed this. He crouches down. "Anna, what is your safe word?"

"Water," I reply licking my lips again. I watch his hesitation. Please don't stop this I plead with my eyes.

"You will use it if you need to," he orders.

I shake my head as I say the word. "Yes."

"You know I will stop if you use it?" he asks again running his finger along my jaw.

"Yes, sir."

And with that he takes my mouth forcefully. This what I need, this will not be gentle. I have had enough gentle lately. I want him to take me, to own me, to claim me, to make me his again.

He picks me up and tosses me over his shoulder, spanking my ass as he walks to the bed. He dumps me in the middle of the bed and watches me intently as he backs away yanking his shirt over his head then slowly dragging his belt out of his jeans. Fuck he is hot. I train my eyes on his movements, reveling at the sight of him. His eyes are dark and smoldering, a hungry beast taking his time to move in for the kill.

Once he is naked, I watch as he walks back to the spot I was kneeling, retrieving the cuffs from the floor. He stalks up the side of the bed. "Lay down, hands up." I quickly do as he instructs. He watches me closely as he clicks the cuffs loosely around my wrists.

He runs his thumb over my neck, pausing over the extreme beating of my pulse. It is a traitor, letting him know how anxious the cuffs are making me. He reaches over to the nightstand and plucks out a blindfold. He leans over me to place it over my eyes. No, no, too much. I need to look at him so that my mind doesn't go to someone else. Shit, I don't want him to stop but I need to see him.

"Water," I say in barely a whisper. He halts and pulls the blindfold back, smiling down at me.

"Good girl. I had to make sure you would use your safe word. I wanted you to know that I would listen to you," he says as he tosses it to the floor.

He bends over and kisses me, trailing them down my neck moving all the way down my torso. Oh, thank god he didn't stop. As soon as his tongue glides over my clit I arch off the bed and writhe like a woman possessed. He brings me to the brink over and over again, stopping just before I tumble over the edge.

He waits until I am a complete mumbling mess, then pushes two fingers into me, curling them at just the right angle. Finding that itch that you just can't scratch yourself. Then he lets me fall, white sparks break behind my eyes as I float in the darkness.

He crawls over and thrusts into me, slowly moving back and forth, waiting for me to focus after my mind-blowing orgasm. I stare up at him and wrap my legs around him driving him deeper, pulling him closer. Our eyes lock on each other, we are one. I will never get enough of him. He is like a life-saving drug.

He thrusts into me and pushes hard until I feel the pain, the burn, going faster, harder, the momentum rises. His muscles tense and he groans out my name as I feel myself reach the summit, then together we fall into heavenly bliss. The world melts away, the only sound our heavy breathing. His body rests heavily on me. I love him. He has said the words, but I have never returned them. He needs to hear them. He needs to know.

"I love you, Dylan," I say breathlessly.

He looks up at me. "I love you too, baby, more than you will ever know." He gets up to retrieve the key to the handcuffs.

I watch over my head as he unlocks the cuffs. He frees me of so much more than the metal that keeps me chained to the bed. He frees me of everything I have been through. I'm so alive. The minute he has them off I jump up and push him onto his back.

"I love you, Dylan Lorenz. I love you!" I say as I straddle him and kiss him passionately. "I would let you lock me in a trunk a thousand times as long as it ended with you being mine."

He laughs and sits up with me still on his lap. He wraps his arms around me, tickling me. I wriggle in his hold enticing him to grow hard again.

"Luckily that won't be necessary. I don't need to lock you in a trunk, you seem more than willing to be with me." He nuzzles my neck. "I love you, Anna Velasquez, I am so happy that I found you," he says as he brushes my hair off my shoulder, gazing deep into my eyes.

"Me too." I climb off him and slink away from the bed. "But, you will have to find me again if you want seconds." I run for the door and glance over my shoulder, taunting the beast…my beast.

The End

Epilogue

It's been two months since Dylan and his team found me. I can't lie, there have been dark days but most of the time I'm blissfully happy. To have a family again, is indescribable. I love Dylan and everyone here on the estate.

We've been working hard at dismantling Oliver Wright's organization. Dylan talked me into claiming my biological father's inheritance. It wasn't easy for me. The money he made had all come from the suffering of others. I sold every asset. All the cash is now in an account dedicated to helping the women that we save. There were many, there will be many more.

The things I've learned have been horrible. I understand now why my father worked so hard. I have mostly focused on the search for one girl, Brian's girl, Addison. We found her. It has taken a lot of convincing, but Dylan finally agreed to let me go undercover with him to get her out. I would be lying if I said I wasn't scared. I am. I'm terrified.

I won't allow him to see it, the fear will only make our story more believable. We are going into a dark underground club. One where girls are sold, traded, or rented. It is a place for the elite. Elite garbage if you ask me.

Dylan is going in with me, nobody should recognize him. Liam and the others will be outside waiting. If anything goes wrong, they will be there. We are trying to do this with as little disruption as possible. We are going to buy her.

Once we rescue her, the second phase will be a complete takedown. Dylan and I will hopefully gain information on the layout of the club. We need to know where the girls are kept. We don't want to risk anyone who is innocent getting hurt. Get Addison out, learn as much as we can…two birds, one stone.

I watch Dylan put on his tie. He is sexy as hell in a suit. He catches me watching him and gives me a smoldering stare.

"You ready, baby?" he asks.

"Yes, sir," I say as I take a final peek at myself in the mirror. I have a little black dress on, with stiletto heels and a diamond collar around my neck.

Dylan walks towards me and slides his fingers under the collar, pulling me close to him. "You will stay by my side the entire night. Eyes down, don't look at anyone and I mean anyone," he growls.

I know he is nervous about taking me, but it makes his story more believable. He is playing the wealthy businessman and I his slave. Hopefully we find Addison, it appears Oliver had been keeping her at this club. I hope that if I am there, I can make her feel better. Dylan is intimidating, I don't want her to fear him. We can't tell her who we really are…not until we get her out.

Liam bops his head in the door. "Ready guys?"

"As ready as we are going to be," Dylan answers.

He turns to me. "Last chance to back out, I can go in alone. Are you sure, baby?"

"I'm not backing out," I say with confidence. I think I will recognize her even though I have never laid eyes on her…I will know. "I want to help save her."

"Okay, baby, let's go save Addison," he says as he hugs me tightly to his chest.

About the Author

LM Terry is the upcoming dark romance novelist of Finding Anna, Saving Addy and Discovering Danielle. She has spent her life in the Midwest, growing up near a public library which helped fuel her love of books. With most of her eight children grown and with the support of her husband, she decided to follow her heart and begin her writing journey. In searching for that happily ever after, her characters have been enticing her to share their sinfully dark, delectable tales. She knows the world is filled with shadows and dark truths and is happy to give these characters the platform they have been begging for. She is currently working on fourth novel Death and Daffodils.

Facebook: https://www.facebook.com/lmterryauthor/

Website: https://www.lmterryauthor.com

Made in the USA
Monee, IL
10 August 2020

37760207R00194